D0571742

Valfierno

Valfierno

The Man Who
Stole the *Mona Lisa*

Martín Caparrós

Translated by Jasper Reid

ATRIA BOOKS
New York   London   Toronto   Sydney

ATRIA BOOKS

A Division of Simon & Schuster, Inc.
1230 Avenue of the Americas
New York, NY 10020

This book is a work of fiction. Names, characters, places, and incidents either are products of the author's imagination or are used fictitiously.

Copyright © 2008 by Martín Caparrós

Translation copyright © 2008 by Simon & Schuster, Inc.

All rights reserved, including the right to reproduce this book or portions thereof in any form whatsoever. For information address Atria Books Subsidiary Rights Department, 1230 Avenue of the Americas, New York, NY 10020.

First Atria Books hardcover edition July 2008

ATRIA BOOKS and colophon are trademarks of Simon & Schuster, Inc.

For information about special discounts for bulk purchases,
please contact Simon & Schuster Special Sales at
1-800-456-6798 or business@simonandschuster.com.

Designed by Karolina Harris

Manufactured in the United States of America

10 9 8 7 6 5 4 3 2 1

Library of Congress Cataloging-in-Publication Data

Caparrós, Martín
  [Valfierno. English]
  Valfierno : the man who stole the Mona Lisa : a novel / by Martín Caparrós ; translated by Jasper Reid.
    p. cm.
  I. Reid, Jasper. II. Title.
PQ7798.13.A57 V3513
863'.64—dc22   2007031206

ISBN-13: 978-0-7432-9793-6
ISBN-10:   0-7432-9793-8

This story is based on real events

As are most

Contents

Prologue

PERUGIA REALIZES THAT EVERYTHING WILL have to be resolved in the next fifteen minutes and tries not to think about how those fifteen minutes could change his life.

Clutching his broom, he walks toward the arcade that gives out onto the Salon Carré. Just before he leans out he hears voices coming from below. He tries to keep calm and finds a place from where he can see what's happening without being seen.

"This is the most valuable painting we have in the museum, the one all our patrons want to see. It is said to be worth millions, if it were ever to be sold, which of course will never happen," intones an old man whom Perugia knows—Georges Picquet, the head of staff for the museum. He is accompanied by eight or ten museum employees wearing new smocks.

"Needless to say, I expect this part of the museum to be kept extra clean," Picquet instructs the recruits. Perugia cannot believe his bad luck. Once again the star has evaded him. He begins sweeping again and looks over at the brothers, across the Duchâtel Gallery, dusting frames with their cloths. Thanks to the sweat on his hands, his broom is on the verge of slipping from his grip. He listens to the voices below. If they are not gone within ten minutes, he will have to admit defeat. Please God, he thinks, make them go somewhere else!

". . . of the museum. I also want to show you this area over here, where . . ."

He hears footsteps. The procession moves toward the Apollo Gallery. The white smocks drift out and the Salon Carré is empty. This is it, he says to himself, and, not really believing it, has to repeat it: This is it!

He finishes sweeping some tiles, telling himself not to rush.

He thinks about the star, his grandmother, and, finally, about the fact that he cannot wait a moment longer. He looks over at the Lancelottis and makes a sign to them to follow him.

He cannot believe that she is up there, alone, hanging on the wall, just that easy, helpless—like a woman who no longer knows what to ask for in exchange for herself, who knows she can't ask for anything. Perugia can't believe that it's this simple, that all he has to do is to reach up and take her down from the wall for the blessed *Mona Lisa* to be in his hands, but there is no one in the Salon Carré, Vincenzo Lancelotti is beside him, Michele is in the gallery keeping watch, and she is hanging right there, ripe for picking. For the first time in all those hours, Perugia smiles: whores, all of them whores, he thinks, and a wave of heat rolls up his face, reddening it. For the last time, he looks to either side. Then the yellow badge comes into his head and he is furious that he had to think of it just then. He again brushes his left testicle lightly, for luck. Then, slowly, as if he still cannot believe it, his hands reach up.

Bollino

1

🦎 I AM VALFIERNO.

Let's just say that I'm Valfierno. Or that I used to be. It was as Valfierno that I pulled off the most amazing caper—the story of a lifetime.

"Why did you choose the name Valfierno?"

"Didn't we agree that you would limit your questions to matters of fact?"

"Yes, of course. Isn't that a matter of fact?"

"My dear fellow . . ."

Tuesday, August 22, 1911. The Paris late edition was selling like crazy. On every street corner, paper boys shouted out the news: someone had stolen the world's most famous painting.

"The *Mona Lisa* is gone! Read all about it! *La Joconde* has disappeared!"

"Mesdames, Messieurs, we have lost *La Joconde! La Joconde* has escaped!"

The heat was unbearable. It had been like this for weeks, and except for the few who were profiting from it, everyone was miserable. The topic dominated every encounter, every café, every ornate salon, every church and fancy brothel. In such a cruel heat, Paris couldn't be its usual festive self, and this made everyone feel all the more miserable, and cheated. Men and women would talk to each other of nothing but the heat. They'd move on listlessly to some other topic of little interest only to mop their faces and return to the subject again. "The world is not what it used to be," they sighed.

"It's progress, my dear, progress. If it weren't for the Socialists and this foul heat . . ."

For weeks, the heat sucked all conversation dry, until suddenly, that afternoon, everyone was talking again.

"They've stolen *La Joconde!* France is a laughingstock!
Extra! Extra!"

I am Valfierno.

I was a very happy child. My mother called me Bollino and
I thought that was my name—Bollino, I'm Bollino.

One time in the street, a woman said, "What a lovely child,
what's his name?" and I told her Bollino, and my mother laughed a
lot, and said, "No, Señora, his name is Juan María," not knowing I
also called myself Eduardo. But I—Bollino, Juan María, not yet Enrique, still Bonaglia, also Eduardo—was a very happy child.

The boy has dark hair, a wide face and delicate features, and
is somewhat short for his eight years. He has a decisive way about
him; he gives an order and the other two children follow. The other
two are both blond, the boy is older—about six—and the girl is perhaps five. Around them the park is dazzling—a sea of lush, perfect
lawn, a pond sprinkled with lotus flowers, hedges trimmed in the
shape of small houses, magnolias, monkey puzzle trees, oaks, islands
of lilac bushes, white statues of animals and goddesses and warriors,
also a peacock. At the top of the park the windows in the French-
style mansion reflect the sunlight. The dark-haired boy announces
that they are going to the statue of the deer. The blond boy objects.

"Don't tell me what to do! You can't tell me what to do!
You're no one to tell me what to do, you're no one!"

Diego is shouting, on the verge of tears, and launches himself at the dark-haired boy. Bollino is half a head taller than him
and stronger, too. Diego tries to hit him, but Bollino dodges his
blows, not hitting back. Marianita laughs. Diego tries again,

swings, and loses his balance. He falls, clutches his eye, and yells from where he lies on the ground that Bollino has hit him in the face. His little sailor suit is dirty.

"Bollino hit me! Bollino hit me! I'm going to tell my Mamá," he yells, his face stained with tears and mucus, as the heavy woman in the maid's uniform rushes over. Her skin is pale, she has blond hair and feet like platters. Up close she looks younger. She picks him up and cleans him off. Diego doesn't like her to touch him, and he recoils, yelling, 'Annunci, Annunci, don't touch me!' Mariana and Bollino watch them, holding hands. The air smells of orange blossom and loquat.

"What happened?" asks the maid, in her Italian accent.

"Bollino hit me! He's bad! I'm going to tell Mamá!"

"I did not! I really didn't! He fell, he slipped and fell. I didn't touch him!" says Bollino. The maid strikes him once across the face, hard. It makes a noise.

"So you learn not to mess with the kids," she says to Bollino, and he looks at her without any expression, all his effort going into not crying.

"But, Mamá, I didn't do anything!"

Suddenly, no one gave a thought to the heat. The painting's theft was a national scandal, and nothing stirs a population more than to be witness to a national scandal. Nothing grabs them quite like being at the center of a real disaster, cast as actors in a real drama—the consolation of knowing they have lived through a moment that many others will for years just pretend to remember, of knowing that this time they have actually felt the touch of history, normally so aloof and disdainful.

My mother raised me valiantly. I remember her feeding me once—it must be one of my first memories—she speared tiny pieces of meat for me on the end of a fork, and with each bite of mine she said, "Bollino, chew each piece well with your mouth closed, or you will hurt both your belly and your reputation," and she laughed. I laughed, too: "reputation" must be a very funny word.

She was always looking after me, and that family was also very good to me. When I was little we spent all our time with Diego and Marianita. Those were long and happy days, swimming, riding the horses, playing games in the park and the playroom, my mother watching over all three of us. The family would give me presents— toys and clothes—and every now and then the father would tell me that he loved me like a nephew, and that I was very intelligent and would do well in life.

Until I turned ten we were inseparable, those children and me. Afterward, when Diego began his studies with the governess they'd brought in for him, his father gave my mother money to send me to study at school with the monks. The day before I was to start, he called me into his study and told me that nothing was more important than education, and that only without it were you truly poor, and that if I had any problems I was to tell the Father Superior, he would take charge of me, and that he wished me all the best things, and that if there was anything I needed I was to come to him, and he gave me a smart leather folder for my papers.

The day that he had Angel take my mother and me in the carriage to my first day of school, I discovered that beyond the walls of that park there was a path that led down to a large town on the banks of a river. It was very ugly. I'd heard people talk about it before, but until then I had never paid any attention.

"But Valfierno, that's not where you were born."

"Are you asking me this, or telling me?"

"You told me your mother was a foreigner. You told me you were a foreigner."

"A foreigner, you say? From where?"

The woman waits at home. Home is a squalid room in a big house that had once been a palace. Ages pass. She sits wringing her hands and waiting, knowing that she will have to wait many more hours. In those hours she will ask herself a thousand times why she wasn't able to find the words to persuade him not to go. Neither words of love, nor threats, nor reminders of his paternal responsibilities could help her, and she will ask herself again and again what could have made him choose that supposed duty that had called him away.

She will also wonder if maybe he was right, as he was so many other times—that she exaggerates her fears, that they are just a woman's hysteria, nonsense. Surely he is right, and yet she is still scared, and she still expects to hear how he left, arrogant as always, bidding a careless farewell with that condescending smile. "Don't worry yourself, woman, these are not things for you." And "you" could have meant her and the boy, but she knows that it didn't, that it meant women, all women, and it saddens her to be mixed in with them all like that, as the smell of burnt grease on his clothes in that room saddens her, the smell he leaves behind for her so that she won't forget that it's him she is waiting for.

The woman is not yet twenty but already heavy from motherhood and her diet of bread and beans. She has unusually light eyes in a face that is dark and streaked from wiping tears away with dirty hands. She sits, and sitting, you notice the weight and roundness of her arms. She would make a beautiful Madonna.

Her name is Annunziata—Annunziata Perrone, born in Trimoli, in Italy, on the twenty-fifth of March, 1850, a Monday, the Feast of the Annunciation. Daughter of Giovanni, wife of Gian-Felice Bonaglia, ex-seamstress, a woman now.

She continues to wring her hands slowly, then dries them on her brown skirt, which is clean but for the small grease spots that won't come out, and she thinks again of the words she couldn't muster and tries to comfort herself. She never knew how to use words; he was the one who knew how. When he was first pursuing her, after work at the dress factory, when she was fifteen and had a smile—everyone agreed—that would be her fortune, she knew that she was supposed to keep quiet and listen to him. She was quiet when he asked her to sit with him beside the dry fountain in the square, and she was quiet each afternoon when he came back to find her again and extended his hand for her—he did not reach for her hand, but would extend his hand so that it was she who, quietly, would grasp his. She said "I do" quietly when the priest asked her, and she kept her screams as quiet as possible for the midwife who told her how happy her man would be now that she'd given him a son. "A healthy boy! Your man is going to be very happy!"

She knew to be quiet, and was learning that her silence could give her power, as well—that perhaps she didn't need words. She thinks now that when she did need them—this morning, for example, those words of love or duty or sadness that she didn't know how to say to him—it was too late, and she twists her hands and dries them on her skirt, and the boy grabs them and asks her, "Are you hot, Mamma? Your hands are wet."

The boy won't stop asking silly questions: "Are you hot, Mamma? Are we having bean soup tonight, Mamma? Will Papà bring me a candy tonight when he gets home, Mamma? Why are you hot, Mamma, when it's so cold?" She tells him to be quiet and concentrates on her waiting. For her, waiting is knowing that terrible news can come at any moment and that if she waits intently enough perhaps she can head it off, prevent it from coming. That waiting like this is the price she must pay so that it doesn't come. And that if it should finally come, the waiting will have made it less terrible; it might be less terrible.

"When are you going to start making the soup, Mamma? It's getting late."

I didn't know where we had come from, but I knew I hadn't been born there, in that river city they called Rosario. At first, of course, I didn't know that; later I thought that if I'd been born anywhere it was in the big house, in the little room I shared with my mother under the roof. In the end, I figured out that we must be from somewhere else because my mother, who was so good and whom the children obeyed and who looked after us all, had a strange accent. It wasn't hard to notice. It was the first real thing I ever noticed, that I remember noticing: my mother spoke in a strange accent. At the time I thought it must be a way she spoke to make the children do what she said.

Sometimes I asked my mother about my father. Or rather, I once started to ask her about him. I suppose that in the early days, while we were happy in the big house, it never occurred to me. Diego and Mariana were the ones with a father because they were the ones who had things; I had some things, too, and they also had a mother who was very pretty and had lighter hair than my mother and I never thought to ask. But later, in school, boys often talked about their fathers, and then I had to keep silent.

One day I decided to ask my mother where my father was. I didn't say "Mamá, why don't I have a father?" or "Who does he think he is, leaving us all alone like this?" or "Why did you leave him?" or "What happened, Mamá?" Instead, I asked her where my father was, and she thought a moment before answering. It's strange, now that I think of it, that she had to take a moment before answering; she must have expected that question, imagined that question and her own answer for years before it finally came. But she thought for a moment and then told me that he was not around because he'd had to go away to work somewhere—I don't remember where—to earn money. I asked her when he was going to come back with the money and she asked me right away if I'd ever lacked for anything. I didn't say, "A father, Mamá." I lied instead and didn't say that.

"The papers all said that a theft like that had to be the work of a diseased mind, or some obscure genius. See that, Newspaperman? It never occurred to them that it might be something much simpler: a work of art."

I am Valfierno.

I was a very happy child. My mother called me Bollino and I thought that was my name—Bollino, I'm Bollino. I was such a happy child. But my father wasn't there. Perhaps I should say that I was a very happy child because my father wasn't there. My father wasn't there because he'd gone to make money somewhere. Because they hadn't let him come with us when we moved to our new city, and he was trying to get there now. Because he had to look after our other house. Because his mother wouldn't let him go that far. Because he was killed in such-and-such war. Because who could love a boy like me, who was so bad? Because he'd left something very important behind and had to go and get it, and he definitely was going to find it and come back.

Once, I asked my mother what my father's name was and she didn't want to tell me. "What kind of a question is that?" she said, as if she didn't know.

2

♼ THE MARQUÉS EDUARDO DE VALFIERNO fusses with the knot of his bow tie to a degree many would consider excessive. Valérie Larbin thinks it is entirely too much, though he is in all likelihood exaggerating his usual meticulousness just to irritate her.

"Aren't you going to get dressed, my angel?"

"What for? Are you taking me out somewhere?"

The music is silent. Valérie reclines on a chaise longue of grey velvet, her long, raven-black hair falling in torrents across her white breasts. Her black silk robe with the red Chinese characters lies slightly open, as if to show that she is very much a woman. Valérie Larbin smokes, her mother-of-pearl cigarette holder held between lilac-painted nails—the vampire queen of some movie she has seen recently.

The Marqués looks at her and smiles to himself. Everything about her is a poor imitation of some bad film. If she knew, he thinks, that he used to do the very same thing long ago—or perhaps not so long ago. If she knew that what appeals to him about her is something else entirely. If *he* knew, he thinks, exactly what that was.

"So now you're going to ask me to parade you around like a wife?"

"No, like an expensive mistress."

"Which you are not."

"Do me the courtesy, Marqués. If I were, you couldn't allow yourself."

Valérie is a vulgar wonder, with her big tits and her fake refinement. He can't stand to be attracted by such commonness.

"I can allow myself what I please."

"Not me, Valfierno, please. You might be able to fool the lovelies in the Bois de Boulogne with your act, but not me. How long since you've paid the bill for this suite? How much longer is the hotel going to be patient?"

"I can also allow myself to be quite without funds."

"Marqués . . ."

Valfierno hates it when she speaks like a character in some cheap melodrama, which is almost always. In fact he hates her most of the time, yet he keeps seeking her out and buying her silly baubles with cheap paste glitter and despairing when she disappears, which is often. He imagines her with her hands on some pig, older than he is and richer, wheedling real jewels from him, and he can't stand it and he despises her and nothing excites him quite as much as that and back he goes, seeking her, sending her bunches of gladioli. She must not know who he really is, he thinks, or she wouldn't do these things to him. No one really knows, he thinks. If they did!

"You don't understand anything."

"No, I don't."

A little past one in the afternoon, humid heat, Paris, the end of summer. Valérie and Valfierno have been in the suite since about three or four in the morning, when they returned from a ball at the Opera-Comique. Valfierno was too tired and drunk then to give her what she wanted, and he asked her to caress him awake later, that this would revive him. But in the morning he fared little better, and now he just wants her to go, soon. Not having the temerity to ask her to leave, he begins to dress on the flimsy pretext of a lunch engagement. He knows, in any case, that as soon as she is gone that he will again begin to need her, their next encounter.

"Marqués, may I ask you a question?"

3

⚘ THE SCHOOL WAS NOT SO bad—the monks spoke almost in verse, addressed me formally, and hit me only when necessary—but it did not suit me. It was full of wild boys, bigger than I was, who disdained me. I was out of place among those brutes; later I learned that they were the sons of poor farmers who had sent them away to school to set them free from the pig muck, the frost on the hands, the days that began before daybreak. It did not suit me, and when I complained, my mother told me that I must get used to it, that I didn't know how lucky I was to be at that school, that Don Manuel had been very good to us and that I must not complain again.

And I did not complain again, but would wait each week for Saturday, when she would come to take me out. We would walk through the city's main square and she would ask me about school and tell me that she would do everything she could to see me educated, a gentleman. So that I would go far, she would say, always so that I would go far. And I think that even then, when she said go far, I thought literally of a different place, of going far away.

"Later, when I started to get a little older, I was embarrassed to walk in the street with my mother."

"Why?"

"I told her that people looked at her too much. That her beauty was a little too garish. That her figure, her makeup—everything about her was too garish."

"What are you trying to say?"

"Let's get one thing clear right now, Newspaperman. I've said exactly what I want to say. When I want to say something, I'll say it."

In the second half of the nineteenth century, in a place like Rosario, a woman like her attracts attention. Rosario has just officially been made a city, though it is really just a messy, overgrown port town trying to secure a future for itself.

The port grows, its main function being to export the grain that the region produces in such enormous quantities almost without meaning to, as if by sheer chance, and to receive the shiploads of poor emigrants who begin to arrive from European ports—especially the Italian ones—eager for everything they have left home to find. They prefer the relative harmlessness of this overgrown town to the seemingly more menacing, disdainful, and standoffish air of the country's main port, Buenos Aires.

The town's streets are made up of low houses with iron grilles over their windows, the occasional oil streetlamp, and mud. Around Rosario's main plaza, with its town hall and half-finished church, a few of the streets have been cobbled. On some afternoons she strolls along them, seemingly unaware of how out of place she is there, how her presence detracts from the picture, complicates it.

In the second half of the nineteenth century, in the center of a town like Rosario, everyone has a role to play within a strict hierarchy. This is still the case, and will be for some years, until the invasion makes it impossible.

The priest has his role; the Governor, his functionaries and hangers-on, the Justice of the Peace, the top eight or ten newly minted grain barons, their various lawyers, the three or four doctors, all have theirs. Also a few newspapermen, possible candidates one day for Governor or a similar post, have their role, as do the old militia leaders who, having risen up against a distant tyrant twenty years earlier, had assured the growth of the town—they all have their place in those streets, as do their ladies, or what those gentlemen call ladies.

And as they have theirs, so, too, do the vendors of rolls and other street food available for dispensing with the occasional hunger, and the peddlers of hair combs and pretty trinkets, and the boys who wait around to help ladies carry home their purchases or get across a puddle. The stable hand, the blind old man, and the cripple at the church, the various other poor who help at the concert, and the few constables who watch over all of it—they all have their places. But she has no place there, on the cobblestone streets of the center of that town, and yet she continues to take her walks there.

She is large, like one of those barrels of cheap wine—young, with a lively smile on her careworn face and clear, penetrating eyes. Her blond hair, already going grey, is gathered up—and she is enormously fat.

She doesn't wear her maid's uniform on her walks—if she did, she would have her place. Instead she wears a skirt that was once black but is now grey and threadbare, a blouse that used to be white and is now also grey, and a red shawl on top.

She walks proudly, as if something about her warrants a look of respect or acknowledgment. As if something about her permits her to leave her role of servant to the richest man in the area to mingle on the cobblestone streets with the cream of the town. She walks, and they look at her—spitefully, indignantly they look at her—and she returns their looks. Always just two paces ahead or behind her walks her son, a boy of ten who looks younger, with thick black hair, delicately drawn features, his short pants frayed, eyes like hers, a patch on his shoes. The boy's name is Juan María and he always walks a little behind or in front of his mother along those cobblestone streets, a little away from her.

Sometimes he escapes his mother's gaze and ventures farther afield. Sometimes there'll be a woman with an expensive coiffure carrying a parasol and wearing an imported shawl, and he'll position himself a little behind or in front of her, as if he were her son. For a couple of minutes, until she notices, he walks as if he were with her and returns the greetings and smiles that the ladies, the gentlemen, the priest, the Governor, the judge, the lawyers, grain barons, journalists, and street vendors all offer up to the woman with the coiffure and in the same movement, to him, the boy, Juan María.

Until he's discovered and escapes again. Sometimes it's the woman with the coiffure who discovers him and says, "Go away, little brat, who do you think you are!" Other times it's his mother who notices him gone and calls his name, looking for him, and when he appears says, "Bollino, what's wrong? Bollino, my Bollino . . ."

I suppose I was a happy child until the day I realized that I had to be. Until I saw how my mother depended on each tiny detail of my happiness and then it seemed to me that, as the way to take care of my mother, it was far too fragile. After that, it was much more difficult to maintain this state that—as my mother's attitude seemed to suggest—was always in danger of breaking.

"Do you think that we only care about things that are in danger of breaking?"

"Don't be an ass, Newspaperman!"

On weekends I went back to my life, to the big French house, to my room, to Diego and Marianita. We were happy to see each other; I told them things about school and the brothers (and almost nothing about the other boys), and Diego showed me his books of drawings. He asked me if they were teaching me French and sometimes even spoke French words to me, and I pretended that I understood them, but Marianita would laugh and I'd realize I'd got it wrong. But I liked it because it was like before, and they called me Bollino like my mother, and I ate their food and it was like before. I liked it to be like before.

The boy's name is Juan María, almost everyone calls him Juan María and he's on the point of not being a boy anymore. It's debatable: who can say that up to this point you're a boy and then beyond that you're something else? Borders, unless they are the borders of a country, tend be gradual. It's not easy to cross a border like that—still harder to know when or even if you've crossed it. It's a journey without clear boundaries. For a boy, the first shadows of a beard, sudden, unexpected slips of the voice, those new pimples, all mark the fact that he is no longer what he was and that he will never be again, as much as he might try. The boy spends years learning something he will have to learn again many times: that what he has just learned—to be a boy, to live like a boy—no longer serves him, for when he has finally mastered it, then he will have ceased to be one. Then he will learn to be something else, something different every time. A way of being that is always the same.

Señor Manuel de Baltiérrez is standing, his arms crossed over his impeccable shirtfront, his small blond wife to his right, his left foot tapping a rhythm on the floor. His voice when he speaks is low and contained, inspiring greater fear.

"You deceived us. You took advantage of our kindness, you tricked us. I don't have much more to say to you. Tomorrow morning at dawn you will leave here, you and your unfortunate son, and I do not wish to see you ever again. Never again, understood?"

Facing him, just a few feet away, the fat woman is drowning in her maid's uniform. Her lips are pressed together, her forehead gathered to prevent the tears from coming, and she struggles for words which, she knows, will not help her.

"Sir, it wasn't me! I swear to you I didn't do it, Don Manuel, it wasn't me! Why would I do something like that?"

"Anunciata, don't take me for a fool. You've done that for years now. It's all over."

"But, sir, please God!"

"Don't bring the Lord into this, Anunciata. The necklace was in your room! Or are you going to tell me it wasn't?"

The greyhound who'd been sleeping at Don Manuel's feet gets up and takes a few steps toward the warmth of the fireplace, where the logs are crackling. Anunciata looks at the fire but finds nothing there.

"No, I know it was there, but I swear that it wasn't me! Why would I do something like that? Where would I be better off than here? Where am I going to find a family that treats me as well as you?"

Now she does cry; Anunciata sobs. Don Manuel makes a gesture of disgust.

"Nowhere, I imagine. But we're not talking about logic, Anunciata, but about cheats, miserable cheats like you. God knows what you must have in your head; I don't care. I said tomorrow morning, and that's all there is to say. I'm only sorry for your son."

"Do you think she was capable of robbing him?"

"No, Newspaperman. How could you say that?"

"But the necklace was in your room?"

"Yes, of course it was in our room."

"So?"

"Do I really to have to spell out everything?"

4

"MARQUÉS, MAY I ASK YOU a question?"

"As long as you don't ask me if I love you," replies Valfierno, and knows right away that it was not necessary. Valérie allows him his life; she does not judge him. She takes a sip of her tea and retouches her lips with a rich vermilion. Then just for a moment, without intending to, Valfierno thinks of Mercedes, Don Simón's daughter, and the thought surprises him.

"What is the strangest thing that you have faked?"

"Faked? Me?"

"Come, Marqués, I'm not a fool. It's useful for me to seem that way, but don't believe it, not you. Come—what is the most unusual thing that you've ever faked, apart from your title, your name, your history, and those pearls you gave me last month as a present? Sometimes I think even your nationality is false. I can't say why, exactly, but I'd bet that you're not even Argentine."

" 'Fake' is not part of my vocabulary," replies Valfierno, but he knows that his lack of indignation says something, and he doesn't mind telling her like this, through his silence.

"What would you call it, then?"

Valfierno plays his gaze over her like a tongue, that languid diva's body draped across the fake velvet couch. The velvet of her skin against the fake velvet of the couch, he thinks, then tells himself not to be so trite.

"I'm sure you don't call it anything—some things are better for not being named, wouldn't you say, Marqués?"

For weeks now he's been asking himself why he keeps calling her, seeking her out. For weeks he's been telling himself that a pair of tits isn't enough, that anyway they're not up to his standards; that they're so animal, so primitive—two dangling bags of fat that females use to feed their juices to their young. Tits are the most prehistoric feature of our species, he thinks, laughing to himself as he looks at them again.

Once again he asks himself why this woman—who could easily find herself more rewarding adventures—keeps on accepting his invitations, tolerating him. That's the word, he thinks—"tolerate." It must be that flaw—the one thing that prevents her from being truly beautiful. I must think more about that flaw, he says to himself, and what about it turns her into a kind of lie.

"Don't try me, Valérie."

Unless, he thinks, she needs this for some reason that he has yet to understand, and now he is alarmed. He recalls that in an errant moment he'd been tempted to think it was his charms that had seduced her, but that something had told him it wasn't, or at least that there was something else as well. Something: a sense, the wreck in the mirror.

"Marqués, may I ask you another question?"

Valérie gets up from the couch, goes up to him, brushes the nonexistent dust from his shoulders, and lets the black silk robe with the red Chinese characters part slightly.

Valfierno wears a suit of raw linen with brown and white shoes, his shirt impeccable, a purple bow tie. His shoes have heels, to make him taller. He finishes his grooming and surveys his expensively cut salt-and-pepper hair, the thin mustache, the green eyes like slits. The straight, aristocratic nose. A modest mouth. The forehead smooth. He has the right face for his role, he thinks: pleasant, neat, nothing particularly memorable.

"Marqués, couldn't we work together?"

"That's just what I need!"

"You'll want to, eventually."

"No doubt, my angel. But now I have a lunch to go to, and if you don't make yourself decent, I shall be late."

"Marqués, don't be an idiot. It's not what you imagine."

"And what is it I imagine? Do tell me."

"I'd rather not guess. In any case we both know it's pure fantasy. I simply want to tell you this: a friend of mine knows a fellow who until just recently worked at the Louvre. He's an idiot, but he's without scruples. That's not that common in an idiot like him. You know what they say: morals are the substitute for intelligence. This fellow can go in and out of that museum the way you do at the Hippodrome d'Auteuil."

"Why would that be of any interest to me?"

"I don't know, Valfierno, but think it over. You're the thinking type. You don't always know how to do things, but you do know how to think. If we work hard, my love—even harder than last night—maybe something will come to you."

He was this close to hating her.

5

🐝 THIS MAN DIDN'T SEEM TO want anything. Valérie was not used to having a man look at her without looking; having his eyes remain so absent. The pianist continued to hammer out polkas. The air was heavy. A client was drooling on her shoulder.

"Hey, you—mademoiselle."

"Me?"

"No, my little grandmother from Pétaouchnoc-sur-Oise!"

"What do you want?"

"What do you mean, what do I want? Shouldn't you be asking me that?"

"I am asking you."

"No, you know what I'm talking about."

The floor is thick with sawdust, the air with polkas, and the walls with paintings by painters who couldn't pay for their drinks or their lives. Valérie tries to remember what the world was like when it wasn't like this, and she asks herself what she wouldn't give to have her own little parcel of memories: a little girl in a pure white dress running through a meadow full of pretty yellow flowers, for example. Surrounded by a litter of golden puppies. A bright pitcher of orange juice waiting for her outside on an old iron table painted white. A strict but understanding father watching her from a distance while he absentmindedly swipes at his boots with his crop. Or at least a modest old peasant house set in a valley—the kind you see everywhere in France—that she has seen so often in paintings, with a mother who cooks in a big pot and a father who trudges home, weary from pruning the vines, and lights a long pipe and sits himself down in front of the fire. The smell of smoke. Many little brothers and sisters. A plaid skirt. Another dog with matted fur who growls. Or best of all, in another house, in a big bedroom filled with light, a bed with a big canopy and lavender sheets, and a mother kissing her forehead while she dozed, so sweetly dozed.

She would kill, she tells herself—though she has no idea whom—for a mother who kissed her forehead, or at least for an aunt who would wait up for her some nights, her hands on her hips, yelling at her that this is no time for a young lady to be getting home, any home, and who would drag her to the bathroom and wash her face to get rid of her makeup and who would shout at her that she was a lost cause for whom things would surely end badly.

But she doesn't have this memory or any other worth remembering, and she is sure that this man knows who she is and what she is—he must see it, as she herself does. She thinks: there are men who would run from this, out of timidity, even while I spend my life taking advantage of the other kind. Escaping from the other kind or flirting with them. Teasing them with what they are never going to get, or perhaps someday, after a long campaign, a costly campaign, a stupid campaign, and so on through days, months, years until I find one who will fill me with memories of a girl singing in an old church choir with her hair tied up in a blue ribbon, her face washed, unclouded, glowing. The silly face of a girl who wouldn't even need to be pretty—who wouldn't care if she was pretty. How easy it would be not to have to think about being pretty, she thinks. Since she was first able to reason, beauty—her own supposed beauty—has been her great weapon for nearly everything. And she's not even beautiful; she knows she's not even that.

"Who will know how to fill my past with memories?" she asks herself, without any great hopes. She looks at the man who looks without looking.

Valérie Larbin was what the chroniclers of society—or their putative sons, the social novelists—would have called a demi-mondaine. The qualification is specious. The first half of the term, the demi, makes it ambiguous: these women were not worldly, they were only half worldly. These were not women with set rates, prostitutes who in exchange for their services received a specific amount of coin (or notes for that matter, depending on the quality of the product). But it was understood that they were—in an era in which women feigned a fundamental indisposition to any romantic encounter that had not been preceded by the necessary signatures—women disposed to exchange their favors for an indeterminate set of favors in turn. These might include money, but more often consisted of gifts, attentions, various invitations. All of which bestowed on the practice the more attractive air of indefinition, since it wasn't an automatic or explicit exchange. The interested party would size up the quality of the offerings and thus avoid the strict rationalism and measurement through which the bourgeoisie typically saw the world. To have a demi was to have a demi-adventure.

"Do you know who that guy is?"

"Which one?"

"That one there."

"Val, there are about ten different guys there."

"Him, with the dark hair in his eyes."

"No, I don't. I've seen him around here a couple of times, but I don't know him. Why?"

"No reason. Just wondering."

Beauty is a weapon that you can never grab by the handle, someone once told Valérie, and she remembers this whenever she lets herself go.

The clientele at the Faux Chien is a mixture of would-be Montmartre artists, slumming bourgeois in search of emotion, con men on the make, the jumble of regulars, and the girls. It's eleven thirty at night, and instead of a piano, an accordion plays, and a man with a raspy voice sings songs about women and animals. A few people dance in the middle of the room; many more drink.

Valérie is used to men who are too timid to approach her, but not to men who ignore her. The man with dark hair and the eyes too close together is sitting alone at a table in the corner, where two cracked mirrors meet. He drinks wine and seems far away, his eyelids drooping over eyes as black as his hair, a sharp, cruel nose, and an uneven mustache. Vincenzo Perugia wears an open white shirt and a blue kerchief tied around his neck. The look could almost be affected but instead contributes to the overall look of disrepair, of a lack of interest in trivial things.

Valérie looks at him and decides that he's a man who knows what's important, and even more, what is not. Perugia takes a swig of his wine as if he were sitting in his own kitchen. Valérie understands that this gesture owes nothing to what's going on around him, to the Chien, to her.

Usually the men in the Cabaret du Faux Chien are afraid to come up to her. Valérie knows this—her secret is to appear just slightly inaccessible. She knows how to project being out of place, how to appear to be above where she finds herself, to find herself in places that are beneath her. In a salon at the Ritz she would be an interloper; here at the Faux Chien she is a young woman who has just mistaken her way home. Here at the Faux Chien she stands out among the fifteen or twenty other girls who haven't thought to make themselves stand out in any way, who thought that to belong one only needed to be like all the others.

Valérie stands with her back to the bar, her ass against the bar, her left foot in its kidskin boot hooked on the brass foot rail, her left knee moving back and forth under her silk skirt, her finger between her bright red lips, and she looks at him. To her, nothing stands between the two of them—the waiters in their leather waist-coats, the regulars who are singing and toasting and spinning promises of wispy futures, the smoky air, the song—everything dis-appears. All that is left is her on one side, leaning against the bar with her left boot tapping and her finger between her lips, and him, there in the corner between the two mirrors, not looking at her. Not seeming not to look at her so as to attract her with the difference of his indifference—just not looking at her at all.

Or a man who will give me a man's memories, she thinks—the memories of a man who doesn't have to wait for things to come to him.

His lips are thin, finely drawn. That fineness is one of the first things you notice about him, the manifestation of an overall fineness that at first glance he seems to embody. His lips are so thin that it looks like he doesn't have lips at all, just a slight downward curve to his mouth, the corners pulled down in an expression that could seem contemptuous, if you believed those lips would ever take the trouble to disparage anyone. Above the thin lips is a thin nose, slightly turned up, the oval nostrils ending in an almost sharp point; a nose seemingly not made for smell, too delicate to come in contact with the smells of this world.

He has a distinct, rounded jaw, and his high cheekbones have a slight flush to them, as if the air had finally managed to reach skin so white that it looks as if it had never been touched by anything before.

His long, lank hair is a perfect black—perhaps dyed—and he wears it pulled back, which elongates the shape of his head and face. His face has the aspect of a bust, a frozen version of Madame de Pompadour or Maintenon or some such character, though his eyes are opened wide, as if in surprise.

Valérie's eyes are also big and dark, open and round, as if surprised, though there is something in her look that says nothing can surprise her, and then something else that says perhaps. She can open her eyes very wide, as if they were out of her control, her way of showing that there's something within her that can open and close. Her way of saying, sometimes without wanting to, that she is not what she seems.

Then, when she can't avoid it, she opens her lips and we can see her teeth.

Beauty comes in many forms—who could have known.

He must know that I am what I am. He must see it; it's obvious. He knows but doesn't know. There are men who are frightened off.

This time, Valérie doesn't worry about his seeing her teeth. She thinks that the man with black hair must know what she is. He sees, and that is why he doesn't look—there are men whom it disgusts, who condemn those kinds of women. As if they themselves hadn't sold themselves out to some crook who makes them do whatever he wants. He must be one of those imbeciles who thinks he's all clean and proper because he works for the owner of a factory, a man I could make crazy if I wanted to, ruin if I wanted to, just as I could ruin him if I wanted, though I have no reason to waste my time on some sanctimonious ass with a dead brain full of stupid ideas about decency and cleanliness and honesty and order and country and how superior he feels even though he doesn't realize he sells himself out much more cheaply. She thinks he must be one of those poor, sad men who hide themselves in other people's ideas so they won't have to think for themselves; terrified of thinking for himself.

Vincenzo Perugia sees that alluring, strange, distant, almost-beautiful woman, and for a moment it seems as if she is looking at him. Valérie Larbin approaches him and hopes she can get her voice to come out like a whisper, even in all this noise: I don't want anything from you, I want to give you everything.

She readies her throat. Don't let him look at me.

Vincenzo Perugia looks at her with something she takes to be contempt—an excessive contempt, almost incomprehensible, as if it would be even greater if it could but didn't know how.

For their part, those women did not consider themselves to be altogether outside of the world. Their name reflected this duality: they were by definition half in and half out, with the constant chance that they would fall completely out and the constant hope of returning to be completely in. They were, in any case, women who had forsaken the path of fiancée-wife-mother, and if they did live by their sex, they did not do so according to the new worker-boss relations that their society now dictated almost everywhere. They were loose women, people said, living bitter lives, though they themselves thought that, compared to many others like them, their lives were better. Loose women, who did in their job what other women wanted to do for fun, and who, in that professionalization, lost any possibility of enjoying play as play, pleasure as pleasure, sex as love. Loose women whom you could simply leave, the way Tholomyes and his three friends left those four demis in *Les Misérables,* with the grandiose letter that ends by advising the four abandoned demis:

Mourn for us in haste and replace us with speed. If this letter rends you, then do the same to it. For almost two years we made you happy. We bear you no grudge for that.

She wanted him to return. Every night she looked for him at the Faux Chien without telling herself what she was doing. Every night her eyes scanned the faces that filled the place but she didn't see him and she didn't admit to herself that yes, she sought him. She did not dare to ask after him—that would have been a confession she wasn't yet prepared to make to herself. Then the next week she saw him again—he was wearing the same shirt or one identical to it, sitting at the same table, drinking the same thing. There was the threat again—identical.

Her white lace blouse has thin ribbons attached to its deep neckline, which she now ties closed, though this does little. Usually she leaves it open, showing her white breasts and the dark beauty mark at exactly the point where her tits begin, where the skin begins to curve out to form them. She ties the ribbons and walks over to the table in the corner between the two mirrors, seeing herself in those mirrors, advancing.

"You haven't told me your name."

"It's Vincenzo. Vincenzo Perugia."

Valérie takes a moment to try to pinpoint his accent but can't quite place it. He does not return the question.

"My name is Valérie."

"I thought so."

Juan María

1

SUDDENLY, I NO LONGER HAD a place. Overnight, I was taken out of what had always been my house, my life. Diego and Marianita hadn't wanted to say good-bye—either that or Don Manuel hadn't let them. And my mother didn't want to tell me why we were leaving. I suspected it was my fault, but I wasn't sure. Some years later she told me. Even then, when she told me, she didn't know, and I didn't tell her anything.

And so we moved to a tiny house in another barrio, to that little shack of Antonio's—Antonio, who was so good to my mother. I began to like staying at school more and more. And my mother no longer called me Bollino—I was now Juan María.

"Mamá, I'm going to look after you."
"Oh, yes? What are you going to do?"
"I don't know yet, Mamá, but don't you worry."
"One day, GianMaria, when you're grown up. Right now I have to sew all these shirts."

Best of all was Saturday. I liked Sunday less because it was only a part day, a day that began full of possibility but turned quickly to waiting for sundown, when my mother would take me back to the monks, and school. It wasn't that I didn't want to go, as I've said—more likely I even missed it. What really bothered me is that a day that began by promising such extraordinary things could end in such a routine and predictable way. But Saturdays did not suffer from this. Saturdays everything was still possible.

Usually on Saturday nights my mother and Antonio would go to the seamstresses' dance. My mother would wear her shawl and Antonio his broad-brimmed hat—every Saturday from the time

we went to live with Antonio. I stayed behind, alone in the house—
we can be kind and call it that: a house. That was my house then,
though it also wasn't.

The boy learned that he lived in a city—or town, or place—
which might have been any other, and learned that the fact he lived
in the city was pure chance, and most of all, that that city was not
the only place in the world, or rather, the city they called Rosario
was not the world. It's a shock; it comes as a shock to a boy when
he learns that the place where he lives is one among many, that he
might have lived in any number of other places. Not that he could
choose to live in other places, for that comes later—at first, the
shock is learning that things could be as they are or a thousand different ways. When it dawns on you that, as a result, everything
might be different. Or, said in words that a boy would not use: that
nothing is necessarily so.

For most of a boy's life, he thinks—though he doesn't really think, for this suggests too much, better to say that he lives
under the belief—that everything around him is decreed, necessary:
parents and places and teachers, his abilities, his toys. Later, bit by
bit—and then finally, one day, all at once—a boy understands that
these are single possibilities among infinite others. The unease that
this discovery can produce is epic—and only survivable thanks to
the short attention span and lack of imagination of so many boys.
Only they survive it.

So it is not the new beard or the voice that now skips, or the
pimples—it is this: the discovery of the intolerable caprice of their
situation that, when it comes, causes a boy to stop being a boy.
Though for the lucky ones, not even that.

"You said that you learned many things in that school."
"Yes, though I don't think they were the things they meant
to teach me."

"For example?"

"Don't you know, Newspaperman? Am I really going to have to spell every single thing out?"

He gripped my hand to guide it on its path around the paper that had once been white and that was now being marred by my markings. First I marveled at how easy it was to spoil that whiteness, the purity of the paper, or of anything else. Later, I marveled at how once it was spoilt, it could not be recovered. I marveled a lot during that time, when each marvel took an effort of imagination. I was a happy boy then, though who can say if I was still a boy.

The priest would grip my hand and guide it. This was drawing class: fifteen more or less filthy boys wearing grey smocks in a high-ceilinged schoolroom, cold in the way of a big room, with walls that had once been white and low desks of dark wood, their foreheads furrowed with effort as they copied the features of a Jesus embedded in his cross. One day, Little Stanislaus asked the Father if we could draw apples and pears and live people, by which I suppose he meant live women, though he said people. The Father replied that we could once we had learned how, but that for now, as ignorant as we were, all we could do was to try with the Lord's help to draw His images. All that year we drew Virgins in cloaks, Christs in loincloths; I suspect we could have gone on drawing them forever.

And the priest would grip my hand and guide it. He would position himself behind me—I would be seated at the high desk and he would stand immediately behind me, his cassock grazing my shirt—and the fug of his breathing would invade my air from behind, his face close to my shoulder, his bitter smell enveloping me. Even now, when I smell cheap tobacco I recall Father Franco's hand on mine, his firm hand, with the hair on the back, clasping my own. I liked it. Of course, I admired the way he was able to make a few unassuming strokes become the thing we were drawing: the long hair appearing, the lines of the extended arms, the two feet appearing, held by the spike, the drawn cheeks. But most of all I liked the firmness of his hand guiding mine across the sheet, making all decisions for me, propelling me along.

"What do you want to be when you grow up?"

"I don't know. What about you?"

"I don't know. My grandmother says if I'm lucky I might get to be a priest."

"A priest? You, a priest?"

"Yeah. She says that your whole life is set, everybody needs them, and they get the best wine."

"But priests can't have any girls."

"Why do you want to have girls?"

"I don't know. Father Franco says that they can ruin a man. They must be important."

"Hey, don't change the subject: what do you want to be when you grow up?"

"I don't want to grow up."

"What an idiot, you don't have a choice."

"Oh no?"

Seven boys surround him in the cloister of the school: "Juanita María, little Guinea pansy." The seven boys chant and dance slowly around him. "Juanita María, little Guinea pansy." The boy tells himself it's not even worth responding, that in their sin they'll find their penitence, that they're just a bunch of poor farm brutes, that he is so different from them, that they do it out of jealousy. That's what Father Franco would have told him. Pure jealousy—because he's so different, and Father Franco helps him and not them; he is the chosen one. Pure jealousy, he tells himself, because he's different and does the best drawings and sometimes Father Franco will make him a present of an apple or an orange, depending on the season, for after dinner. But not them, and the seven of them keep dancing around him and chanting "little Guinea pansy," keep on like that for days, perhaps weeks. They are like ghosts, chanting and dancing slowly, on the edge of silence. No one sees them. The Father in charge of supervising their break does not see, and the boy knows that if he were to tell anyone his life would become a complete hell. Then again afterwards, the chanting in the dormitory, when the Father on duty extinguishes the lamps and tells them that it's bedtime. Pure jealousy. An old, rotting apple left in his bed: pure jealousy.

"You mentioned that you were smaller because your mother had forged—"

"No, I was smaller because I was younger."

"That's what I meant—the other boys were twelve or thirteen and you were just ten."

"It was because my mother wanted to get me into that damned school and the priests had told her that they wouldn't take me before I was ten, so she managed to get someone to fake some papers of mine so that they said that I'd been born two years earlier. I gained two years with the stroke of a pen."

"Do you know who did that, how it was done?"

"I have no idea. I think it's strange that my mother managed to do something like that."

"It wasn't her style?"

"It's not that. I don't know where she would have found someone to do the forging."

"Perhaps she did it."

"Maybe. I hadn't thought of that."

Pure jealousy, and the anguish of nights: not knowing what he was going to find in his bed, one of thirty in that silent dormitory; of the daybreak; and of the days: being always on the edge, the silences, the feeling of an overall helplessness while he tried to think of a way he could escape. Beginning to ask himself what he had done so wrong and finding too many possible answers. Until one afternoon, as Father Franco grips his hand in his own—with his tobacco breath, his cassock brushing him, his other hand resting on his shoulder or neck—to draw the serene curves of a Virgin in a heavenly shawl, the boy discovers that it's not him, that neither he nor his classmates have understood. Suddenly, the boy discovers that it's not true that Father Franco has been holding his hand to lead it here and there—that he hasn't been doing it to him but that he would do it to anyone, to any eleven-year-old boy with down on his legs and a skipping voice and skin still soft. That it isn't him; it could be anyone.

It's something the boy doesn't yet know to call a revelation—or in lay terms: intuition. He understands without knowing—he simply understands. He understands—without knowing how, without words, without the showiness of ideas. In a flash he understands, without having to go through nouns, verbs, prepositions, words of time and place. He doesn't like the way this happens; he's disconcerted by the idea that this understanding happens to him, that he has not really played a part in it. He doesn't like the feeling that he's not in control, but now that he's learned in this uncontrolled way, he tells himself he must control the priest; he thinks he can. If the priest isn't doing what he does to him—if it is not to him specifically but to anyone—then it won't be him who will be using the priest, and as a result, he need not fear punishment, for he will have done nothing wrong. He has an enormous power and he vows to use it: he has discovered that he is not who he is, and that is power.

"Son, you're big now, all grown up. Now I can tell you the truth about your father."

"The truth, Mother? What about what you told me already?"

"I've told you what you could hear."

"Then don't tell me any more, Mother. Now I'll be the one to say what the truth is."

That his father was a gentleman like Diego and Mariana's father who lowered himself to marry his mother because he wanted to join his life to the life of the poor. A son of a bitch who got his mother pregnant and then ran back to the comfort of his rich family. An artist so exquisite that he decided that nothing was worth it and gave himself up to the cause, to meet his death however it should come. A naïf duped by that bastard Garibaldi. An idealist, who gave his life so that his son could one day be proud of him. An agent of the Pope, whose lie he lived out to its ultimate conclusion. Who says you have to have a father, anyway?

He considers all of this, and promises himself that one day when he's ready—or perhaps when he has no choice—he'll decide which is the true story of his father, even though his mother keeps insisting:

That his father was a hero. His mother insists on telling him the story of his father and she tells him over and over that he was a hero, that he died for what he believed, and that a con man left them—him and her—high and dry, out in the world without help or food or a future, with nothing. That his father abandoned them but didn't want to—he wanted the world to be a different place, dreamer that he was. And that it's easy to be a hero, a dreamer, a valiant knight like his father, dead like his father, gone like his father. That what is difficult is not being a hero but putting food on the table every day, and that poor Antonio was no hero or dreamer or anything like that but at least he kills himself working every day so that she—and of course him, too: the boy, not Antonio's boy either, not really poor Antonio's responsibility, as she won't stop pointing out—kills himself working just like her so that the three of them can live, can eat every day, can just stay alive in this world, which is the way it is, even though to your father it was all fantasy. And Juan María refuses to listen as his mother keeps repeating the same thing over and over and Antonio is never there when his mother tells him these things, or rather his mother never talks about his father when Antonio's around.

This happens many times: she talks while his stepfather is out, then he returns drunk, and some nights he hits her and the boy hides behind the curtain that divides their room in two and thinks, huddled behind the curtain, that one day he's going to bust that swine's head open. Then, still huddling, he hears Antonio crumble and start to cry and ask Juan María's mother to forgive him, sniffling, and he hears him promise her that he won't drink again, she'll see, and please to forgive him, and then that boy behind the curtain thinks that in spite of everything he's really a good man, just as well his real father is dead; that he's a happy boy, or at least a lucky boy.

2

"SO HE WAS THE ONE who gave you my name?"

"I don't know if I can tell you that."

"Then I can't really tell you anything, can I?"

"I understand."

He had a point. If I withheld this piece of information then there was no reason for him to tell me what I'd come to find out. This was an exchange, after all, and he at least wasn't going to pretend to give me any more than I was prepared to give him; he was not playing any games.

"Yes, it was him."

"That son of a bitch! It's been a long time; hard to believe he's still the same son of a bitch," he said, and he looked me in the face, defiant. I guessed that Yves Chaudron didn't normally look very defiant, but that afternoon he was trying it out. He didn't look like he used this kind of language regularly, either.

"Still a real son of a bitch!"

I realized then that he didn't know. I didn't think it was time to tell him yet.

"Yes, he was the one who told me about you," I told him, and it was true, even though it had been some time ago. Yves Chaudron leaned back in his flowered armchair. He had just turned sixty but he looked older, his thin body too thin, no meat on him, deeply wrinkled, his features too sharply drawn.

"And you really want me to tell you the story?"

"No. Well, yes, but actually I'd prefer it if you would first tell me a little about yourself."

"About me? Why would you want to know anything about me?"

"It's important. If I'm going to tell the whole story I'll need to know as much as possible about all the main characters."

"Sure, the main characters. But I'm only a minor character. I was always just one of the minor characters."

"You were quite a forger in your time."

"I was no forger," he said, and he looked toward the kitchen door. It was as if he were practicing—no doubt he practiced every day of his life; that's what they call marriage.

The door opened and his wife appeared with a wooden tray: two cafés au lait and a plate of pastries.

"Don't even look at the pastries, Yves. They're for the gentleman," she said. I took her accent to be Polish or Russian. It matched her round face and her round and watery eyes. She was a good ten years younger than he was and had just begun to go grey. Later Chaudron would tell me that they had married more than ten years earlier, when Ivanka—he called her Ivanka—had arrived in Paris on the run from the Soviets and without a penny, willing to give herself to the first man who could provide food and shelter. He was nudging fifty then, and he thought this might be his last chance to secure himself an old age in which he might actually be well cared for.

"And you know what? To my big surprise she turned out to be the perfect wife. She doesn't bother me, she knows her place, and I don't bother her too much. In the beginning I did want certain things, but later I learned to adjust," he would tell me, much later. For the moment, he continued stirring his café au lait; staring at it as if nothing else existed.

"I was never a forger."

"Monsieur Chaudron, please excuse me if I offended you somehow, but . . ."

"But nothing. If you can't call things by their proper name, then we're not going to have anything to talk about."

My punishment was another five minutes of silence in

which he sipped his café au lait and showed me who was boss. But I was used to this kind of situation. I know from experience that someone without much excitement in his life—a nobody—can rarely resist the temptation of an interview, of having a real reporter focus all his attention on listening to him.

"You were telling me you knew Valfierno in Buenos Aires."

"I didn't tell you that!"

"I think you did. What were you doing in Buenos Aires? You were born quite close to here, weren't you?"

"Close depending on how you look at it."

Chaudron seemed capable of qualifying every single point. He was a man used to weighing pros and cons, to considering every possible nuance for as long as necessary—sometimes, it seemed, his entire life.

"But yes, it's not far—a few kilometers northeast of Lyon. I grew up in a family of glaziers. My father, when he saw that I could draw, decided that if I learned a little more I could help him on the job, so he sent me to school in Lyon."

I'd like to be able to say that the start of Chaudron's painting career was exciting and full of hope, and even successful, or at least promising, and that but for his rejection at the hands of stuffy, tradition-bound art institutes, or a personal disgrace, or the demands of a rapacious woman—but I can't. From the very beginning, Chaudron told me, he knew that he would be a copyist. He used that word, "copyist," and he accompanied it with a faint smile.

"You know that I had a stammer then," he told me, as if that explained a great many things. Upon starting school—as soon as he had his first brush in his hand, he said—he discovered that he was quite incapable of reproducing anything in three dimensions: a room, a body, a face, two apples, the Ródano hills. If, on the other hand, he wanted to reproduce a drawing, a painting, a tapestry, then there wasn't a single shape or color or texture that he couldn't master.

"Some people can copy certain things, other people other

things. Some things have more prestige and some have less," he told me. And that anyway the world had one too many dimensions.

"And too many people who believe they've invented something new. Not me, thank God."

Chaudron referred to himself in the past tense; some people think of themselves that way. Chaudron had trouble in school. His attempts at drawing models failed time after time, and his adviser threatened him with expulsion. Professor Falaise was an old alcoholic who somehow still managed to pass himself off as a painter with a future, one of those fools, Chaudron told me, who still think the world owes them something when it's quite clear that in fact they are the ones with all the debts.

The young Yves Chaudron dedicated himself to studying his professor in detail. He watched him paint and asked him questions, learned to imitate his walk and gestures, drank the same Pernods that the old professor drank and all the while painted pleasant fields full of cows and cowlike peasants for the annual show. When he was finally able to conjure up the old professor's memories without meaning to, he began to paint one of his landscapes. It didn't imitate any one painting in particular, but it had something of all of them.

Chaudron finished the painting, and one afternoon in March he crept into Falaise's studio and left the painting tucked in amongst the others. The effect was remarkable. The fake Falaise was hard to distinguish from the real ones except that it was in some undefinable way better. As Chaudron told it, Falaise must have noticed this, for that year he submitted the fake Falaise to the annual show.

For the first time in his life, after more than thirty tries, Falaise won first prize.

"Sir, what you have done is criminal."

"What I have done?"

"Yes, Professor: to pass off someone else's work as your own."

"What are you talking about? The impertinence!"

"I'm talking about the landscape that I painted and that just won first prize in the show."

Chaudron told me that Falaise denied everything right up until Chaudron produced an irrefutable proof. He didn't want to tell me what the proof was, but he did say that the Professor immediately changed his argument:

"You're the criminal, Chaudron, to forge a painting!"

"I forged nothing, Professor. I simply painted as if I were you, that is all. And you gained by it. That is the crime."

"Don't be a fool, Chaudron, the crime is yours for what you've done and because I am your professor and I say so!"

"If this comes out, Professor, you're finished."

"You as well, Chaudron."

They had reached that point in chess when neither player can make a move without forfeiting the game—the danger of every con. A few days later Falaise told him that he could put him in touch with a copyist in Paris who could give him work. It was a good offer—if he didn't accept, Falaise said, he would turn Chaudron's life into a hell.

"You don't know what it was like for a timid kid like me to think about going to Paris. I was nervous, terrified. But I couldn't see any other way out."

Falaise gave him the money for the train, and Chaudron left one morning without saying good-bye to anyone. In spite of everything, he now dreamed of conquering the city. But Falaise's friend the copyist wouldn't give him the time of day.

"I went hungry. Do you know what it is to go hungry, really hungry?"

I was about to tell him that yes, I did, but thought at the last minute that this might earn me another rebuff. I've learned to be careful, especially in interviews. An interview is a contrived situation—both sides pretend to be having an amiable conversation when in fact their real interests are quite different, and often at odds.

"No, the truth is I don't. What happened next?"

"What happened next was that for months I didn't know what to do. You see, I couldn't go back to my village because my father would have been furious."

"Furious?"

"Well, I don't know; that's what I thought then. And I couldn't stay in Paris. I couldn't find any work. Paris was full of good copyists; there was nothing for me in that terrible place. I decided to emigrate."

Ivanka was running a duster across the shop window and appeared engrossed in her work. But I had the impression that she wanted to hear the story that her husband had never told her. Chaudron didn't look at her. Or me. His eyes were fixed on a distant point, as if he needed to look far, very far, to see what he was telling me.

"Why Argentina?"

"What do you mean, why? Have you ever emigrated? You know how these things happen, Mr. Reporter? It's not like you sit down and think and figure out where you're going to go. Or like you read about different places in guides and magazines and then, after careful consideration, choose one over another. How do I know why? Because I saw a picture in a magazine. Because someone you meet in a café tells you about this place where their cousin is doing real well."

"But—if you don't mind my asking again—why Argentina in particular?"

"Don't you know anything? Lots of people were going there then. Or do you think the place just appeared now? Even then, almost forty years ago, you could see it was going to be big."

Chaudron arrived at the port of Buenos Aires in 1898. He was twenty-five.

Ivanka had stopped pretending. She stared at us now, the duster idle in her hand, her eyes as big as saucers. I realized that

Chaudron was using me to talk to her. Maybe he wanted to comfort her: telling the story of his emigration was a way of telling her that he had also been through humiliation like hers.

"And it was there that you met him?"

"No, not then. Years went by."

"What happened in those years?"

"That I'm not going to tell you."

"Go ahead, tell me. We have plenty of time."

"I don't think I will."

Now Chaudron was looking at her, too. He had stopped looking at me and spoke directly to her, although in a very quiet voice, causing her to lean toward him to hear what he was saying. When he'd stopped talking, he directed his gaze at the ceiling for a bit. Then he turned again to me.

"You're not going to remember me."

"What do you mean? How can you say—?"

"Listen to me; I know how it is—I've been learning my whole life. You won't remember me. No one ever remembers me. Maybe you'll remember this house, or my wife, or this chair, but not me. No one ever remembers me. Maybe you'll even remember these words I'm saying. We can prove it: remember this now, and in a few days, maybe next week—whenever it is—try to remember my face, or one of my gestures. I'm telling you, no one ever remembers me. That's how I could be so many others: Falaise, Ribera, Zurbarán. That's how I could even be Leonardo."

Having said this, Chaudron fell silent. I fell silent, too: it was a stupid duel of silences. He won—I asked him again if that was when he met Valfierno. But I suspected that he was right, that I would need to write down all my impressions of him as soon as I left that house.

"So. You want me to tell you how I met him."

"Please."

"I can't tell you. But I'd like to explain who Valfierno was then: he was a panderer. What do you call it?—he was a pimp."

Chaudron looked at me with the hint of a smile on his face: the player who launches an attack from an unexpected corner of the board. I didn't know whether to believe him, or rather, I didn't believe him at the time. Valfierno had not told me this—and I still believed his version of the story. Moreover, Chaudron had every reason to be angry, to resent him.

"But I don't want to say bad things about that son of a bitch. When all is said and done I owe this house to him. If it hadn't been for the whole business of the *Mona Lisa,* I could never have bought it. Really in the end I owe him everything," he said, and then fell silent. It was clear that he didn't know. If they hadn't seen each other in all these years, he had no reason to know that Valfierno was dead.

3

HE DISCOVERS THAT WHEN FATHER Franco rubs him hard it's not the same as when his prick gets hard for no reason. He discovers that it's also different when he himself takes hold of it in his hand and squeezes it and strokes it and goes faster and faster until he explodes. He discovers—actually, a neighbor tells him—that you can lose it in another person's flesh, and it scares him, at first it really scares him. He tells him that a piece of his body has to go into the body of a near stranger, and that scares him, too. For months he shies away from the invitations from the other guys in his class to go out with them to the Mecha Ranch and become a man. Though they are just brutes, he has to do something; he knows that it can't continue like this. He is fourteen now and once again the target of ridicule from the boys who say the most savage things that come into their heads. They say that Father Franco has convinced him, that now he's one of those. They warn him: be careful, he'll do us all! They tell him he's a real, first-class, ass-class fag now. He doesn't believe them, but he starts to question himself, and he delays—he's still scared of losing that part of himself in someone else's body. Until finally Ruano takes pity on him: "Juanma, don't be an idiot, it's not a big deal, Juanma!" "I don't know, Ruano—how do I know that? I don't know anything!" And Ruano—out of mercy? out of scorn? out of pride?—offers him an out: "You know I'm having it with Dorita, right? Next time I take her out to the field you follow us—dead quiet, and slow—and you'll see everything. You'll see—you won't be scared no more."

He feels as if he's walking on a tightrope. A branch snaps, and he shrinks back, but they go on, unaware, occupied only with each other, with their rubbing against each other as they go, tasting what's to come. They stop and hide themselves behind a berry bush, and him on the other side and the two of them on the ground, and her on the ground and Ruano on top of her and he's pulling down her slip and unbuttoning his pants, and he grabs his dick and with his hand around his dick he searches between her legs for her opening. Juan María watches them, afraid to breathe, afraid to miss any vital detail. He watches while Ruano finds her opening and starts in, moving rhythmically, like the rhythm of the hand but with his whole body, forward and backward and forward and then suddenly harder, more roughly, more quickly, forward and backward and forward, and watching, his eyes get bigger, are like two saucers, moons, tits—eyes straining to get everything, to learn everything push by push, so that later, alone, he can replay for himself every single movement, sound, face.

Quiet again—later that night, in his own bed and quiet once again—he thinks he will be able to do it himself. And that Sunday he goes with the boys to the Mecha Ranch and they come back one stronger; he comes back one of them.

4

HIS HEAD LIES DEEP IN a pillow of goose down, his body on the soft mattress. His lips are apart, his eyes half-closed, and his blue silk robe open. Valérie, on all fours, plays with his cock. She leans on her elbows and knees, her ass high and ripe, milky-skinned, splayed with its pores and tiny blue veins; juicy. From it, her back swoops down and then up in a great curve to her head—a tumble of dark hair like thick waves—which is buried between Valfierno's thighs.

She goes to work on his cock, cradling it in her left hand, squeezing it with her lips, licking it with her tongue—great loud wet licking. In a low voice, Valfierno groans and watches, especially the quivering of those tits, which hang low now like an udder, suspended from the chest; her slight belly hanging down as well.

Her ass sticking up, her tits hanging down, two and two, flesh and flesh, white and white, a balance to be broken over and over. Valfierno watches her ass rise up as her head descends further. Being sucked off is sex without working, he thinks, without effort—either a pure gift or a business transaction, and his eyes close as her lips close on his cock. As he closes his eyes, he gives himself over for a moment to ecstasy, the promise of ecstasy, but no—he grabs a handful of her hair and pulls her head away from him and covers himself with the robe.

"Wait, wait."

Valérie straightens up and wipes the back of her hand across her mouth; she looks at him, her lips full and swollen.

"What is it? What do you want?"

"Not me—I want to know what it is you want."

"Marqués: isn't it obvious?"

"No, I mean from me. What is it you want from me?"

Valérie remains looking at him, her mouth agape. He can see her teeth, crooked, yellowing. Valfierno tries not to look.

"You sound like something out of a cheap magazine, or more like one of those naughty posters you can get for fifteen centimes!" she tells him, forcing a smile.

"Don't play around, Valérie. Women only suck men for love or money, and with me, love is too much and the money's too little."

"Did you ever consider that I might like it?"

"Don't be stupid, Valérie. We all know how this works."

Valérie looks at him and sees that he's struggling to control his hatred. Valfierno knows he picked the worst moment to come out with this, but for days now it has nagged at him, bothered him. In the beginning, his nights with Valérie were like so many others, often much better than the others. But lately he has noticed a change: she attends to him too much. It is no longer the equal exchange of two willing bodies; she has become his slave, an awkward geisha, and Valfierno's suspicions are aroused.

Very slowly, he repeats: "I ask you again, Valérie: what is it you want from me?"

Suddenly, he understands, though "understanding" is not the word. He knows, in that inexplicable way that one knows certain things, that he is old for her, soft and affected; a prissy, middle-aged fool. He knows too, that that ass is looking for something in particular. That he was stupid to think that because he had no money to give her she wanted nothing from him. How stupid he was; how could he have believed that?

"Nothing, Marqués. Nothing you can't give me. Nothing that'll cost you even a penny, don't worry," she tells him, teasing now. Valfierno's own fears prevent him from taking the high ground.

"Don't screw around, Valérie," he says, unable to come up with better.

"I already told you: I'd like us to work together."

"You're just being ridiculous."

"No, listen—at least listen. There's a lot of money in it."

"You're completely insane."

"No more than you. And this is the sanest thing I've ever said. Maybe the only sane thing."

"And what makes you think that anything like this would interest me?"

Right away Valfierno comes up with an answer he doesn't want to consider: what would interest me is that it could be a way to keep her. But I mustn't love, I don't want to love. If she uses me I can use her, too, for my own ends, he thinks, though he knows it's not that easy. He wishes she would desire him; he wishes he wouldn't desire her. It's not that easy. She goes on talking to him with his cock in her hand, his defused cock.

"Come on. Marqués, don't say anything, just listen for a moment. Listen like you were listening to some silly girl's story."

"That I can do."

"If that makes you feel better."

"My love . . ."

"Your love. Perhaps more, Marqués. It's very simple: do you remember my telling you about that man the other day, the one who works at the Louvre?"

"Yes, I think so."

"Don't pretend, Marqués, I saw that you paid attention. It's quite simple: I have the in, and you have the contacts. All we need is a plan."

"A plan for what?"

"Marqués, please," she says, and takes his spent cock in her mouth. Valfierno looks up at the ceiling. He feels himself hardening and tries to resist. He will show her that she cannot make him do anything he doesn't want to. Valfierno extricates himself from her mouth, gets up from the bed, and ties his robe. He understands now why he has never let himself undress completely in front of her. Him so old, close to fifty. How could he have been such an idiot?

"Don't you realize? This could be the chance of our lives."

"Our lives?"

"My life. Your life."

Valfierno forces a smile. The best way to get through a bad moment is to move to the next one.

"Do you really think your friend could be useful?"

"Not for many things, it's true, but yes—for some things that you don't much care about, and also maybe for taking a couple of paintings."

"And what on earth makes you think that I'd be interested in, as you say, 'taking a few paintings'?"

"Valfierno, please. Don't. Are you interested or not? You don't have to tell me now, but think about it, please. Don't be silly. A chance like this comes only once in your life."

Perrone

1

It cost me dearly to stop being Bollino—Juan María, too. And still more, later, to understand why I'd done it. Back then, I still wanted that kind of thing—reasons, I mean.

A father can be either a path or an obstacle for a man, but not both. If he passes his own achievements on gently, he can be a path, but if his history becomes a burden, then he will be an obstacle. He will be a path if his own failures offer the secrets to their avoidance, an obstacle if they loom still as dangers. The burden can be to do what the father wanted to do but couldn't, or to do what you think the father wanted you to do, or to become your father to take on his dreams.

In fact, a man with the name Juan María Perrone shows up as having been arrested in Rosario for belonging to a group of anarchists some sources referred to as "Los Errantes"—the Wanderers. The police registry shows this Juan María Perrone to be nineteen, which coincides with the age of our man, as does the name, if we consider that he could still have been using his mother's name then.

The file gives few details about the circumstances, but we know that the arrests came in response to a bomb plot against the offices of the newspaper *El Municipio*. The homemade bomb exploded, dislodging the plaster around the door of the large house that served both as the newspaper's offices and the home of the owner. The plot appeared to be linked to a demand to make Sunday a day of rest. Rosario's stores and businesses were open every day of the year for fourteen to sixteen hours a day, and workers worked every one of those hours. The more activist unions—including most of the anarchists—were trying to get the workday shortened. But every attempt to reduce the length of the workday was opposed by the store owners—and by *El Municipio*—as an attack on commerce. The paper was a declared enemy of the unions and was also suffering its own financial difficulties. Some said that the owner had been trying to muster the support of his own kind—Rosario's well-to-do bourgeoisie—by showing himself to be a victim of the anarchists. Many more saw the plot simply as another criminal attack by anarchists.

For his alleged role in this attack, a Juan María Perrone was arrested, along with various accomplices. It seems likely that this is our man, though later, Perrone shows up as having died in 1888, which at the very least raises some doubts.

"Was it you?"

"What do you mean, 'you'?"

"Valfierno, please—don't play dumb."

"Becker, we could go on like this forever. Just because you lack subtlety doesn't mean that everyone else does."

According to him, he was dead, and it could be true. Actually, he claims that Juan María Perrone is dead, and that's probably true, though he undoubtedly suffered for a few more years. There are deaths that last a lifetime; others are quicker, more definitive.

The cockroach climbs up the flaking plaster of the wall. The youth tries to concentrate: up the flaking plaster of the wall. To climb up, to ascend, as Father Franco would have said, to climb, to scale, to mount, to reach great heights. He tries to become the cockroach, to imagine the cockroach without feelings, or meaning, to climb just because. He tries to think of the cockroach not suffering, to close his eyes and see the cockroach in his mind, to close his ears and hear in his mind the scratch of the cockroach's climb up the flaking plaster wall and not the screams. "Worthless little crook, you'll talk, everybody talks here. Miserable scum, wait till you see how you talk." As if the screams were far away. As if the screams were just a memory. As if he could simply fall to the floor, a cockroach, or change direction or retrace his steps, a cockroach. "Little shit, you are going to talk." To be a cockroach, just climbing.

"Me, Señor? What do you want to know?"

"There are some things you don't need to understand, Newspaperman. Just hear."

"Which things?"

"I thought that I had to be Bonaglia."

"Bonaglia?"

"Bonaglia. Truly my father's son."

It feels like the very end of the night, of what has been a very long night. The youth is bleeding from several wounds on his face. He is tied to a chair. His shirt is ripped, stained with blood, spittle, mucus. His black hair is matted, his eyes blackened by blows, the pain from his hand twisting his face in a grimace. "Everyone talks here, scum; you'll talk too, little shit." "Me, Señor? What do you want to know?" "Don't play the moron—the same thing we've been asking you from the beginning," says a monster of a man with stiff hair like horsehair, and he asks his henchman to bring him another cup of yerba maté. "Yes, sir, since the beginning of time," he says, "or do you think this is going to go on forever, little shit?" He slurps the maté and then spits on the floor of uneven tile and greenish mucus. "I said a maté, Ramirez, not this crap." The youth looks for his cockroach; he hasn't seen it for a while. His neck hurts when he tries to move his head.

"It's unbelievable the way these punks try to be heroes. Imbeciles! Hurry up with that maté, Ramirez, we're waiting!"

The flames of the lamps flicker and the youth's mouth trembles. He's afraid that once again they'll yell the same things and hit him the same way, and he can't think anymore, not even about his cockroach, he is too terrified now even to envy it.

"Me, Señor? I already told you everything. I placed the bomb. I did it. I placed it, I told you: the twenty-second, Sunday, at six in the morning, right after the watchman made his rounds."

"Do you take us for retards, you little scum? You think we don't know you couldn't have done it on your own? What's going on with that maté, Ramirez, the maté! You're not even really part of the group, are you, you little creep? You hardly know them—we just grabbed you so you'd give up the German, you little moron! Fucking Ramirez!"

"It was me, Señor, I put the bomb there. You don't believe me but it's true, Señor."

If only he could be convincing, thinks Juan María, if he could just sound like he believed what he was saying. He is afraid even of thinking the truth, of remembering details about what really happened, because he can't believe that the police won't hear him if he thinks it, and he doesn't know if he can think in a voice low enough that he won't be heard.

His hands are crossed and tied behind the back of his chair. His eyes, cheeks, lips all burn with pain. The monster tells him that he's going to ask him one more time, that he's going to give him one more chance because he's a good guy. Juan María considers not going on with his story—he doesn't know if he can keep it up. He thinks he can, he hopes he can, but he doesn't know, he can't be sure and then the monster whips, snaps, smashes, crunches his head back, no word able to describe how his big hand demolishes his face, buries itself in his face and snaps his head backward like a whip, producing unimaginable pain.

With extraordinary effort Juan María brings his head back upright and says once more, "I was the one who placed the bomb; I did it."

And the monster, "Fucking Christ! Tell me where the German

is! Tell me what happened, don't be a moron! You imbecile, don't you realize that if you don't, you're going to get yourself killed?"

He says "get yourself killed" as if he's talking about an external force—death? simple gravity?—that operates inevitably beyond will or desire. The monster tells him, "You're going to get yourself killed," and he thinks that if he dies now his friends will know that he was strong and resisted until the end, that they can rely on him, that now for sure they'll know that he's trustworthy. And Don Manuel will know that he died fighting injustice and his class, and his mother will think he died like his father and she'll hate him. Once again she won't have understood anything, he thinks, once again. And how easy it would all be if I could just kill myself, if I knew how to do that, how easy . . .

"Kid, I'm going to ask you one last time—Jesus, I've had it with this!"

It would be easy if I could just kill myself, except that for that I'd have to think something important right before. If he knew he was going to die he would have to think of something important right before, he thinks, and once again he tells the man, "I did it, Señor, I already told you, I was the one who armed the bomb."

"Oh yes? Why don't you tell us how you did that," says the monster, willing to amuse himself now, and the youth spins a tale filled with holes and errors of fact, and the monster has fun asking him for details, which the youth makes up, in haste, badly, inventing sloppy details until the monster finally gets bored. "Ramirez, get me a cigarette, he's boring me," he says, and with a sudden, violent kick he sends the chair flying with the youth in it, and it crashes to the tiled floor, the uneven tiled floor, the sickening smack of those tiles against his side, and once on the floor, more kicks. "So you think you can just tell us any old crap, you little scum? What do you take us for?" And on the floor, with his bruised and beaten arms over his broken face, his injured, lacerated, broken face, he thinks— amazingly, he is still thinking of these things; incredible that he thinks of these things now—that it was strange that the best defense of liberty was to lie like a criminal. Though badly, like a stupid criminal; he would have to do better.

"Were you ever in such a position of helplessness, Newspaperman? So vulnerable? So much at someone else's mercy?"

"No, I don't believe I ever was, Marqués."

"I trust it never happens to you. Except now, perhaps. Now that you have to listen to everything I'm telling you and you don't know what to make of it."

"Is that how it seems to you?"

"What about you? How does it seem to you?"

One thing kept occurring to him afterward—actually two. First, that not once throughout his entire interrogation did he think about the famous cause of liberty, but rather about the admiration, or at least the respect that he would earn in the eyes of his few accomplices, whom he considered his friends, who were defending that famous cause in the Argentine city of Rosario in 1884. He thought a little about Don Manuel and his kind of people, but most of all he thought about his father—that if his father had been able to see him in that moment he would have been proud. It surprised him to think this. He'd never thought much about his father before—his real father, a man now dead whom he never knew—as someone who might have thought about him, had feelings about him: pride, disdain, sorrow. He'd always thought of him as someone who thought and felt only about himself, until that night, and from then on. And one other thing: that he could never again let them catch him so unprepared.

Even then I knew that one day I would have trouble remembering all of that. That I would try very hard to forget it, and then one day I would try again to remember it. I suppose memory is something you can manage; I'm sure that later it gets away from ordinary men—those who don't know how to manage their memories. I knew that even then, though I had not finished understanding it all.

"I don't believe that it is possible to become rich without being ruthless; a reasonable man will never make a fortune. In order to get rich, you must be fixated on one single, immutable idea: the desire to make a fortune. And to make that fortune you have to be a usurer, a shark, obsessed, tough—a killer. To bully in particular the weak and the small. And when you have amassed your mountain, you can climb to the top and from your peak survey the valley of the miserable that you have made," reads the youth, alone in his cell with the candle flickering, and he is visited with a rare smile.

Sullen—you have to appear sullen.

He learns that the German has also been arrested. A thief from Rosario tells him this, not one of his supposed colleagues. A thief who took pity on him, who also tells him that the anarchists are in no doubt about who gave the German up. He knows that the only way to prove to them that it wasn't him is to show them who did do it, and he vows to try. He has a suspicion and wonders how he can prove it. He knows it will be difficult, but also that if he doesn't his life will not be worth living.

He learns to seem sullen. In the public areas—the cafeteria, the yard where prisoners spend two hours in the morning and two hours in the afternoon—he gets in the habit of appearing sullen. He walks with his back very straight, his legs extended, erect, trying to make himself taller. Later, he will remember this as ridiculous, but at the time his main preoccupation was his bearing.

For several days he is determined to figure out what he has to do. It takes him that long to realize that he no longer makes decisions, and that for a long time he will make almost no decisions at all. He despairs. His muscles tense up by themselves, the effort of relaxing them making them tenser still. He is in despair. He must appear sullen.

The prison he's been taken to—the National Penitentiary— is too big. In the suburbs of Buenos Aires, it is a huge building, re- cently inaugurated, with battlements and towers and all the latest prison advances. When he first saw it—the only time, when he could look at it from a distance as he arrived in the horse-drawn wagon, surrounded and guarded—he had a moment of content- ment at the idea of living inside this great medieval castle that looked so much like the photographic plates Father Franco used to show him. Immediately afterward, as soon as the great metal gates opened and then closed, the castle became a series of corridors, yards, and his cell, above all his cell. Prison is no more than the re- duction of possibilities to the minimum possible. A form of perfect concentration, where the outside world can't distract you. In prison—as he came to think much later—the world becomes some- thing each inmate can invent as he wishes, according to whim and personal taste, something that does not present a threat or impose any unnecessary reality. In prison, reality is so small, so spare that there is a lot of room left over. Prison, and especially his cell, is the ultimate framework, the model for all invention. In that cell, the youth—though he wouldn't realize it until many years later—began to construct the person he would later become: his persona.

But for the moment he only knows how to look sullen. It bothers him—suffocates, even scares him—the barely restrained en- ergy he feels during the spells in the yard with dozens and dozens of other delinquents like him. Delinquents like him, he repeats to him- self, tasting the sound of those empty words.

In the yard he talks only to the Frenchman, who some call Bernardo Dasset, others León Daván, still others Juan Pablo. The Frenchman is about thirty, and is described by the police as "being in charge of all the French thieves in the city, who work as hotel waiters, painters, or coachmen, and act as his spies. He maintains several addresses to avoid becoming known to the police. He dresses elegantly, is well mannered, and has refined tastes." He does seem to have refined tastes. He must have, to be able to enjoy Juan María's various qualities—the shy look, delicate features, lean buttocks, that wariness caged animals have that makes them mistrust almost everything. Dasset/Daván doesn't seem to care, or perhaps cares especially, perhaps it excites him. He takes advantage of his standing in the prison to visit Juan María in his cell three times a week—an hour or two, never more. The youth cares less about it all—his submission to the inmate, the inmate's cock in his ass, the inmate's saliva on his neck and shoulders, his cock in his mouth, having to bend to his desires—than he thought he would. He never reaches the point of enjoying it, but it doesn't bother him. It's one of the ways in which that sparse reality claims your rights without bothering to acknowledge them.

Dasset/Daván visits him, guides him, forces him to submit—"submit" being, far too much, the word—and teaches him how good manners and the right name can be critical tools. He also teaches him to read his French books—this is their deal: in exchange for what I want and what you can't refuse me, I'll teach you French, what little use it is—to recognize some of his own overlooked qualities, and, no doubt without intending to, to simulate pleasure. Consequently, he comes to understand that there is nothing that can't be faked; that you can feign anything.

"So what? If it wasn't me it would be someone else, someone who wouldn't be as good to you as I am. Don't be stupid—*bête*—*chéri*. In here, nothing is free. There are the protectors and the protected and nothing else, and you are nothing without a good protector. Now, enough words, *chéri*. The time for talking is over for today."

"Why? Who says?"

"What is this 'who says'? Your protector says—the only voice there is."

⅜

Almost every night in his cell his fantasies accompany his hand. Never about him, or the Frenchman, or María, always about Ruano and Dorita. Once in a while—by accident, without meaning to, immediately remorseful—he thinks of Mariana, who must by now be all grown up, a proper blonde. There is little room in prison for blondes.

"There are natures that are purely contemplative and quite removed from action, but that can nonetheless be sparked into motion by some mysterious impulse, with a speed that appears quite alien. Like the man who, afraid of encountering bad news in his mail, paces fearfully for hours in front of his door before daring to go in. Or who will leave a letter unopened for two weeks, or who delays six months before finally resigning himself to doing what he should have done years ago—they are thrown abruptly into action by an irresistible force, like an arrow loosed from a bow. A friend of mine will light his cigarette next to a barrel of gunpowder just to see, to know, to tempt fate, just to spark his energy, to play, to know the pleasures of feeling anxiety, for nothing, whim, out of boredom," he reads, alone in his cell with the candle flickering, and he finds again that rare smile. Perhaps it's at that moment that he decides he doesn't give a damn what all of those people—he says "those people" —think he is.

His mother's letters are few and say little—that her eyesight is weak, that she doesn't feel well in general, that poor Antonio is drunk a lot, and why did he do what he did, what they say he did? From time to time he thinks of the necklace. And hopes there will be fewer letters. At last they stop.

"You said that you learned a lot in jail."
"I learned that in order to change anything you first have to

change yourself, to become someone who has the power to change things."

"Anything else?"

"There were other things."

For his involvement in the attack on the offices of Rosario's *El Municipio* newspaper, a man with the name Juan María Perrone served a four-year sentence in the National Penitentiary. When he was released, he was given a change of used but clean clothes by the Women's League and a letter from his stepfather announcing the death of his mother. Newly free, he was twenty-three or perhaps twenty-four and was to learn, among other things, his real name.

I was searching. I know I did things that I wish I could forget, but I remember them—far too much. What's the point of forgetting things that are easy to forget?

2

❧ "WHAT DO YOU KNOW ABOUT *La Joconde?*"

"What?"

"You heard me, Yves. What do you know about the *Mona Lisa?*"

"That's not what I heard—*Joconde, Mona Lisa* . . ."

"You know the strangest thing about all of this, Yves? It's that from time to time I find myself almost liking the way you believe your role in life is to annoy your fellow man. I've come to think that perhaps this will end up being my role, too."

"What an honor, Marqués. As you yourself say: you become your neighbor."

"Enough of this, Yves. Now I'm serious—what do you know about the *Mona Lisa?*"

"The same as everyone else."

They speak to each other in Spanish. Yves Chaudron's accent mixes French *r*'s and a Río Plata lilt. Eduardo de Valfierno blends the pure Argentine with a Frenchified rhythm.

"Which is?"

"Nothing."

Yves Chaudron never knows anything—on principle. It has been some time now since he decided on a path of ignorance, and he has stuck to this scrupulously. Especially since he became executor of Valfierno's schemes and ideas, a partnership that affords him the ability to be, as never before, the hand—and a most able one—directed by another's mind. The perfect situation for him.

"You'll need to find out soon enough."

"About the *Mona Lisa?*"

"What do you think we're talking about?"

"If you won't tell me . . ."

Chaudron tails off and then does something that for him seems like an abrupt gesture—he wipes each joint of his fingers with a rag soaked in turpentine. Valfierno wrinkles his nose at the smell. Centuries could pass, he thinks, resignedly, and the smell of turpentine will still always remind him of that priest who was not what he seemed. Chaudron dries his hands on his white painter's smock and looks at him for a moment before speaking.

"Eduardo, we need to do something. Since we've been in Paris, the business . . ."

"Let me remind you that you were the one who convinced me to come."

"Me?"

Chaudron looks around him with an expression of Who, me? To come here? The studio is bright in the morning light but very small and crowded: half a dozen half-finished paintings—mostly religious scenes in the Spanish baroque style of Ribera or Zurbarán—two easels, palettes, little knobs of paint, three small tables crowded with brushes and more paint, a tottering bookcase with a few books on art, and a narrow cot in the far corner.

"That is something we are not going to talk about."

"Right. It's not worth it."

"Valfierno—I'm worried."

"Have you ever been anything else?"

"Please, Valfierno. I am really worried. We need to do something. Have you seen how the world is now? It's unbelievable: streetcars, the Métro, electric light in houses, phonographs, automobiles. Soon we won't be able to do anything."

"Have you been drinking already? It's morning! What do aeroplanes have to do with us?"

"It's obvious, Señor Marqués. You should be the first one to see it. Soon they're going to have machines that will analyze paintings, the materials, I don't know what. We're not going to be able to do this anymore. We have to do a big one before it becomes impossible, Eduardo. Progress is going to kill us—we'll end up in a museum."

"What was that?"

"We're going to end up in a museum."

"That's not a bad idea. I have to think about that. In a museum."

"I'm serious, Eduardo."

"So am I."

Valfierno loosens his black bow tie and takes a look at the paintings Chaudron is working on. They are perfect, copies that cannot be improved, and once again it surprises him that his copyist could be so unambitious for himself, that someone of his ability should be content just to be Valfierno's hands. And once again he asks himself why. It has to be because he is a copyist, that is the word. I am the forger, he thinks, and smiles to himself. Occasionally Chaudron asks himself the same question, and the answers he gives himself alarm him, and he tries to forget them.

"How's it coming with that Murillo virgin? I see it's almost finished."

"It just needs a couple of touches and then the whole aging process. A few more days, and meanwhile . . ."

"Bustelo's impatient. He asks after it every time I see him. But in the meantime, you must steep yourself in everything that has to do with *La Joconde*. Go to the Louvre, look at her, make a couple of copies, buy some books."

"With what money, Marqués?"

"I'll get you the money, don't you worry about a thing. Leave that to me, as usual. You—become Leonardo."

Chaudron smiles to himself, and that little smile is almost a boast: he knows that he can. That he could, if it were suggested, begin preparing the same pigments, the same palettes, imitate the very same brushstrokes of the master. But he doesn't know why, and he is not sure that he wants to.

"You're not thinking of selling copies of *La Joconde*, are you, Eduardo? Even your ignorant Argentine ranchers know that it's in the Louvre. Certainly everyone in Paris does."

"I'm not thinking of anything, Yves. It seems that the one thinking is you. Now that's a joke!"

3

"YOU HAVEN'T TOLD ME YOUR name."

"It's Vincenzo. Vincenzo Perugia."

Valérie takes a moment to try to pinpoint his accent but can't quite place it. He does not return the question.

"My name is Valérie."

"I thought so."

He says it as if there really was some way he could have known it, as if knowing what couldn't be known was something he did, or as if he couldn't think of anything else to say.

"Why did you think so?" she asks, and regrets it. While she's saying it she regrets it.

"Just because."

"What are you drinking?" she asks, and again regrets it.

"Nothing. Wine."

She despairs. She looks to the side—the mirrors. Silence reclaims them. And goes on. And on. She thinks that if she were just to grab his head in both hands and give him a furious kiss, hard, like that, perhaps that would get him out of his shell. She doesn't do it. She asks herself if it's because she doesn't dare. Doesn't dare? The very idea seems strange to her.

"And you?" Vincenzo Perugia now asks, though as someone who doesn't really want to know. He is sitting with his back very straight and his hands on the table on either side of his glass of wine. She stands, close but not very. The rest isn't happening.

"What about me?"

"Nothing, it's an expression."

She grabs his glass and drinks some. He watches, still not seeming interested. Her vermilion lipstick stains the glass. Now he grabs the glass and—wanting to? not wanting to?—places his lips on her lip marks and finishes it. She can't tell if it was a drink or a gesture.

Valérie was not even thirteen—living with her Aunt Germaine in that room: the run-down building, the shabby working-class suburb, the sorry youths—when her neighbor told her he'd give her whatever she wanted if she'd let him kiss her.

It was nighttime. Her aunt was never there and the neighbor must have been at least twenty or thirty years old.

"A kiss, or anything you want?" Valérie replied, and the neighbor looked taken aback.

"So what do you want to give me, a kiss, or anything you want? It's not the same thing—could be the opposite," she said, with just the right smile, and the neighbor didn't know how to respond. He left without saying a word, and Valérie could finally turn her attention to the trembling of her legs, which were jumping around now as if they were separate beings. This passed as she realized there was another side to the coin. That night, she began to see that she could get things from men in exchange for something that she believed wasn't important to her. She felt very powerful, rich, like those rich girls she had seen that time in the Jardin des Plantes—even richer. She also assumed she would be able to manage them.

Some time ago, a poet had written:

Love orders, in extremities
That we but feel, and hold our peace
But what is surely more appealing
Is to give voice, and hold back feeling

Valfierno would recite this to her much later, during one of their talks. Valérie smiled.

Valérie Larbin had it all clear in her head: none of it had anything to do with love. Love—or whatever the novels meant by that silly word—was either a luxury or folly, she was not always sure which. Whereas this exchange was quite precise: to give so that she would get, to give without giving, to provide what they didn't have and what she didn't know. Valérie told herself that what she was giving was counterfeit, not the real thing, not what her friends—her clients?—expected or were paying for. Much later, she would tell this to Valfierno: "They want love and I give them a pretty good substitute, something very similar. So you and I are both fakers."

Valfierno wasn't having it. "No, my dear, not at all. Not me, and not you. First of all, we're not even sure that they want love, but we do know that they want what your body has to offer. The real faking here is what everybody does for that: to promise love so they can get sex. Faking is what so many bourgeois call love: sex with flowers and chocolates," said Valfierno, and the word "bourgeois" in his mouth sounded contemptuous—not aggressive or envious, just contemptuous. Valérie was surprised; she had not heard that note before in his voice. Not envious but contemptuous, she thought. And aristocratic, it occurred to her.

"Do you really think so, Marqués?"

"I don't just think so. All the rest is a lie, I know that. While on the other hand you, my dear, deliver the real thing without any disguises. That glorious, creamy ass is the genuine article," he concluded, and she could not decide if he was being serious, and in truth she couldn't quite shake the thought that he was. In those cases she kept quiet.

"Isn't that your Italian over there?"

"My Italian?"

"Come on, Val. I saw your face all those days that he didn't show up."

"Really, Gigi—you think I'd ever be interested in a guy like that?"

As she gets closer he seems different. The same, but changed somehow. She looks more closely, seeking out details: he has the same white shirt with the open collar and the blue kerchief tied around his neck and the glass of wine on the table between his hands, but this time—she makes a mental note, though she knows you can never really know in these cases—his eyes, which are not looking at her, are making an effort not to. As if now he didn't know how not to look at her. Valérie takes this as a good sign and walks toward the table. As if there were nothing separating them, she walks toward the table. She knows that her footfalls make no sound, that she is a queen, that when she approaches someone in the Faux Chien she is a queen, that as long as she doesn't open her mouth, she is a queen. She touches the ribbons that keep her deep neckline closed, that never keep her neckline closed.

She is almost there. Without looking, she sees herself in the mirrors. Now he does look up at her. He gets up. She stands still while he gets up, pushes back from the table, walks around it to her, takes her hand, and tells her that they're leaving. "We're leaving," he says, a murmured instruction, a slight tremble, and they start walking. Valérie lets herself be led by the hand, and for a moment she has the suspicion that this is something he's rehearsed many times over. She doesn't ask herself why his grasping her hand and leading her out gives her that chill, that feeling of suffocating. Why now, this man? Together, they walk toward the door. There's a door. It's raining.

The purpose of a cabaret like the Faux Chien—like all the others—is to create a world separate from the world outside. Outside, it might be raining, snowing, icy; inside, the heaters maintain a constant, different temperature. Outside it can be day; inside, the tightly closed velvet curtains create a perpetual nighttime. Outside there are rules, and norms; inside also, but they are very different. Outside, there is class; inside, there is sex—these are similar, if not the same. Outside, money can buy just about anything; inside, money can buy the kind of things that can't be bought in other places, and again, not everything. Outside, the world appears to have limits; inside, it does not, because the limits are different. Inside—truly inside—some come to believe that the world is an illusion from which you can wake up.

This is why it's so harsh to come out of a cabaret. This is why some never leave, even when they leave. This is why the rain that greets them at the door of the Faux Chien feels so exaggerated.

What if that was just how it was? At what point does one thing become another?

Neither one speaks. They walk.

Until they get to Perugia's room and go in, and he says, "This is it, come in," playing down the trace of embarrassment she hears in his voice. He does not say, "This is it—I'm sorry," though that's what she hears.

Perugia's room in that cheap pension is a ten-foot square with a chair, a table, a trunk, and a narrow bed. A kerosene lamp sits in a corner of the room on the edge of the trunk. The wallpaper had flowers once. Perugia's room smells of sweat, of a man enclosed. To Valérie it smells of the world of a man who doesn't know—or has forgotten—that the world has smells. The room of a man who has forgotten himself—and once again that chill and the feeling of suffocation. Not the room of one of the others who want me to make them a man. He lets go of her hand.

He remains silent and so does she. There is a bottle of pastis on the table. He fills two glasses without a word. They raise them and toast in silence. She braves a smile, opening that big mouth. The flame of the kerosene lamp flickers. They are standing in the only free space in the middle of the room, and for a long moment they do not look at one another. Valérie thinks that she must make a move but hates to think that she has to—she's there because she didn't think she'd have to—and she remains standing. She remembers that she knows how to make a man jump with pleasure, arch with pleasure, ache with pleasure. She aches but stays quiet, savoring the wait, standing there. He will do what's required, she thinks, and shudders. He will do what's required. Now, the silence does not threaten.

He grabs her face in his hands and kisses her mouth and runs his tongue across her teeth—one by one, her teeth with his tongue, either he knows or he has no idea. Her broken teeth with his tongue, someone who knows, accepts, buys. Someone who says "everything, everything." Even the teeth.

There are moments when time gets confused. These muddled moments are time at its best, when it can no longer be used as a measure.

You think that if you hear that question you'll give this answer, and you're surprised when the answer appears ready, on the tip of the tongue. You think that nothing would be better than to close your eyes and let yourself be enfolded sweetly by dreams, to feel the sleep creeping over you and the muscles' release, falling further and further, but then, suddenly, you're waking up. You think that if you stretch out your hand to brush that cheek, and catch that curious or inviting look with your own, and bring your eyes closer to those eyes, lips to those lips, all the rest to all the rest, that the bodies will all finally come together, but then you discover, not knowing how, that all that has passed and that you're just remembering it. And you begin to think of time as a friend.

Much later, she would hear:

Love orders, in extremities . . .

Valérie is strewn across the narrow bed, disheveled, flung there, her body still, arms by her sides, tits spilling down her sides, legs stretched out, slightly open. Sitting next to her, naked as well, hair matted, his cock dangling between his thighs, Perugia looks at her—not as you'd look at a live person but rather a portrait or a statue. He looks at her as if he owed her no explanation. He smokes, says nothing, looks at her, smokes. Now he really looks at her. As if, she thinks, she existed only to be looked at. It's a peaceful tableau, outside of time, or trying to be. It lasts—because of this, surely, it goes on and on.

If only we could stay quiet, like this, for hours upon hours, for days, she thinks. Then he speaks.

"I could stay like this forever."

"Do you think it should take hours to say words like 'forever'?"

"What?"

"Nothing."

Valérie gets up and starts to dress. It makes her shy— shy?—to have him watch her dressing, and when she's finished she leaves without a word. It's what he intended, and she goes. Outside, in the street, it is still raining. She can't believe it; it's still raining.

Bonaglia

1

THAT OF COURSE THE FIRST thing he did when he got out of jail was to get on a ship. He'd been locked up for so many years that he thought he had to get out into the world. He found a French clipper taking purebred horses from Buenos Aires to California and signed on as a kitchen boy. That's all he wanted to know—just that his next stop was to be San Francisco and after that the captain would decide, though he was prepared to give himself up to whatever course chance set, whatever uncharted courses. It had been the hope of something just like this—he hadn't known exactly what but it could easily be this wandering clipper—that had kept him alive during those four years inside.

On that first voyage—which was not really his first but his second, only he was so little on the first one that he didn't remember anything about it—he learned a lot of things, some of which he liked more than others. He learned that when someone dreams of the thing that will save him and tries to get it, most likely what ends up saving him is not at all what he dreamed, but something else; he learned that he had a knack for getting seasick; he learned that he had a knack for picking up languages and gestures and poses and mannerisms that sometimes surprised him; that when he did that, it scared him when he couldn't go back; that when he did that, he forgot what he was before.

He learned that two distant ports could be a lot more like each other than two neighboring towns; that two men from distant places can have a lot more in common than two compatriots. He learned that there was nothing he missed, and it pained him; that it was important to make memories; that life on a ship is too much like life inside, even though they seem like opposites; that sometimes what seems the opposite is really the same.

That there are lives in which you don't think of any other life, and that on that boat he came to think of himself doing the same thing always, on a boat like that one, always him, like that, surrounded by all that water. He learned that there are nights when you would give anything for a caress you hadn't paid for; that on those nights a man can be very fragile and do things that he doesn't usually do; that a man like him can do a lot of things he doesn't usually do; that it was difficult for a man like him to know what he wanted, to understand what made him different from other men, or at least what made him who he was—now Enrico or Enrique Bonaglia.

In this way—little by little, port by port—he learned a great many things. But his real revelation came on a later voyage one humid night in Malacca's Chinatown.

Two or three days before, as we were coming into the Malacca Straits, we had been attacked by pirates. You know how that little finger of sea was—and still is—rotten with them. They have a reputation for ruthlessness, which they've no doubt earned. More than once I've heard stories of the calm with which they throw their victims into the sea, and of their wealth. But the ones who attacked us must have been the dregs of the buccaneering world, a ragged bunch that boarded us from a sampan on the point of sinking. You might think that their miserable state and very desperation would have made them fiercer and more frightening, and I suppose our captain thought the same.

Captain Burton was an imposing Englishman with the small sharp eyes of an eagle, of the sort whose bearing and manner embody the entire might of the Empire, and who serve as a warning. Like a good Englishman, he ruled by the use of contempt and the lash—forms of refuge that often serve well.

It was already past dark when we realized that our vessel had been overrun with bandits. Our Malayan attackers carried rusty

scimitars and were so gaunt that even a light wind ought to have dis-
patched them, but they were Straits pirates, and perhaps felt that
they could take advantage of this reputation. There are many who
do this, usually very successfully, and I don't only mean pirates.

To our surprise, our captain fell for it. When he saw that we
were surrounded he told the pirates in a most unimperial voice to
take whatever they wished, only to spare our lives—certainly his, and
perhaps ours as well, it was never quite clear. The poor man looked
quite terrified. The pirate chief agreed but did not look at him.

Luckily for us, our bosun, Mr. Hopkins, didn't share the
same trust in the promises of bandits, and he had reason to know.
With a very British name and mound upon mound of black muscles, he was a wild beast escaped from the depths of God knows
what jungle. He had a scar that crossed his entire skull and would
turn white when he was about to attack; that night the scar was
gleaming. Suddenly the black Mr. Hopkins roared out something
unintelligible, launching the attack, and the rest of us—two dozen
desperate men—attacked with him. I could embellish what happened, but in fact the skirmish was over so quickly that it barely
merits the name. Within minutes, our attackers were feeding the
sharks, if indeed there were any such undiscriminating sharks in
those waters. And though you may not believe me, I can tell you
that I was quite scared.

In the morning we arrived at the port of Málacca. The sun
was shining, and there was a pleasant breeze. Amidst the smells and
shouts from the docks, Captain Burton gathered us on the deck and
said a few words about our courage and a well-earned extra week
of shore leave. I suspect he needed it as much as anyone, and more
important, that he wanted the crew to have the chance to drink
enough to forget his cowardly conduct in the face of danger. Perhaps this way he could recover some measure of his authority. He
never did, but that's another story.

As soon as we got ashore I attended to the essentials. A

small Hindu girl cost me little and attended to me for a couple of hours. Afterward, I took a turn through the town. You probably don't know it—what's good about Malacca is that hardly anyone does. But Malacca is a labyrinth of tiny streets that would surprise you. By that point I'd stopped in at a great number of ports, and after a while they all resemble one another.

I took a room at a pension, bought myself two bottles, and passed the next few days that way. The hardest thing for a sailor coming ashore is the journey back to becoming human; some never manage it. I ate, I drank, I listened, and I told those tales that sailors tell and twist and turn into fiction. There was an old man at the inn who must have been German or Scandinavian, who was in the final stages of delirium tremens, and who, for the price of three or four bottles, sold me his last possession, his sea trunk. Don't think that I bought it out of any interest; I didn't imagine I'd find anything useful in it. I merely felt like helping him. This happened to me from time to time. As it turned out, the trunk held nothing of interest except for a uniform that more or less fit me.

The next afternoon, I rose, bathed, and put it on to go out again around the town. The streets were empty, or so I remember them, strange and quiet. I didn't know what I was looking for— probably nothing. But my attention was caught by an establishment with a sign filled with Chinese characters. No one is more disposed to passing time than a sailor in a distant port, and I was no exception. On the contrary, passing time has always been one of my favorite occupations.

The Chinese who greeted me spoke to me in a form of English, and I replied in another. He looked at my uniform, called me Captain, was deferential, and led me to a room that, he told me, was reserved for those of my position. You know how these people are, all they have to do is see a white man wearing a cap and they treat him like their master. I'm sure you'll tell me that we're no different. Perhaps, but sometimes you need a little distance to allow you to see what's in front of you. The more I traveled the more I became convinced of how easy it was to become someone else.

But I'm getting ahead of myself. The room was barely illuminated by a couple of kerosene lanterns with tortoiseshell shades, and with every breath there was that unmistakable smell. Chinese girls wrapped tightly in silk ran among six or seven cots hung with tapestries. In most of these, men lay sprawled with long pipes dangling from their hands. As you have no doubt guessed, this was an opium den. I had been in similar places before; I must confess that I didn't find it an entirely disagreeable way to pass the time. But I had never had opium like this.

I cannot say how many hours I passed in that den. During that long night, I was a fat woman who tried to get up but couldn't, and fell under her own weight. I was a father who was looking for his son and got lost each time just as he was about to find him. I was a dog—I believe I was a dog. I was an earnest Italian who planted a bomb in a confessional which then exploded—then afterward, I was the bomb. And interminably I was a man whom every new interlocutor called by a different name.

A French serving girl spoke to me in a German that I tried to understand. An American banker called me Count and told me he knew my country, especially Florence, trying to sell me shares in a railway. A Basque priest advised me to be wary of men, and I in turn remember telling him something terrible that I tried to forget but that kept returning to me. A Japanese fisherman yelled at me in a language I did not know but that I understood perfectly. He admonished me for the fact that my Chinese ancestors had invaded his bay with their marauding junks. And there was more. It isn't difficult to recount, but in fact the journey lasted an eternity and was strewn with traps, pleasure, despair, and tedium. I was on the point of speaking to myself—of saying something out loud to myself so that I would discover my true language—when I awoke. Or perhaps I did not awaken, but rather the opium's waves ceased carrying me along and produced that effect—the illusion of an ending.

Afterward, I slept for an entire day, perhaps longer. When I managed to get up and eat something I was able vaguely to remember some of the scenes I've just described to you. It took a great effort later to reconstruct them all. I went for a long walk through the streets of Malacca. There were street peddlers selling chicken with rice, Malays tottering under huge and impossible loads, Muslims without their veils, and everywhere that insistent odor. I couldn't identify it.

I walked until I thought I finally understood something—without words, without knowing exactly how. The way I had understood, as a young boy, that what Father Franco had fondled was not really me. This was a revelation. I had known from the beginning that I would not always be a sailor, but I had supposed that chance would carry me from one place to the next, from one profession to the next. That morning, I decided that I would be that chance—I would decide all the places, I would do what was needed always to be someone else. And also that I needed to choose who to be, and dedicate myself to being that person, since it is nothing but cowardice to keep being the person you drew in the first lottery. I decided that morning that there is no better enterprise than to build the person that one is going to be.

I never returned to my English ship. I had some friends in Malacca. First I traded in gemstones from Borneo, later in other, less prestigious goods. I had various women; I sold some of them. I made money and bought myself a reputation. The years were going by. Life was calm and pleasant, but with time I was beginning to need something more. I didn't wish to end up a rich colonial of dubious origins, tucked away in some lost corner of the world. I traveled, started new ventures, made more money. You'll excuse me for not being any more specific, but there are some things I'd rather not tell.

What I do know is that I was almost forty when I began to

feel the pull of nostalgia. Perhaps it was something else. In any case, I wanted to be the man I'd wanted to be in Buenos Aires, where I had only been a convict before. Call it vengeance or a second chance, as you wish; for me it was now my main challenge. I believed—let us say that I believed—that the ultimate test of being who one wants to be is to be that person in the place where one began. Only there can one really be who one wants to be. In order to complete my project and build my persona, I needed my country, so in the month of June of 1903, I arrived at the port of Buenos Aires. I wore an impeccable white suit and had a trunk that contained many more, as well as some gemstones and documents showing my true name: Marqués Eduardo de Valfierno.

Valfierno related all this to me during the first conversation we had after he'd offered me the chance—asked me?—to tell his story. I believed him; I had no reason not to. We met again the following day. We were both having a glass of Cointreau when he asked me if I knew what it was like to be on a sailing ship in the Indian Ocean.

"Do you know, Newspaperman, what it is to be on a clipper in the middle of the Indian Ocean with menacing dark clouds beginning to gather in the western sky?"

"No, but I can imagine."

"Sure, sure—you can imagine. So can I. That's what I'm telling you, Newspaperman."

"It is a fever, a convulsion of pleasure, the strangeness of the possessed, which ceases to govern the body's movements and abandons itself to another soul, which performs these superhuman feats, undreamed of," wrote Don Domingo Faustino Sarmiento, and which Valfierno might well have read. Though Sarmiento, as usual, was talking about a ballerina.

Sometimes I can still recall the shapes of those clouds—the way they formed into different shapes. The way it seemed to be the wind that was molding them, only it wasn't. How their outlines can disappear and yet remain in people's eyes. How, as fluid as they are and as many shapes as they take on, the cloud is still a cloud—even in the clearest of skies, precisely by its absence. And how none of that matters.

"The truth, Newspaperman?"

"I don't understand what you're saying."

"I'm asking if you want me to tell you the truth."

"Yes, of course—why?"

"I don't know. The truth is, I didn't leave Argentina until 1908, when I went to Paris."

"And all that about the sailing ship and the pirates and those opium dreams?"

"Exactly that."

That when he left prison he was like a stray dog—lost and with nowhere to go. The streets of the capital are too much for a young fellow who has lived only in the provinces and in jail. He spent three days walking through those streets with the feeling that he was worse than a foreigner—he was nobody. He could walk and keep walking for years and neither the streets nor the people on the streets nor the owners of the houses on those streets would ever notice him, he was nobody—more than in the big house when he was a child, much more than in the streets of Rosario after they had thrown him out, more than in the school with the priest, much more even than in jail.

He went hungry those two or three days since he didn't dare to beg, even though he saw lots of others do it; he didn't want to think of himself as part of that ragged pack that ran up and down those streets as if they owned them. He wasn't the type to beg, though he was hungry. He was better than that, even if he was a nobody. Hunger wasn't the worst of it—he didn't understand who he was, how to think of himself, what name to use.

And it was hot—it was high summer. He went down to the banks of the river and watched the movements of the washer-women—not the women, but their movements—until he was ready to explode from hate, from distance, from disgust for his situation, not to mention for him, for himself. Then he scraped together the courage to play his one card.

That card was the name of a woman that the Frenchman Dasset had given him. He found his way to the boardinghouse she ran at the end of the Calle Bolívar, facing the Jesuit church. The smell of food made him sick, and he had to sit down on a bench. He thought they might be looking at him but maybe not. The lady, Berta, was almost as fat as his own mother, her arms probably even fatter. Armed like that, with her potato masher and her knives, she was a monument to the limited power of women, to the supremacy of woman over a dominion that men pretended not to want, and when he saw her he didn't want to talk to her, something stopped him from talking to her. Maybe it was fear, though there wasn't any reason, but he left; he couldn't play his one card.

He went back to wandering—three days, four days—through those streets where he didn't exist, thinking many times that it shouldn't really be all that difficult to talk to the woman Berta, but not doing it, and he went on not doing it until finally his hunger caused him to oversleep in the vestibule of another church, where a beggar spotted him and told him that if he went down to the port he might be able to get one of the scraps of dried meat that sometimes fall from the carts taking them to the ships. He also told him that if he felt like it he might be able to sign on to a ship that had lost sea-men in the bars—they were always losing sailors in the bars and were always looking for young lads who were willing to go to sea.

He went to the port and wandered for hours without finding

a single scrap of meat and without daring to talk to the bosuns from any of the ships, and there in despair he finally worked himself up to ask the waiter at one of the inns that feed the day men and stevedores if he could give him something to eat, even just a scrap of bread, and the man told him that if he wanted it he'd have to work for it. So he went back to the lady Berta's pension.

He couldn't say why he decided then to go back there, but he talked to her and she told him that if he was a friend of the Frenchman—if this kid telling her his name was Enrique Bonaglia, was a friend of the Frenchman, and she said "friend" with a smile that he didn't get and didn't want to—why, then she'd be glad to give him a job in her kitchen and a cot in the attic. That evening he ate as if possessed and spent the whole night throwing up.

I no longer called myself Bollino. Or I should say, I only occasionally did. But no one else called me Bollino, or any of those other names.

He said that he didn't stay too many months at the boardinghouse. Life was pulling him in a different direction, according to him. But he liked working at the stove. Berta's house fed thieves, immigrants, whores, and thugs, and the food they served was not always in the best condition. He enjoyed learning to cook, or learning how to use the fat woman's tricks to hide the taste of a rotting fish, the worms in a piece of meat, a lettuce that was too far gone. Learning to rescue something nature had given up on and bring it back into the circle of life. Learning to fight against time and beat it back, though he didn't put it that way. While working at the inn he came to believe that nothing is what it seems, that what everything is really about is learning how to transform one thing into another.

One night, after a few months of this, the fat Señora Berta told him there was no reason that such a good kid like him should spend his whole life behind a bunch of dirty pans. He replied that he didn't understand, and she smiled and told him not to worry, that she didn't do that anymore, but that she had a friend who'd seen him there a few times and wondered—she'd seen him and wondered if he . . . she wanted to know if he would visit her at her house. This friend was a young widow— still quite young, she told him—and she'd know how to treat him right. Several days went by before he said that he would go, and he would never have believed it would be that easy. It took him a long time to find out that some things came easily to him.

He said he lived with the widow for a few years. That I'd be surprised to know who she was—someone well placed in society there, well respected. She gave him a room in her house and he never wanted for money and he didn't have to go with her any-where. She didn't want him to; she didn't want people to know about him. Out of respect, or shame, she said, she didn't want any-one to know about him. She would just call on him some nights, not even that many, and in all that, somehow they got to be friends.

He learned there that it was never difficult to get a woman to give him money. All he had to do was to tell a good story, some-thing that would let her tell herself that it wasn't in exchange for the loving, but out of the goodness of her heart. He made good use of this lesson, and by knowing that he could cook up that loving as easily as the food he used to make at Señora Berta's inn—the rot-tenness of the meat, the decay in a fish: time vanquished. And he re-alized that, seen from here—not then, perhaps, but from here—they were very good years.

"We could go on like this for quite a while."

"But really, Valfierno—what did you do in those years?"

"What good would it do you to know, Newspaperman?"

"Well, isn't that what we're doing? Reconstructing the story of your life?"

"Do you really think it needs to be reconstructed? Whatever

story I tell you—especially the real story—would be much more inane and trivial and boring than you or your readers could imagine. Believe me—much more."

Buenos Aires in those days was impossible to describe: a city that was not the same from one day to the next; that every day, every minute endeavored to become something else, something new. A city to which thousands of men and women escaped from their own cities and towns, having heard that this would be the city they wanted, that it was there to be made, and that they could make it. A city that was already its own promise.

A city where the high and mighty who had lived there before when it was all so different—days before, a week before, twenty, fifty, seventy-seven years before—were looking for a place for themselves, where they could escape the incoming hordes and the grime and the changes and the different languages. They moved on so that they could keep on being the same—just like all those other immigrants.

A city that was already starting to have paved roads, and on those roads, streetlights, and under those streetlights, dresses of organza. Jungle cats, a few madmen, its own accents, thieves, lawyers, prisons, covered wagons, fewer dogs. Its own hotels, restaurants, the beginnings of its own music, a tram, second stories paved entirely in French tile, rich men, millionaires, presidents, senators, ministers, perfumes and colognes, portrait photographers, an opera singer, choristers, writers, poets, more poets, policemen in uniforms with hats. Newcomers who considered themselves indigenous, newcomers who fought for their place, thinking it was theirs. Sailing ships, steamships, cows and more cows, walking to their sacrifice, tongues, mothers, memories of other worlds, a national flag, fewer churches, a profusion of inns, of beggars, even more cows and above all chaos, perfect confusion, a whirlwind; a night turning to dawn—so many believing that a new day was dawning, and dawning for them. Buenos Aires was a premonition, a hallucination. Buenos Aires, in those days, was the future made present.

"Man himself does not know what it is he pursues. He searches, he looks, he walks, he passes right by it, goes gently, takes detours, moves forward, and finally arrives—sometimes at the banks of the Seine, or some Boulevard, more frequently at the Palais Royal" —so again wrote Don Domingo, and each time it's more likely that Valfierno knows this.

He says that no one cared what his name was; they called him Quique. They'd started to call him Quique at the inn, the boardinghouse, and the widow kept on calling him that, with her little bedroom variations. That he could have gone on like that for years—and for a few years he did—but something kept tugging at him. If I want him to, he can change his story. If I want it—he can change it.

"If you want me to I'll tell you the true story. But you're going to see that if I do, you'll miss these stories, you'll see that the truth doesn't do you any good. You know how this works: one of the most common ways to prove that a false story is true is to tell an even bigger lie and confess that the first story was a lie but that this new one now, this one I'm telling you now is the real truth. It's the old trick, where you discover my trick and believe that there aren't any more. Do you know any magic, Newspaperman?"

"I thought I did."

He says that he spent several years trying to learn who he was. And that all those years he lived like what he was—an outcast, a poor kid from the provinces who couldn't find his place or his identity.

2

🌿 THE MARQUÉS EDUARDO DE VALFIERNO arrives just as the Mass is finishing. He has never liked these religious ceremonies, and for years now he has carefully avoided them. But on this morning, the twenty-fifth of May, 1910, a glorious spring day, he needs to find someone without seeming to look. As he crosses the threshold of the basilica of Sacré-Coeur, on that highest of the Montmartre hills, and steps through those enormous doors, he respectfully removes his Panama hat. Valfierno walks with a straight back on his slightly elevated heels. There are days—like today—when he feels almost tall.

"*Ave María purísima,*" he murmurs as he enters, and he wrinkles his nose. The church smells of construction: whitewash, cement, paint. Though it has been more than thirty years since the Bishop of Paris decided to build the church to thank God for the defeat of the Paris Commune, the construction continues. On this morning it is the Argentines of Paris who are adding their own contribution to the project, using the occasion of this Mass celebrating the first hundred years of their nation to unveil the great stained-glass window they have given to the basilica. Or perhaps they are using the occasion of the gift of the stained-glass window to have the basilica celebrate the first hundred years of their nation with a Mass. In either case, they are proud—they are leaving their mark on Paris's most ambitious monument. Argentina is showing France her power.

"*Ite missa est,*" intones the priest, and several dozen bejeweled women and aristocratic men rise and begin to walk toward the exit, greeting each other with hands, and arms, and the occasional cry of recognition. Most of them have known each other forever— they are among Argentina's most wealthy, who spend the better part of the southern winter in the northern summer. Almost all of them have houses in Paris—and to say "house" here is to be modest. Valfierno greets four or five of his compatriots with smiles and nods; he has seen them recently at the embassy gathering, leaving the Opéra, at the Chantilly racetrack. But he is uneasy. He knows that every time he mixes with Argentines he runs the risk that one of them will know him from before, or that Aliaga will have talked. While he doubts it, he can never be sure. This morning he has no choice. If he wants to launch his operation, he has no choice.

"Sebastián! Sebastián!" he calls out to a young man of thirty-some years, whose baby face shows exhaustion, his blond hair smoothed down with paste, blue eyes smudged with dark violet circles, creases in his fine cotton suit.

"Eduardo! How good to see you!"

"And the same to you, Sebastián. What a miracle that you should deign to appear here at such an hour!"

"Miracle is the word, but I couldn't escape it. If my father were to get wind of the fact that I wasn't here to manage his part of the donation, he'd cut off the flow in a minute."

"So I imagine. In any case, it is good to see you. What do you say to lunch at Fouquet's? Now don't look at me that way—it's my treat."

"It's not that, Marqués. I still have something left. But, yes, I'd love to. Why not?"

The lunch is long. The two Argentinos order English roast beef with a Pommard, and Sebastián recounts in unforgiving detail his stay in Deauville, his run of bad luck at the casino, the breasts of the harlot who ended up with his money, the subsequent arrival of his father, the harlot's buttocks, and his father's threats to cut off his allowance if he didn't resume his studies or return to Argentina to manage some family land.

"I wouldn't go back under any circumstances, Marqués. As much progress as we Argentines may have made, there's no comparison between life in Paris and the boredom of the pampa. And with what Father gives me I couldn't do anything there."

"So I imagine, though it's getting quite bad here as well. As soon as they know you're an Argentine, they charge you double!"

Valfierno is delighted with himself: he's able to reproduce exactly the phrases of his companion and his friends. At times even he is surprised by how easy it is for him; at other times he doesn't even notice it.

"You see, Marqués? Chalk it up to the price of fame."

"If you want to call it that. I must say I am not at all tempted to return either. In fact, if business continues this well I'd consider staying in France forever."

Fouquet is one of those restaurants with a regimented style: armies of mirrors, mauve velvet curtains, the cutlery gleaming. The waiters dart like shadows, and one smells more cigars than one does cuisine.

"Ah, how I envy you, Marqués! But of course a man of your station, with your experience, doesn't need to go and rot in Buenos Aires. If I had your means . . ."

"Now, Sebastián, don't be modest."

"No, really. It's true. By the way, we're planning to go to Santiago's Château with the Baron Longueville, his cousin d'Ale-main, Colorado Lynch-Dubois, and maybe my cousin Calzadilla. Would you like to come? We're going in the Baron's *voiture*—a Daimler, you remember. We'd be there four or five days—who knows, perhaps a week."

"I might. Let me see if I can cancel some appointments."

"Of course, you . . ."

The waiter serves them their coffee in porcelain cups and offers liqueurs. Valfierno thinks that this is the moment but that he must go carefully. He pulls a strand of hair back from his forehead, worried that someone will notice it's dyed.

"Are you still buying paintings for your father's collection?"

"Yes, every now and then he has me buy something, though as little as he can—he says I get too attached to the cash . . ." Sebastián makes a gesture with his right hand as if he were trying to shake off something sticky. His polished fingernails have a pearly shine.

"And the collection keeps growing?"

"Yes, bigger, better, faster. A real painting Olympics, if you get what I mean."

"Of course. It's one of the best collections I've seen."

"You're familiar with it?"

"Hadn't I told you? Naturally, I've seen it a couple of times. The thing is, I may have a couple of paintings that I should sell . . ."

"And you'd like to sell them to him."

"No, no, they're not up to his standard. But I did think you might be able to put me in contact with any American buyers you might know of."

"Oof—Americans will buy anything."

"Not like us, so careful and selective," said Valfierno, and he smiles.

"Well, we do buy almost anything, but they're even less cultured. They let themselves be taken like lambs all the time."

"That is not my intention," says Valfierno, and the ensuing silence builds for a moment too long. Valfierno stares at his signet ring.

"No, Marqués, please excuse me; it didn't even occur to me. What I meant was that they're so eager, so hungry," Sebastián says, and he begins to recount in great detail the epic battles in the auction houses of London and Paris between his father and three or four American collectors.

"And through all those battles, they call each other friends now. For years they've argued over paintings pound against pound, franc against franc, and my father does not always win, so you can imagine the caliber of these guys."

"Indeed I can. Do you think you could introduce me to a couple of them?"

"Certainly, as long as . . ."

"Of course if the negotiations are successful, you would be compensated, needless to say."

"No, no, I didn't mean that, but since you insist . . ."

"Please, I do insist. Some men are only generous when it serves them, but I assure you I'm not that way. As you'll see."

3

"WHAT SHALL I SAY ABOUT those years when nothing happened, when there was nothing to distinguish them except their numbers?"

"Perhaps the problem is thinking that nothing was happening. Something is always happening."

"Oh, really? It's clear that you were never Bonaglia, working for Don Simón in San José de Flores."

We now know—we're fairly sure that we know—that upon his release from the National Penitentiary, Bollino, Juan María Perrone, became Enrique Bonaglia. There was no particular reason, or if there was, he didn't know it. There was just the feeling that he had to leave behind everything he'd been—whatever it was that he had been—up until that point. This was accompanied by the feeling—even more confusing—that there was nothing in front of him. And it's difficult to know—there are too many possible reasons—why, for this next journey, he took the name of a father who was virtually a fake.

We know that he wandered through that strange city for several days without finding lodgings. It's not clear just who directed him to Don Simón, but he seems to have been almost happy to be exiled in that way. There certainly wasn't much else to encourage him, and it's also true that he had little choice. Perhaps he didn't think that he'd be able to leave prison behind overnight, but that he'd have to wean himself from it.

Don Simón Coutiño was a Galician in his fifties who had worked every day of his life since he was ten or eleven to be able to have this shop that sold fabric, wool, and thread next to the main plaza in San José de Flores. The shop did respectably well, though it was still quite modest. The *porteña* women of Buenos Aires who summered in the town would bring their linens in, and the local farmworkers, peasants, and maids made up the rest of the clientele.

Don Simón had just dismissed a man who worked for him, so when Enrique Bonaglia—twenty-four years old, with a clear attentive face, a smile still free of arrogance, and a certain intelligence—showed up and asked for the job, the shopkeeper saw no reason not to take him on. In fact, without wanting to say what it was, he saw a very good reason to do so.

He didn't ask any questions. In those days in Buenos Aires, no one checked anyone's stories. One more, one less—everyone was from somewhere else. To Enrique's relief, the position required thirteen hours a day of work, six days a week, meager pay, the right to two meals a day, and the use of the little room at the back of the shop for himself. Enrique Bonaglia told himself this was a good way to stop his seeking, and by then, that was all he wanted.

It was very strange to be Bonaglia—some nights, it was terrifying. Bonaglia, my father's name, being used for this: the refuge for a wretch no one was looking for, and who was looking for nothing.

Clients whisper. When they come into Don Simón's shop, and especially when they leave, they whisper. Shopping is one of the few diversions for the farmhands and peasants and maids of San José de Flores. They also have the choice of going to Mass, or to a dance once in a while, a stroll through the plaza in the late afternoon, an occasional roast on Sundays, but shopping is the activity that brings them closest to their masters, allowing them for a moment to see themselves as similar. The town doesn't offer much to buy, and so it is not uncommon to see them at the shop, looking for a spool of thread, twenty centimeters of lace edging, some yarn.

But the farmhands and peasants are not ones to whisper. They are still very much *criollos*—creoles—which involves a way of being based on a kind of silence. The farmhands and peasants only go to Don Simón's shop when they can say that they were sent by their wives, or their bosses. Even then, they wear an air of distance, distraction.

On the other hand, the maids of the farm owners and their wives come eagerly, and they whisper. They ask each other—as they have many times—who this young man could be, so attentive and smart, though not that tall, who serves each of them as if she were the one woman in his life, but who looks delicately off into the distance when they each lower their eyes for him, or pout invitingly, or say something faintly provocative. Whenever they do that, the young Bonaglia seems to be in another world.

After a bit of this, Don Simón's female customers console themselves, whispering that that boy simply can't be that much of a man. And that if Don Simón took him on hoping to marry off his daughter, as many suspect, then he's picked the wrong horse.

He says that he spent several years trying to learn just who he was, and that he still thought it was something he needed to learn. Or could learn.

Little Mercedes Coutiño is now past twenty-four, the age, according to godmothers, when a girl ceases to be a girl and instead gets dangerously close to becoming a spinster. Mercedes Coutiño is not exactly pretty. Who can really say, since, as we know, beauty is in the eye of the beholder, and it's the eye that is the most capricious, but the young lady meets none of beauty's usual requirements. She does not have the fresh skin of a new rose, nor the litheness of a willow by the river, nor breasts rounded like ripe fruit, nor the grace of a gazelle. She has instead a round face, not unlike a muffin, a single, imposing eyebrow, and a short, rotund body. She is a woman in the wrong vessel, her subtle spirit a prisoner in coarse flesh.

This inadequacy has rendered her timid. When Enrique Bonaglia began working in her father's shop, Mercedes feigned illness in order to spend the next two weeks in her own room on the top floor. Her mother had died years before. She was an only daughter and the only woman in the house, which she ran diligently, and her father hated—perhaps feared—the thought that they might be separated. Which is why he refused her utterly when, at eighteen, she told him that she wanted to become a teacher. No, he said: she was his only daughter. She was not to go off and do anything strange; she was to marry, and her husband would take over the running of the shop when Don Simón became too old. He never said, "When I die," but always, "When I become too old."

As was her duty, Mercedes accepted her father's decision. So that when Enrique Bonaglia showed up, she became quite alarmed, shutting herself up for those two weeks, but then had no choice but to come out. Now, the two young people greet each other politely every day, avoid each other quietly, and try to find a way to live together without any intimacy.

"I see, Señorita, that your book is in French."

"Yes. I don't read French very well."

"I could help you, if you like."

"Do you know French?"

"Yes, well enough."

"Where did you learn it?"

"Well, I spent a few years working on a ship and picked it up there."

For some reason of his own that he has not yet fully understood, Enrique has vowed to himself that he will lie to her as little as possible. The very idea of this surprises him, and he asks himself why it should even have occurred to him. There are degrees: his vow includes everything to do with work and domestic life but it does not—cannot—include his past. He—Enrique Bonaglia—has no past. What doesn't exist cannot be measured according to whether it is true or a lie. Though he would not yet put it like this, he is learning unconsciously about the prerogatives some men assume for themselves in writing about their pasts.

None of which gets in the way of his being a very good worker. Don Simón is delighted with his new charge and spends more and more time playing cards with his chums in Canedo's café, long afternoons during which the two young people search for a way to be with each other; they do not find this easy. For a start, they are enveloped in the heady smell of the fabrics.

It's understood that Enrique should be the one to attend to customers. Unless she is needed, Mercedes remains on the stool, where she embroiders or reads. When Enrique doesn't know something, he asks her as respectfully as if she were the owner, otherwise, they might pass the entire day without speaking. To anyone else—to the whisperers, thinks Enrique—they look like an old married couple that had never been new.

The truth, he thinks, is simpler. (He is still permitting himself to think about the "truth.") She had rebuffed, that one time, his thinly disguised offer to teach her French, and he does not wish to make any more overtures. Something in her makes him feel that he can't talk to her about the silly, day-to-day things about the shop or the town's gossip. To him she seems to be above all that; it would be rude to bother her with it. She deserves better than to have to trifle with such petty things, yet he can't think of what else to say to her.

For her part, Mercedes does not think it proper to converse with a man with whom she has no formal relationship. Most afternoons, the silence is comfortable enough, but occasionally the tension spills over into surreptitious glances, meaningful coughs, an awareness of that heady smell. This is how their time passes.

"I promise, dear friend, that I will mend my ways. I don't wish to keep on, as I have until now, lingering over each tiny bitterness that life delivers. I will enjoy the present, and the past shall always be the past. How right you are! How much happier we would all be if, instead of dwelling forever on our slights and ills, we worked to make our mediocre present bearable," says the book.

Months go by before it occurs to Enrique to ask her what the book she is reading is about, though he thinks later that he must have wondered long before.

It's a novel, she tells him, called *The Sorrows of Young Werther*, by a German writer named Goethe. Enrique is quiet for a moment and then asks her what it's about. Mercedes blushes, and recounts the story of an ill-fated love. Enrique asks her some more questions, then finally plucks up the courage to ask if he can borrow one of her books. She says of course, and the next day she comes down to the shop with a book called *Amalia*. The light is dim, and Enrique can't be sure, but as she hands it to him he believes he sees her color.

I became a reader. Ever since then—all these years. I might have seemed like some fellow, perfectly pleasant, a little bored, who served the customers in Don Simón Coutiño's shop, who'd resigned himself early to Lord knows what, but that wasn't who I was—I was a reader.

Just as I used to in the big house with Diego and Marianita and Don Manuel, I read.

Soon, the shop starts to seem to him like an accident, a trick of the eyes or of a world that wasn't supposed to be there, in that space that was reserved for stories. Soon everything seems to him to be an accident or a confusion. Everything except for the stories he reads and the young lady who gives them to him and comments on them. She is now the only thing that seems real—her and the books, so alike.

Now, afternoons in the shop are perfect. Afternoons in particular, the hour of the siesta, when Don Simón goes off to play cards, when the customers stay away, when Enrique and Mercedes settle themselves to read. Mercedes in the room where the bills and accounts are kept, Enrique in the straw chair behind the counter. They can't see each other; each knows the other is there, and from time to time Mercedes will get up and offer him a yerba maté, or he will wander over to say something to her. Most of the time, though, they read   each in a chair, not looking at one another. Enrique has the strange feeling that he is finally with someone. He believes— wants to believe; so many doubts—that it's the same for her. He wonders how it must be for her, and how it is for him, too. He searches for the answers in the books and sometimes finds them.

"The man of whom I spoke yesterday—that happy madman—was secretary to Charlotte's father, and the cause of his madness was an unseemly passion that he harbored for her. For years he kept his secret until finally, one day, the old judge learned the truth and threw him into the street. You will understand through these small, dry words," says the book.

It was during one of those afternoons that I came to believe that I had finally discovered love. I'd like to know what it was I was reading then—I seem to remember a scene in which a man looks at a woman and suddenly sees her as elderly and thinks that he is the old man walking with her, trailing behind the parasol she carries. He looks at her again, no longer considering her so attractive, surveying her anew with disparaging eyes. When he then shuts them, he sees her again as an old woman, this time with no parasol, and himself beside her. He recognizes himself instantly, though he is stooped and wrinkled—something in his face comforts and soothes him. I remember that I then closed the book, stood up without a noise, and went over to watch her, without her seeing me. Mercedes was immersed in her book, and I understood.

I had a sudden flash of happiness, like a fire flaring up. I hadn't had much experience with love. I'd found myself in jail very young; to say I hadn't had much experience is really to say that I hadn't had any. Marianita was a memory from another life. I had of course spent time in the brothels, but nothing more than that. This was as different from that as it could possibly be—this was love: a pure meeting of souls. This was a joining without impediments, unimaginably elevated from the impulses of the flesh. And I now knew—without my having to tell her or her telling me—that she shared this feeling, that without needing to say a word she felt the same for me.

Love has its rules. What each place and time refers to as love is in fact a set of rules that is recast over and over. Love has many meanings: serenity, chaos, a prize, a goal, the impossible, a basic right, a reason for being, an insurmountable wall, a blanket. You can only speak the word—presume love, discern love—when you know those rules and think your situation fits them. Enrique did not know them, but he devoted so many hours to their study that he began to believe that one day he would.

She didn't exactly tell me, but yes—in the silent way she handed me my maté, the way she remarked on an author's phrasing, or the fate of some poor character, or the beauty of a description, Merceditas was telling me how deeply we understood each other and what a privileged form of love we'd somehow known to build. We spoke to each other in the words of others; no one else could know what we were really saying. It was our own secret, one we hadn't even needed to talk of, or give a name to: an infinite respect.

I would watch her. Sometimes I'd watch her for ages, without her noticing me—without her noticing me?—and it would delight me to see that nothing clouded that purity, that what I felt for her was not sullied by the flesh. She was not sullied by her flesh. Her teeth were prominent, she had a broad and curving forehead, her cheekbones stood out—her flesh did not hide the bones beneath. The flesh was not what mattered in that face, which was so honest, so close to the skull.

From time to time—once—I considered broaching the topic of our feelings, asking for her hand, holding her close, but I amazed myself with my ability to control these impulses. Any of these seemed like a betrayal—they would ruin everything in one animal moment. There was no doubt that we were so much more than that.

From time to time—more than once—those impulses of the flesh would come back to plague me. I was confused and disoriented, until I realized that she was not responsible for it. That it was just the freight I owed for my animal nature. And that it was easy to pay. Twice a month, on the first and third Sundays during the siesta hour, I would take the train to the center of town, and there I would spend half an hour in a room with the same stocky Calabrian woman in Doña Anunciación's brothel, like someone who returns to his sunnier side upon completing an onerous task. The Calabrian woman was the complete opposite of Mercedes—extremely vulgar, a coarse mouth, a riot of flesh. She was the dark mass above which Mercedes' bright soul shone. When I left the brothel—sated, content, without the least remorse—I would stroll about the center of town. Seeing the lively, hurrying crowds distressed me, and I would feel compassion and feel reaffirmed in the refuge I had chosen.

On those nights, I would return home—I called it my home

now—brimming over as never before with love. She never asked me where I went; she trusted me, she never asked a thing. And if she had—if we had needed to reach out to one another with such murmurings, I'd have been able to tell her that what I did I did for her, so that our love could continue at its most pure. I knew that such perfection could not last forever—nothing good ever does—but both of us were intent on trying to have it last as long as possible, on having nothing change.

It was a very happy time, though the master Rousseau would call that a contradiction, the reward of happiness coming from making time beside the point, meaningless. I felt this: it required a real effort later—after what happened—to remember just how many years we spent living through that placid, moderated passion.

"Marqués, forgive my interruption, but did it ever occur to you that she simply did not attract you as a woman?"

"Of course it occurred to me, Newspaperman—I already said so. And I told myself I was wrong."

"Do you still think so?"

"What are you saying? What would you like to hear, the story of my life or my opinion on the story of my life?"

It's odd how easy it is to believe that things will always be as they are now. By always I mean for far longer than the longest time one lets oneself imagine. Into another time.

The morning that he first felt doubt was hard for him. Don Simón had risen in a foul mood—something that happened from time to time, and that almost always ended in drink—and shouted at him over something. It didn't matter what, perhaps some yarn in the wrong drawer, a length of embroidery gone yellow in the sunlight, a speck of dust. It didn't matter, but the shouting was severe. Enrique didn't care—he viewed these outbreaks as a part of his job—but while the old man was shouting he thought he might have seen a little glow of pleasure in Mercedes' eyes. That morning he felt his first doubts, and for days he was on the point of asking her about it. Luckily, as he thought later, he didn't know what to ask. Because it could have spoiled everything. Surely that hint of light had been an illusion, a mirage, and surely his question would have ruined everything. Luckily, he didn't ask, and he would always tell himself that in not asking he had really learned something.

4

"SO, ARE YOU GOING TO make me a extraordinary offer?"

"Well, I don't know that I'd call it extraordinary."

"Come on, Marqués. Merryl-Addams told me that if you made an offer it would be a surprising one," says Colonel Gladstone Burton, and Valfierno is surprised to see that, in spite of Burton's apparently stolid character, the idea of a surprise brings a little shine to his eyes. Colonel Burton is about seventy and looks like someone for whom surprises have never been necessary in getting what he wanted in his life. He has hands like spades and that square jaw that Americans seem to consider a requirement for certain achievements, and sports a blazer of crimson velvet, which only someone who needed nothing would wear. Too solid to be certain—the type of man who has to show that he's in control; the best type of person for this game.

"I trust I won't disappoint you, Colonel."

"Please, Marqués—no need to be modest."

"I have worse faults," Valfierno replies, giving him his best between-you-and-me smile. He learned many years ago that nothing works so well at overcoming suspicion as telling a truth about oneself while pretending it's a joke. But Colonel Burton does not look like a man who bothers with subtleties. His study is one of forty or fifty rooms in his new Fifth Avenue mansion, which overflows with every kind of art object of every conceivable origin: half a dozen classical busts—probably Roman copies of Greek originals; a winged lion that could well be Assyrian; two enormous wooded landscapes that appear to be Flemish; a half-dozen Spanish still lifes; and a street scene by Renoir, or one of his more gifted pupils.

"Let's play a game. If you could choose to have any of the paintings in the world, which would you choose?"

"Well, I suppose it would be something Italian. I did once almost get my hands on a Raphael . . ."

"That's all? Colonel, you'll forgive me, but I expected a little more ambition from the man who covered the entire United States with telephone cables!"

"Well, if I really could choose any painting at all . . ."

"Yes, of course, any painting! Imagine that you have power—true power!"

Burton shoots him a dirty look. Valfierno is having fun; he is surprised to discover that, on top of everything, he is having fun. His script is working better each time he tries it; this is the fifth time using this formula—the same introduction, the same feints, the same measured tones—and he thinks he now has it close to perfection. Though there is always the possibility of a stumble, or even disaster. He cannot relax his attention for a second.

"The truth, Marqués? If I was really that powerful I wouldn't have to buy any paintings."

"Touché," replies Valfierno and decides to try another approach. The stone in his tiepin sparkles as if it were real.

"That Syrian piece belongs in a museum, one of the great museums."

"I agree. That's where it'll end up, once I'm gone. My kids have no interest in this stuff."

His gambit is a dead end, and once again Valfierno decides to switch tactics. He is beginning to worry, but he takes care that it doesn't show. He has spent years of his life taking care that things not show, and much of the time he succeeds. For now, he chats with his host about a concert in Carnegie Hall, the winter's snowfall, the possibility of war with Europe. After a few minutes, the Colonel edges a toe into the trap.

"But, my friend, surely you didn't come to see me to talk about these things."

"No, but I'm not convinced it's the right thing . . ."

"Please."

"No, truly. I think you may not be the person I'm looking for."

It's a risk. But while he might be risking too much, he feels he might otherwise forfeit the pleasure of having someone this powerful beg him.

"Look, I'm not in the habit of having to ask for things, but I demand that you tell me what you came to tell me!"

"Very well. I came to ask you what you would be prepared to do to possess something that all the world wants."

"Something all the world wants?"

"Hypothetically: if you were to learn that *La Joconde* could be yours, what would you be prepared to give in exchange?"

"I think you might be making a mistake here, Marqués."

It's the critical moment, and Valfierno is on the point of admitting defeat. He starts to raise his hands as if to say not to bother, but the American stops him and finishes his sentence:

"Everyone knows that *La Joconde* is in the Louvre."

"Yes, of course. But it could be somewhere else."

"It could?"

"It could indeed. I could find a way for it to be here, for example, in this very room. Are you interested?"

It's a calculated risk. In preparation for his meetings with each of his clients, Valfierno has researched them carefully and found that, in almost every case, they have at least once bought a stolen work of art. So he pays little attention now to Colonel Burton's protests.

"Do you know what you're proposing?"

"Exactly what you heard, Colonel. Are you interested?"

He knows, too, that this is the moment when the client realizes that he is supposed to have ethical misgivings, and that he will transfer these to Valfierno and disparage him to keep himself clean. It's a small price, thinks Valfierno, and waits for it.

"I'd have to see it," says the Colonel. His gesture of disdain is his small alibi.

"You're not going to see it. This is hypothetical," replies Valfierno. "But if I were to show up here with the painting, would you be prepared to pay half a million dollars for it?"

"Half of that would be too much!"

Valfierno makes an effort to hide his smile: his client is caught, like three of the last four.

"No, a quarter of a million is insulting."

"Then three hundred thousand, let's say. Though I see no reason to keep discussing hypotheses!"

"It doesn't have to be one, Colonel. It doesn't have to be," replies Valfierno, and thinks that he might have rushed unnecessarily. Colonel Burton, too, knows how to mount a distraction. Realizing that he's exposed himself, he attempts one now.

"If you don't mind my asking, where is it you're from?"

"Not at all. I'm from Argentina."

"Now I understand."

"What is it that you understand, if I might?"

Valfierno tries to show some wounded honor at the question—it's what would be expected. The Colonel is not paying attention.

"Now I know who I'm talking to. You guys are like us—you don't let details hold you back! That's why our two countries are going to be countries of the future! But I didn't know, Marqués, that there was an aristocracy in Argentina."

"Well, Colonel, you know how our countries are: it's important to us to be seen as republics, but without our aristocracies—without men like you and me—we'd keep on being just a band of savages, unable to appreciate true art, for example, as you and I do."

"*La Joconde,* eh? You did say *La Joconde?*"

"That's what I said."

"And what is the chance that your hypothetical will become real?"

"That depends, Colonel, among other things, on your three hundred and fifty thousand dollars."

The Colonel is quiet now for several minutes, which begin to feel uncomfortably long. Valfierno lights himself a cigar. The Colonel remains quiet. When he finally starts to speak, his voice is almost a whisper.

"A personal question, Valfierno: We both know that painting is pure gold, that you could offer it to anyone you wanted. Why did you choose me?"

The Colonel strokes his mustache slowly and his eyes shine. Now is the time to stroke him. Valfierno knows only too well that what he is selling his clients is an image of themselves: "I have something that no one else has. I knew how to get it. I deserve it."

"Well, first, because I was told that your discretion is faultless. Obviously, whoever had this painting would never be able to let anyone know."

"Obviously. That would also be necessary to avoid . . ."

"And above all, because it's important to me that whoever has it should know how to appreciate it," says Valfierno, and for a moment he fears he has played this last part too crudely.

"Marqués, I don't know how to thank you," says the Colonel, from within the trap.

5

THEY SAID THAT IT WASN'T the Basque's fault. It had been his horse, but an accident, pure bad luck that the dog had barked just at the moment when Arispe the Basque was riding by in his cart. Bad luck that the horse, who was normally used to dogs barking, should have taken fright and bolted just at that moment, just when she was coming out of the church and crossing the street. They were going to say that the Basque wasn't usually there at that time of day, that just on that afternoon he'd been delayed at a customer's, but they knew it made no sense to go on, fate having been so cruel, so unbelievably stupid.

They said that the Basque was desperate with regret—unimaginable the regret that that poor old man was feeling, they said, but then it felt unseemly to keep emphasizing the old man's pain to the wounded girl's father and to the other one, the shop boy, and something had to be the matter there, his face had gone all chalky and white, like the full moon. Maybe all the rumors were true, after all.

Then they told them that Mercedes was in the infirmary and that Doctor Firmin was there and that, yes, it had been a hard bump but that there was hope. That she might pull through, they said. That God would take pity on her.

The very first thing I thought was: why did I never think to kill that dog before, avoid the whole chain from the beginning? If only I'd thought of it before—before!

Accidents are little flashes of only seconds that change hours, months, years—everything. We tend to think of an accident as a skip in the normal order of things, in which certain people and things—the dog, the trap, the young lady—don't cross, wouldn't collide. This is what we tend to think, because we think that there is at base a natural order, a normal succession of events that doesn't include accidents, a normal succession that has been organized by someone or something. But everything is an accident; we only register a few of the more abrupt of these as such.

So that what we tend to call accidents are where the randomness of chance reveals itself and where chance takes on an epic cast. What we call accidents are where the chance of any given moment defines years—a life—in just a few seconds, and seems to change the shape of time. Like a brushstroke, for example, which is made in seconds but then lasts for years. Accidents partake of the essence of art: we see life as made up of those moments that don't change anything substantially, of the moments of chance that have no extraordinary manifestation; art and accidents are made up of the other ones.

Accidents are terrifying. They show that chance rules everything and will often choose not to let you slip by unnoticed. We cannot bear that arrogance, that randomness, so we invent fictions, philosophies, religions to help us bear the randomness of chance. Our history is the history of these inventions—invented to make chance less cruel. Invented so that things have meaning.

Afterward, I tried over and over to remember what I was doing when they gave me the news and especially at the exact moment that the horse ran over her. The worst thing was knowing that while she lay there, I was going on as if nothing had happened. That our connection was not, therefore, what I'd thought.

Mercedes Coutiño's eyes are closed. She has a bloodstained bandage around her head and bruises all over her face, but most serious are the blows to her chest. Of the two kicks, the one that injured her lungs was the worst, or seems to be, says the doctor, "though we can't be entirely certain."

Mercedes breathes as if she didn't know how—slowly, irregularly, hesitantly. Standing beside her bed in the infirmary, Enrique Bonaglia inhales and exhales as if to show her how—he inhales so she will inhale. What used to be routine seems to him now superhuman. Each of the young woman's attempts to gulp air seems to require an effort that completely overshadows all the other, quiet efforts of that body. The body is usually selfless in its modesty, he thinks, never seeking recognition for all its work. Suddenly, the accident has taken away that pretension, as well as his notion that bodies were not all that important. He thinks that if they get a chance—for he does not want to say, "if she lives" —they will have to learn another way.

For a week, the two of them—Enrique and Don Simón—go to visit Mercedes every day at the infirmary in San José de Flores. They each go at different times, so as not to leave the shop unattended. Don Simón is there in the mornings, when the doctor tells him again not to lose hope, to be strong. Enrique is there during siesta and hears from the nun about the small improvements in the injured young woman. Enrique is convinced that the nun is lying to him; he sees no improvements, and on the sixth day he catches himself trying to plan for the time after Mercedes' death, but nothing occurs to him. "For now," he murmurs, "I can't think of anything—thank goodness," and he watches her mouth and her efforts to breathe. He wants to feel worse than he does, more abject. One afternoon he tries to imagine how his mother died.

On the eighth day, in the afternoon, alone in the infirmary, Mercedes opens her eyes and babbles a few words. When the nun arrives she is not able to understand her, and she calls for the two men, who now close the shop and come, running.

"What are you thinking, Don Simón?"
"Nothing, my boy, nothing. What should I be thinking?"
"Be careful, Don Simón."

"O, Charlotte! If I could only have had the joy of dying for you, of sacrificing myself for you. I would have gone to my death filled with joy if it would have brought you happiness and peace. O, but only a few privileged men were lucky enough to shed their blood for you," said the book he'd read some time before, that he rereads again now. The one he's not now sure that he understands, in the midst of his unease.

They told us that we could take her home. Not that she was better, nor out of danger, but that what she needed now was not medical care but rather rest and peace and God's help. Later, it occurred to me—many times, whenever I couldn't avoid thinking about it—that Doctor Firmin simply didn't know what else to do. Don Simón gave her his bed and arranged for another nun to come and be with her all the time. Mercedes spent all her hours dozing.

Every so often she would wake up and try to speak. That night she tried several times; I failed, in amongst all those awkward grunting sounds, to recognize any words. With her face even tighter now to her skull, and her eyes staring out wildly, Mercedes looked at me desperately. When I held her hand it gripped mine; she was trying to tell me something.

She stopped trying, and slept, and I remained by her side for one or two more hours, watching her struggle in that room. I thought that the flesh that we'd disdained was now taking its revenge. I thought that if she recovered I'd ask her to marry me, that I'd surrender to the banality of a union of two bodies. I also thought—I hate to admit it, but I did—that if she survived she would be crippled, would in some way be prevented from being herself. I couldn't stand that idea. Even less could I stand the idea that, had she been in my place and I in hers, she would have cared for me with all the devotion her generosity made her capable of. And that she would have felt a certain pleasure in having me be her cripple, dependent on her, at the mercy of her kindness. This thought made me shudder.

Mercedes died a few hours later, in the middle of the night, fast asleep. I, too, had been sleeping. I died considerably less. Although you never really know.

6

VALÉRIE LARBIN IS BORED. THE night is just beginning and, as usual at this time, the Faux Chien seems an unlikely proposition. It's at this time—as usual—that Valérie thinks that no one is going to arrive, even though she knows they will. She thinks that feelings don't count in the face of experience, though that's not quite it. She thinks, How strange that I think that every night even when I know it's not true. How different what I feel is from what I know, or something along those lines, and she orders a Pernod. She likes Pernod because it leaves her fresh-tasting, as if she hadn't been drinking.

Valérie Larbin sips her Pernod and discovers that there is someone there—at the table by the door, a man of a certain age, his distinguished grey hair glossed back, a perfect mustache, perfectly composed, sipping champagne. It surprises her—sharing the empty bar with him feels indecent, an intolerable intimacy. She looks at him again. Something about him attracts her, and so she launches an attack:

"This doesn't seem like the right kind of place for you."

"And what would be the right kind of place for me?"

"I don't know that—yet."

What attracts her most of all is a style—the way he moves as if he were keeping still, the way he speaks, as if the words themselves were speaking. That was class, status, distinction; there are many words for it but none is exactly right. She'd like to be able to say what they mean. Usually it's enough for her to know that they refer to her more appealing clients, but on this night that won't get going she wants to know more, and she stays with Eduardo de Valfierno.

"This is a place for me, not for you."

"Exactly, Mademoiselle."

Valérie doesn't answer. This is obviously a trap the man has set and she prefers to have the control. She doesn't reply, she doesn't smile. Valfierno continues anyway. Valérie has on a great deal of makeup, and he thinks he can see a bruise beneath it. He hasn't yet seen her teeth.

"That is why I would like to see you somewhere else," he says, and he hands her his card.

"Love orders, in extremities," he recited to her, not long after.

Vincenzo Perugia went to pick her up at the exit to the Faux Chien sometime after three in the morning. Occasionally he would simply show up, but that evening they'd made a date—Valérie had invited him to stay with her until Sunday at the house of a friend who'd gone to see her family in England.

They met occasionally. Each time Valérie told herself that it was the last time, and each time she'd capitulate. Perugia bored her. She was excited by the quiet of his strength, his seeming lack of motive, his apathy, the way he didn't chase her—but she was also bored by it. Most of all, she didn't yet understand him, and she would have liked to know what he wanted from her.

The last time, they had spent a particularly intense night together of perfect silences. In the morning, as he left, Valérie gave him a hundred francs "for a shirt, my love," she managed to say, before some beast in him lashed out and landed a hard blow to her face. She screamed at him to go to hell and asked him if all he wanted from her was her body, and he replied no and shut his mouth. She yelled at him again and told him to go to hell, that he was a thug and peasant and he didn't deserve her and that was it, no more. "No more?" he said. "Alright, I get it," and he didn't go back to the Faux until Valérie sent him the invitation. She hesitated before writing it. First she didn't want to, then she wondered if he'd understand it. If he could even read, to begin with. Perhaps.

Next, she loses all time, it dissolves: he has his left hand—stubby, those thick fingers—in between her legs, his thumb in her cunt, the other four fingers moving against her mound, the movement stronger and stronger and in rhythm, and she arches and with his other hand on his cock he moves with her. She yells out, sighs, and he gets on her, climbs onto her, is on her, moves with her and now their two bodies are moving fast, together, in rhythm, a gallop; suddenly time is back, she arches and yells, yells and collapses, breaks. He no longer matters.

Now she doesn't give a damn about him.

"You don't know what it's like to be born in a town and then live there, thinking you're never going to be able to get out."

"You think I don't?"

"No, it's not the same, it's different here. In my town, the guys, all they can say is 'I hope I can get out,' but you look at them and you just know they won't, they don't have the balls. I have balls; I'm here now."

"You call that balls, huh? So you're the one who's got balls?"

"That's right, Mademoiselle. That's why I'm here—'cause I got balls. I'm going to get to do what those guys want but they can't. I'm going to do it, going to make money here, know what I mean?"

"If I knew what—"

"You know. Here in the city you can. I'm going to do it. Even though you don't think so, I'll be able to. Then you'll see, I'll go back to my town."

"You're going to go back to your town?"

"Sure, I'm going to go back with money and I'm going to set up my own carpenter's shop. I'll be famous all over the area 'cause I know how to make things nobody there knows how to make, modern things, from Paris. Then I'll make even more money and I'll find myself a good lady, decent, from the town, and we'll raise a family together, a family . . ."

"Great. You thought of all this yourself?"

"Let me finish. I'm saying a good family, my kids won't have to get into any trouble, I'll teach them the business from when they're young, and they'll grow up to be great carpenters, even better than their dad. You're looking at a real good carpenter."

"I'm sure I am."

"I am—a real good carpenter. Hear me? Real good. The Louvre even hired me—the Louvre—to be a carpenter for them."

"The Louvre did?"

"Yup—the Louvre. Surprised, huh? You thought I was an idiot. Nope, I've worked in the Louvre. It's been a few months now. I left 'cause I got some other work, but I can go back whenever I want, me, just like you see here. I can go back if I want to."

"Really?"

"Yup. Whenever I want."

Even the way he said "Louvre" —the thick accent he had when he pronounced the word—irritated her. Everything about him irritated her. And she couldn't get him to shut up. Or to leave. Or not call her again.

When he gets Valérie's call, it takes Valfierno a moment to remember who it is. Then comes that little primitive jolt of triumph—she called! I got her, the idiot—she called me! She pretended to play dumb but she called. He is often surprised—ashamed even—by how much he still enjoys these small victories. He's surprised by how difficult he finds it to be Valfierno.

"Do you remember me, Marqués?"

"I implore you, don't toy with your prey!"

"But, Marqués!"

꽃

They meet that night and Valfierno takes her to a dance at the Opèra-Comique. There are lights, a cascade of lights. Valérie looks at everyone—it is so cosmopolitan, so elegant—and Valfierno hopes she doesn't notice that everyone is also looking at her. Valfierno takes pleasure in their looking, in their envy.

Cosmopolitan and elegant, a pack of strivers like me making their way, thinks Valfierno, though some of them began their striving two or three or even ten generations before him. Everyone dances. The band plays one of the latest favorites: "*Ma Tonkiki, ma Tonkiki, ma Tonkinoise . . .*" Dancers move to an impossible rhythm, people moving fast, the thumping of the beat, the movement of the air, the perfumes that can't mask the smell of warm sweat: "*Son Anana, Son Anana, Son Anammite . . . ,*" the smell of bodies in the air.

Valérie wears a lilac dress with crimson sequins, a neckline plunging all the way to the bottom of the sea, to those two great waves, the kind of vulgarity only a true gentleman could allow himself, thinks Valfierno, then he is suddenly alarmed—perhaps they are all looking because it's too much, because she's so out of place. She's had a drink or two and laughs loudly, her mouth open and those teeth showing, marking her out, and she's so young—that's why they're all looking.

The smell of bodies in exertion, and he thinks: they're looking at how coarse she is, they're laughing at me behind my back. Damn them! These are all ways of disguising envy, he thinks. The ones who know me know that I can do this and they are jealous of me for it. As for the rest of them, what do I care what they think? But he doesn't convince himself. That stunning body, tits like melons—who cares about the rest? Screw them! This is mine.

More smells, fast-moving bodies, "*Il m'appelle sa p'tite bou'geoise, sa Tonkiki, sa Tonkiki, sa Tonkinoise . . .*"

"Marqués, take me somewhere else."

"Somewhere else, my dear?"

"Somewhere we can be alone," she says.

They are all moving with abandon now, and the smells—above all those smells. You didn't need to say anything, thinks Valfierno as he gloats in anticipation and she spins and spins: "Marqués, take me somewhere where we can."

"Maybe the worst mistake I made was to include that girl Valérie."

"Did it cost you?"

"It depends. I'd say so, yes."

"Tell me how you came to include her."

"I don't know if I should."

"You did agree to tell me all the facts."

"I know that. But that was just an agreement."

One night much later it occurred to him that the probability of their meeting somewhere in the world—a demimondaine orphan girl from a working-class Paris suburb and the son of an Italian seamstress who'd ended up in the city of Rosario—was infinitesimal. But then it occurred to him just how amazing it was that even things with a high probability ever actually came to pass.

First I have to make him feel like king of the world, like a real man; that's never been any problem. And then right afterward, right then, when he feels like he could do anything—then. But first get rid of those airs, get him to where he's just like anyone else, have him lose his crown, mess up his hair, mess up his mustache, the little cocked eyebrow. Where the careful expression on his face drops as he gasps for just a little more air so that he can keep moving, touching me, finding me, and then the escape that's also entry, the entry escape—in and out and in and again until it's done, he's undone and stays undone, a contented idiot, satisfied, a real man, feeling like he can do anything—then. Then how do I find a way to talk about the museum.

If I could do it myself everything would be different. If I could get that Italian going by myself and get everything else going by myself it would be so different, but I can't. I need him, and so I need to undo him, make him a contented idiot, a king of the world. But that's never been a problem for me.

"Marqués, couldn't we work together?"

"That's just what I need!"

"You'll want to, eventually."

"No doubt, my angel. But now I have a lunch to go to, and if you don't make yourself decent, I shall be late."

"Marqués, don't be an idiot. It's not what you imagine."

"And what is it I imagine? Do tell me."

"I'd rather not guess. In any case we both know it's pure fantasy. I simply want to tell you this: a friend of mine knows a fellow who until just recently worked at the Louvre. He's an idiot, but he's without scruples. That's not that common in an idiot like him. You know what they say: morals are the substitute for intelligence. This fellow can go in and out of that museum the way you do at the Hippodrome d'Auteuil."

"Why would that be of any interest to me?"

"I don't know, Valfierno, but think it over. You're the thinking type. You don't always know how to do things, but you do know how to think. If we work hard, my love—even harder than last night—maybe something will come to you."

"Maybe."

"Or I can tell you what I've been thinking."

"You?"

"Yes, me."

7

SHE HAD GONE; WE REMAINED there—Don Simón and me, two men missing the same person, such different things. Mercedes' death had joined us somehow, victims of the same event who seemed destined— destined?—to suffer together. I could have left, of course, but I couldn't find any reason to. The old man treated me with a strange affection, made up not of words or gestures but rather of a kind of shy maintenance of our silences, as if he knew of the pact that had bound me to his daughter and wanted to make up to me what I'd lost. In another way, it was also as if the woman's disappearance had removed a weight from us, and a barrier.

Don Simón continued his card games, which became longer, and lost interest in the shop. I read and read and tried to cover his absences, though we both knew—without saying it, since we didn't say things—that we didn't know why we kept on with it. A death is not so hard for what you lose—it's terrible because it makes you create a new life when you thought you already had one.

They were interminable days, and there were so many of them. In those days, during those years, I couldn't stand for things to finish, and I always left a little of whatever I had so that I could go on with it later if I wanted: a last bit of soup I'd take to my room each night, a sip of wine left in my glass, five or six pages left to read in every book. In this way, I made a life that didn't seem to have beginnings or ends; it was always the same; time didn't cross it. I was busy all the time without knowing why. Nor am I sure that I was unhappy.

Though I had inherited all her books, I nonetheless got in the habit of buying one or two books whenever I went into town, which was every Sunday then. I was not only reading her novels now, but also history books, tales of journeys to the most exotic places, biographies of some of the important men who were changing our world. It pained me sometimes to think that in reading these new books I was leaving her behind.

My Sunday outings were the only times I went anywhere, my times for peering over the precipice. Every Sunday I would get up at eight to shave and wash and then take the train into town. I would have lunch in one of the inns there—Berta the Frenchwoman's, Narcis the Catalan's, one of the Italian ones—and drink a couple of glasses of wine. In this state I would make my way to Doña Anunciación's brothel. Sometimes I had the Calabresa, sometimes others. They all shared the same floral smell of their disinfectant, and they all made more or less the same gestures, probably on purpose, so that the client would think he was causing them, that they were his.

On more than one occasion I considered not going, but I never missed it. It continued, in a way, to be an homage to Mercedes, a way to renew our communion, to assure her that the body was not what was important and that no one could take her place in my soul. When I finally left, refreshed, I would walk along the Calle Florida and occasionally end up in a theater. I had discovered in those depictions a way of not thinking that was not so different from reading.

In the evening, the train would take me back to San José de Flores. Each Sunday I'd arrive tired and satisfied. I'd have savored that other world which others envied and desired, and confirmed to myself that I could still reject it; I had no need of any of that.

There is a certain contentment attainable in the imagination that does not anticipate any change; that does not expect ever to have to confront reality. Such an imagination, which needs nothing but itself, contains great pleasure within.

Those were days in which Enrique Bonaglia used to imagine things that he would never do, and be happy. Ideas would come to him: he would go to sea, become a cat burglar, live off a rich widow. He'd be a sailor who became bosun on a sailing ship that crossed the world's oceans, braving storms and savages and taking his courage to its limits. He'd come up with the perfect scheme to con coarse nouveaux riches by selling them bonds in a small central European monarchy, which would return them enormous financial rewards and other, irresistible benefits. The young widow of a pampas land baron would come into the shop one day by chance and fall prey to his charms, offering him the world and more to tempt him to come away with her.

The stories he thought up became more and more elaborate, full of adventures and risks and triumphs. Sometimes during his siesta he'd even indulge in defeats from which he would recover, and avenge himself.

On one of his voyages, he'd be almost shipwrecked but would save his crew and go on to perform amazing feats, discovering a trade that would make him rich—would make him, for example, into the most powerful opium smuggler in Southeast Asia, and he'd build a secret empire that would spread its tentacles across pagodas and jungles, across slums and palaces. Later in his life he'd write his memoirs and show the world of the bored just how different a life could be—more different than they could have imagined—though to protect his high position, the memoirs could not be published until after his death.

He'd exploit the greed of those nouveaux riches by selling them bonds in the Kingdom of Belgravia. Thanks to the promise of enormous wealth—bolstered by some initial small but encouraging returns, and especially by the bestowing of various Belgravian noble titles on the more important buyers—he would begin to frequent the most aristocratic salons and eventually become one of them himself.

Thanks to the widow, his life as a rancher would be peaceful and happy—summers in the country, winter trips to Paris, and autumn nights at the opera—until, finally tiring of this idleness and inspired by the prospect of inheriting his wife's lands upon her death, he'd experiment with breeding different types of cattle and would create a new breed that would revolutionize Argentine ranching and propel him to a position of power on earth so far only dreamed of. He'd make a fortune, buy himself Argentine citizenship, launch a political career noted for its intelligence, make even more money, run for senator, become a minister and perhaps even, finally, president.

He would be, he thought, a captivating millionaire, an aristocrat, a leader of men, the object of great envy. He had legions of ideas and with them the great pleasure of knowing that he'd never have to realize them. The comfort of their being only ideas—unassailable perfection.

It occurred to me then that Don Simón must have some peace of mind, knowing that he had come to this country to achieve something and had achieved it. I, wanting nothing, could also achieve that if I put some effort into it.

Until the night that Don Simón said that he had something important to tell me. This was unusual, and I think I was scared. Later I concluded that it had scared me because I thought I knew what he would say and I was afraid he might not say it.

It was hot, a summer night. Mosquitoes circled the kerosene lantern; the smell of kerosene was in the air. Dogs barked nearby. The old man served wine and spoke to me carefully: of course I knew that, like me, he was alone in this world, that everything he had done he had done for his poor daughter, and that now that she was gone his world had crumbled, he said, and then was quiet. He took a drink of wine. It seemed to me that he was heading in the direction I'd predicted, meaning that I would no longer need to worry about my future. Meaning that, though he hadn't said anything, he was worried about my future, about what would happen once he was no longer there to run the shop. Which all meant that I no longer had reason to worry: if the old man kept on in the direction I thought he was going, I'd never have to worry again, and I could continue with my fantasies in peace, without a care.

"Son, everything I imagined for my life is now destroyed. But I don't want everything I managed to build to be lost. Tell me that after I'm gone you'll look after the shop, you'll make sure it survives."

"Of course, Don Simón, if that's what you want."

"Of course that's what I want."

"That's fine then, Don Simón, we don't need to talk about it again."

It gives him a funny feeling, that night, in his bed, sweating, knowing that his life—the question of his future—has been solved. He searches for the joy he should feel at such monumental news but doesn't find it, and he suspects that he's stupid, lacking in imagination. That he'd never thought about what his life could have become after the old man died if what had happened had not happened.

His life has been solved, meaning that he can keep doing what he has been doing for years. What from this distance seems to him like his fate, or his nature. His fate or his nature, he thinks to himself.

One day it came into his head that Diego de Baltiérrez— Diego, from his first life—must now be grown up, and he was surprised that he hadn't thought about him before and decided to try to find out about him. He must be in the papers, he thought. He must be someone important.

I memorized Greek history, and then Roman history, and was, in sequence: Leonidas and Brutus, Aristides and Camillus, Harmodius and Epaminondas. All this while I sold maté and sugar and scowled at anyone who would try to pull me out of the world I'd discovered to live in. "I was reading, as I used to, on mornings after the shop had been swept, when a woman named Laora passed by on her way to church," read Enrique, delighted: a story about a man—a shop attendant—who'd invented himself to perfection.

Reading like that—not just reading but reading a lot—I came to see that Argentina was the perfect place for this. Argentina was an idea that was being created, made, and in a country that was making itself its men could also make themselves, even make themselves into other men.

Those Basque hawkers who spread over the pampas with their little wagons, living like Gypsies until they'd amassed enough land deeds to trade them to the soldiers for gin. Within a few years they were the new lords, the nobles of a new aristocracy of cattle. And those countrymen or near-countrymen from Italy who arrived with nothing more than their hands and their hunger and used both to build themselves a house and family. And the Jews who, aided by the support of their brethren, launched themselves in business and money lending and became wealthy merchants not long after arriving there. And those blond women who, once here, entered the profession they wouldn't have dared to enter in their own cold countries, and who after a few years retired with enough money to allow them to purchase a near-spotless reputation. And, finally, the poor local *criollos* who rose to heights on the strength of hard work and study, like the late Sarmiento, a shopkeeper who became president. If anyone had led the way, it was Sarmiento.

It came to him out of sheer boredom one afternoon in the shop. He had the idea of selling certain items they'd never sold before. He told the customers—certain customers, the ones who gave him looks—that there were only a few left, that they were the latest thing from Paris, and that they were very expensive but that for her he could offer a special price, and he'd quote an inflated number and usually the lady would buy. Until one day Don Simón discovered that he was selling more than usual and asked why. With something like pride, Bonaglia told him what he'd been doing and the old man forbade him from doing it anymore. Bonaglia said that no one was getting hurt. Don Simón said that it wasn't about that, that in the shop they did what he said. For the moment, son, I'm still the one in charge here. He said this calmly, without any anger. Bonaglia told himself he didn't care, that the old man was an idiot; no one understood him and he didn't need any of those fools to understand him.

He has put on weight. He looks at himself in the full-length mirror that Don Simón put in to attract more of the maids who like to shop there, and he's pleased. He, Enrique Bonaglia, who never paid much attention to his body, now has the slight paunch that reflects the comfort of his new station. He likes it. He likes the word "comfort," which he sees in magazines. It has a modern, European, sophisticated air. He now reads magazines as well. Since he's learned that he's to be the owner of a shop, Enrique reads them, studies them, especially on those Sundays, on the train into Buenos Aires.

It occurs to him one afternoon as he comes out of the brothel that when he becomes the owner of the shop he'll be able to pay a shop attendant of his own, which will allow him to come into town two or three times a week if he wants. After everything he's been through, he's going to end up a prosperous businessman. He smiles, but is alarmed at the same time. Perhaps he'll even marry— as a shopowner he won't want for that kind of attention. He smiles again and is more alarmed. He does not want any dramatic changes in his life.

But that afternoon in the theater, watching a play in which an aristocratic family battles with the daughter's dishonor and sinks into tragedy, he thinks again of the Baltiérrez family and realizes that he could also sell the shop and use the capital to launch himself on one of the lives he's imagined. Afterward, he leaves the theater and, without deciding to, goes into a bar and orders a grappa. He drinks a great deal that night, becoming drunk.

That it is nothing but cowardice for a man to stay in the role he drew in the big lottery. That there is no greater endeavor than to create a man. That there is nothing more difficult, no greater art. That there is no greater folly.

I spent the next months in a state of anxiety that I wasn't used to. Don Simón grew worse every day; the moment when I would have to choose my life was fast approaching. And though I told myself that it didn't have to be this way, that there was no reason things couldn't go on as before, I had already changed course. No one returns to paradise after having left it. Doubt had decided to pay me a visit; from that moment, nothing was as before.

Reading was now perilous for me. As soon as I would enter into those fantastic lives—which I did almost as a reflex, having subsisted on it for so long—the unease of knowing that I might try that life if I wanted would take away all the pleasure and turn it instead into an interminable struggle. I suffered, but I kept going back. Time and time again I returned to reading and imagining and turning over my options. I hated it, but I kept going back.

I found him dead one morning. It was autumn, though not yet cold, and I'd noticed that it was already after eight o'clock and he hadn't come down to the shop. Before I did anything else I tried to feel grief and was on the point of succeeding before I got distracted. As I was going back downstairs it dawned on me that my story was now about to start. Now, at last—my story.

8

🦂 "I WAS WITH THAT FRIEND of yours yesterday."

"Friend of mine?"

"Whatever he is; I'd rather not know. The Italian mason, that fellow Perugia."

"I thought he was a carpenter."

"Does it make a difference?"

"It depends on what you want him for," replies Valérie, and Valfierno thinks that it must be hard to be twenty or twenty-one and all alone competing in a world full of crooks, and that it's not surprising that she always presents this stupid and improbable façade of certainty, but it still irks him that she does. That she stops short of understanding that at that age you can't begin to know everything. As if she didn't realize that she didn't have to pretend to know everything, he thinks, and he smiles to himself.

"What? Now what?" Valérie demands.

"Nothing. I was just thinking that it's sometimes much easier to see other people's faults than one's own."

"I don't know what you're talking about and I don't care. You were telling me you saw Vincenzo."

"Vincenzo?"

"Perugia."

"Oh. So you call him Vincenzo."

It's hard to say if this is a question or a statement; probably neither. Valfierno decides on a momentary truce. Lifting his champagne glass, he waits for Valérie to join him in a toast. He looks into her eyes and smiles. She responds with a textbook indifference. Around them the hubbub of the brasserie is slowly dying down. It's after midnight, a time when he is less likely to encounter someone he knows, when Valfierno will dare to go out with her to a place like this.

"I saw him last night."

"You already told me."

"I know. Do you really think he can be trusted?"

"As much as you can trust any man."

"How far is that?"

"Only a little bit more than a woman," replies Valérie, and she opens her vermilioned lips to stick her tongue out at him, showing her teeth at the same time. Valfierno looks away, or begins to, but then makes himself focus on those teeth. They're the price, he tells himself—seeing them, knowing that they're there, can help me.

"I asked him what he could do, and he told me that if the money was good he could do anything."

"Don't take too much notice when he says 'anything.' He should have said 'anything I can think of,' which is much less."

"That's what I thought. He doesn't give the impression that he's any kind of genius."

"I suppose you want him to teach you Ancient Greek?"

"Seriously, Valérie. I'm worried that he may be too stupid, even for this."

"Even for what?"

"For what I want him to do."

"Which is . . . ?"

Valfierno reaches over and grasps her hand—the one with the costume jewelry resting on the tablecloth—but lets her question hang in the air. He feels the way her fingers contract out of either nervousness or disgust.

"You know what I remember, Marqués?"

"I'd rather not think."

"I remember the time I asked you what the strangest thing you'd ever faked was. Do you remember what you said?"

"Yes."

"You didn't say anything. You acted all proper. And I thought you were even faking that. But now you can't do that. I'm the one who told you Perugia worked in the Louvre. I'm the one who came up with the idea that we could get up to something with him. Don't think now that you're going to give me the shove!"

"I would never trick you, Valérie, if that's what you're talking about."

"My love, you know I could find out so easily . . ."

Not only does he know, but he guesses that she has already found out. That she is pretending to ask him these questions but already has all the answers from Perugia. He would like to know what kind of relationship she has with the Italian.

He is calmer now. He's decided that it doesn't bother him if Valérie thinks she is using him; he doesn't care. As long as she behaves and he can use her, he doesn't care. As long as I can let off steam with her, he thinks, and the phrase sticks: let off steam. But there are moments when he's not convinced. He should stop seeing her, forget her once and for all, just forget. And above all not get her mixed up in this. That will be difficult.

"It's better for you not to know anything, Valérie."

"Better why? For who?"

"Better for you. And for me."

"So you're going to keep me out?"

"Out of what?"

"Marqués Eduardo de Valfierno, or whoever you are, I'm young, and it's useful for me that people like you think I'm not smart, but I am. And I don't think it's a good idea for you to treat me as if I wasn't."

There's something in her tone that annoys Valfierno. He wipes his mouth with the white napkin, coughs, and lifts his head. And says what he hadn't planned to:

"In that case let's be clear. From now on we're going to stop seeing each other. It's not working, neither for you nor for me, and it's not helping us, either. You're to stay out of this business. Leave it to me. Of course, I recognize your contribution and I'll make a pledge to you: if everything goes well you will get from me an extraordinary gift, more than you ever dreamed."

"Valfierno, you can't keep me out of this. You can't leave me, either, Valfierno, that's stupid!"

Valfierno looks at her with something close to tenderness. He asks himself if it's true that he's just left her.

"It's for your own good," he tells her, but he worries. Valérie is a child; she has nothing to lose and she doesn't know the way things work. She could make trouble.

"You don't know who you're playing with," she says and bares those teeth.

9

"So you didn't see Valérie again?"

"Who?"

"Valérie. Valfierno's woman friend. The one who helped him . . ."

"Ah, her name was Valérie."

"Did you forget? From everything I've heard, she wasn't the type of woman you forget easily," I said. Chaudron looked toward the kitchen before he replied. For the moment, Ivanka was nowhere to be seen, but she could have been behind the kitchen door, and he needed to know.

"You said 'wasn't,' Becker. Is she dead?"

"I don't know. I was hoping you could tell me something. I haven't been able to find her anywhere. But if you don't even remember her name . . ."

"Remember? I never met her. He never introduced us. Divide and conquer was one of the Marqués's specialties, you know." He smiled to himself as he said this and drew his hand down his face as if he was tired. The way he said "Marqués's" sounded strange.

"There I go again, letting him have his way. I would never say 'divide and conquer.' That was the way he talked, always so pompous: 'divide and conquer.' "

"Then if you don't mind my asking, why do you care whether she's alive or dead?"

"I don't. Of course I don't. Why would I?"

He made a point of this. Up until then Yves Chaudron had seemed like someone who'd resist any kind of emphatic statement. The kind of person who worries that any assertion is going to get him into trouble. But now he was emphasizing too much. I was intrigued, but I hadn't come there to get to the bottom of his relationship with Valérie Larbin, or whatever he used to call her.

"Why do you say 'divide and conquer'?"

"You don't know how he was!"

"Who are you talking about?"

"Him, Becker—Valfierno. Who do you think we're supposed to be talking about?"

"Valfierno, right. Sorry, Chaudron."

"Well, I think he was always worried that we'd gang up on him. It worried him. Stupid. Why would we have done anything like that?"

"Why would you?"

"I don't know. To steal his ideas, I guess. That's what he was afraid of: that we'd steal his ideas—as if he had any. He always believed that people around him couldn't help envying him and that they would try to take whatever he had. Or maybe he was afraid we'd found out something about him, I don't know. That he wasn't what he said he was. That we didn't really need him. The truth is, I don't care. Don't think that I care."

"Don't worry," I said, but Chaudron had already slipped away. The old man went back and forth between a friendly distance and complete absence.

He was still now, his gaze on a painting that hung on the opposite wall of the little country house. The house was so cheesy, so French. It was funny to think that this elderly man had taken part in one of the great art cons of the century to furnish his house with fake country-rustic chairs and fake flowers. The painting seemed familiar: a Virgin on some rocks with a chubby infant, done in dark tones. It was a large painting with a gloomy and imposing kind of beauty, and I wondered to myself if it was one of his.

"Yes, I did that one," he said, without my asking. "I did it when I was Leonardo."

"What do you mean, 'when I was Leonardo'?"

"What I said. Do you think that the way you paint someone else's painting is to grab a brush and try to copy each and every brushstroke? That's what I thought when I started, when I studied with Professor Falaise in Lyon. You don't know what it cost me to find out I was wrong. The truth is, I owe that to Valfierno. He showed me that if you want to do what someone does, you have to become that someone else. That's what he was best at. Think about it—we talk about him now and we call him Valfierno."

"I don't see your point."

"I could explain it if I weren't so tired. Though I shouldn't. The thing is, I'm not old enough yet to be this tired. But it's what I said—to paint like Leonardo I had to be Leonardo. I had to study his writings, eat his food, feel his frustrations, live . . ."

I didn't dare ask him if he'd also adopted his sexual habits. Sunk there in his armchair with its flowered cover, he didn't look like someone who would ever have been involved in such a thing. Perhaps he was right when he told me that no one ever remembered him, that he didn't stay in people's minds. His work was memorable, but he himself had no distinctive feature apart from that. I wondered how you could remember someone who had nothing memorable about them, but this was silly—I was wasting time on distractions. Ivanka bumped the kitchen door to let us know she was coming in. Without realizing what he was doing, Chaudron sat up and straightened himself in the chair.

"*Chéri,* it's time for your medicines."

"Yes, dear."

I asked him if he was ill, and he looked as if he had expected the question. Then I asked him to tell me what had happened when he got to Buenos Aires, and he replied that he'd already said he wouldn't give me any details.

"That's all right, I don't need details—just give me a general idea of what happened."

Yves Chaudron asked his round Russian wife for water to

wash down his medicines and told me that in the beginning, Buenos Aires had intimidated him as much as Paris had, only for different reasons—it was a jungle.

"It was a completely wild place, where you could do anything, or so it seemed. You don't know the energy that ran through the city. All those people who'd just arrived from somewhere, who had brought with them the force of their hunger or their hope and were poised, ready to leap at the first opportunity. Believe me. It wasn't only me, it was a frightening place."

It took Chaudron a couple of weeks to find his first job: he was taken on by a Portuguese photographer to paint watercolor portraits of his subjects which they could have along with their photo for a reasonable sum. It was a good idea—he told me they came out better in the portraits than in the photos—and the Portuguese began to make good money while Chaudron had to content himself with a wage that barely covered his room and board. He wouldn't have minded so much, he said, had he not been half in love with a Serbian seamstress who used to throw his poverty in his face. Across the room, Ivanka again interrupted her sewing to pay closer attention. She was sitting just below the big painting, and it occurred to me suddenly that the face of the fake Virgin looked a lot like Valfierno's description of Valérie. Something prevented her from smiling.

"I decided that I didn't need the Portuguese, that I could do portraits for myself, and I had some cards made up offering my services. I thought it would be hard to get customers, but in those days in Buenos Aires everybody needed everything. The problem was when I went to paint their portraits. I'd get them to pose and try to paint them, but I could never get the portraits to come out looking like them. I had no trouble copying photographs, but when they posed for me I couldn't make it work. I shouldn't really have been surprised, it's exactly what happened to me before I left France. I must have thought that by changing countries and starting a new life, I'd be able to paint models, but I found out that I couldn't, that I was still me, just on a different continent. It was very dispiriting."

Chaudron then found another photographer with whom he could have the same deal he'd had with the Portuguese. It took him months to get things back to the way they'd been before his split, but then he resigned himself to it, working for years as a second-hand portraitist. He made enough to rent a small apartment, woo the Serbian girl, and even save a little. He had no great ambitions, and he thought his life would just go on like that for a long time.

"Or forever. I really thought things would be like that always, but you know how it is, there are words that people like me don't dare say."

I didn't ask him what he meant by "people like me"; I was beginning to understand. The new century had just begun when he got a new job with more money and above all more stability—he heard that the Post Office was looking for an artist to design stamps.

"I'd never done that before, imagine, but in those days the Argentines were still kind of naïve—they thought a Frenchman could do anything. I showed up and they hired me. After a while, I got hired by some other people to do the same thing."

"What do you mean?"

"What I said, Becker. Don't be an idiot. There were other guys who paid me a lot more for the same designs."

"Collectors?"

"Becker, please. I did it. I made good money. Maybe you just don't know—there's not much difference between working this side of the law or the other. Why would you know? Luckily, most people think there's a big difference. If it wasn't for that, the world would be a big mess."

"Excuse me, Chaudron, I don't really understand what you mean."

"Makes no difference to me," replied Chaudron, paying no

attention to me now. Sometimes his humility would transform itself into a quiet contempt. For a few moments, it was clear that he wasn't speaking to me, that he didn't need me for anything.

"The problem was, I was bored. I had a lot of time on my hands and I was bored. The Serbian girl had gone and married someone from her own country. I was grown up now and still alone, and I was bored. If it hadn't been for that, I guess I would never have met him."

"Met who, Chaudron?"

"Who are we talking about, Becker?"

Ivanka had appeared silently—a benefit of wearing the plush slippers she wore in the house. She seemed to exaggerate her accent as she offered us dinner. I told her she shouldn't go to any trouble, and she replied that it was no trouble, that it was all ready. Chaudron smiled.

"Enjoy it, Becker. My wife cooks like an angel and isn't usually so generous. She obviously likes you."

The table was in the kitchen. Ivanka served us dumplings that she called pirugies or pierogies, filled with something I couldn't identify and smothered in cream; I had to struggle to finish them. We drank wine, and the talk wandered to the state of the world. The Russian woman didn't say a word. Chaudron seemed to be well up on the effects of the crisis, unemployment, the dangers we faced. He ate as if he wasn't paying attention, but he came back twice for another serving. Ivanka smiled. Chaudron spoke with his mouth full:

"I don't know what you think, Becker, being an American, but more and more people think that capitalism won't make it through this crisis, that this time it's finished."

"That's just foolish."

"Don't you believe it. Look at Germany here, right next door. The Communists are almost ready to take control, and then we really are finished. If somebody doesn't stop them, the world we know will be over in a few years."

I couldn't tell if this prospect scared or exhilarated him, and I didn't want to investigate. It still seemed ludicrous to me. During the month I'd been in France I'd heard the same story a number of times—European hysterics, the nightmares of countries that had been weakened by complacency and a surfeit of ideas. When Ivanka offered us coffee, I asked Chaudron if we could have it in the sitting room so that we could return to our discussion before it got too late. She wasn't happy about it but she said nothing.

"So you were telling me that you met Valfierno because you were bored."

"In a sense, but yes, it's true," he said, and he lowered his voice. "I used to go to this whorehouse in the center of Buenos Aires, a modest place, nothing expensive. The girls would dance the tango, and then there was the rest of it. That's where I met him."

"So you became friends because you were, how do I put it—partners in adventure?"

" 'Friends' is a bit strong. With him, 'friends' was always a bit strong. The Marqués isn't the kind of guy who really knows how to have friends."

Chaudron was still talking about him in the present, and once again I wondered whether to tell him. It bothered me that I didn't know whether he'd think it was good news or bad.

"No, we weren't friends. And anyway, he wasn't there for fun; he worked there."

I don't know if it was calculated, if he'd planned for the impact, but I had the impression that he enjoyed the effect his words had on me. I tried to hide my reaction, but I suspect I didn't do a very good job.

"What do you mean he worked there? Didn't you say it was a whorehouse?"

"Sure I did—it was Señora Anunciación's brothel. Kind of a second-rate whorehouse. Just right for him."

10

"YOU'RE GOING TO HAVE TO do six."

"Six?"

"What'd I say? Three? Nine? Twenty-four?"

"Steady, Marqués, don't have a fit. And remember that you told me it would be five."

It's ten in the morning. Valfierno has had nothing to drink but he paces nervously back and forth from one side of the studio to the other. He doesn't have much room, perhaps three or four paces. He thinks it might be Chaudron's studio that is making him nervous, the crammed little room, dingy in spite of the sun and fastidiously organized. Or perhaps it's Chaudron himself—his quiet, and his increasingly timid look—these irritate him to a point that is frankly worrying. He has to control himself; he needs the painter.

"Yes, you're right, I did say five, Yves. But I just received a letter from Philadelphia: the last one has fallen! I thought he wasn't interested but he writes that he is, to excuse his changing his mind, that he begs me . . . Don't for a moment think that it's not appealing to have the most powerful oilman in the United States of America begging you."

Chaudron wipes his hands on a rag soaked in turpentine, and the smell startles Valfierno. It's cold. Though he's at home, Chaudron wears a brown scarf around his neck over a paint-spattered smock. Valfierno has not removed his black woolen coat with its fur collar.

"Three more copies, in that case. That could take months."

"We don't have that long, Yves."

"I don't care how long you say we have. I have a job to do and I'm going to do a good job. What do you think of these?" he asks Valfierno, showing him two identical *Joconde*s leaning on two easels. Chaudron knows that the question is purely rhetorical. In the last weeks Valfierno has been to the Louvre various times to see the original and he has it now in his mind. At first glance, Chaudron's *Jocondes* are perfect. It occurs to him that there is a risk that they are too good, that they are more like the original than the original itself.

"Astonishing, Yves, as always. I suppose you're taking the same care with the details as you are with the way it looks?"

"You know very well, Valfierno. Boards of the same kind of wood, well aged, the paints made according to the same methods, the same cracks . . . You know what my dream is? To have Leonardo himself come and try to tell the difference!"

When he talks about his paintings, his abilities, Chaudron is transformed, and Valfierno once again realizes his incredible luck. On a third easel is another *Joconde*, partly finished. The landscape is almost complete, but the face of the Mona Lisa is just an outline.

"So three more now, not two."

"Yes, Yves, and quickly. In a month I have to leave for New York, and I have to have all the paintings with me."

"Won't you have problems with the customs people there?"

"Yves, what's wrong with you? You know very well that there's hardly a single American who goes to Europe and doesn't come back with a couple of cheap reproductions. Like ours."

Valfierno smiles to himself. He'd been about to say "like yours," but by saying "ours" he both moves from his initial false aggressiveness to a camaraderie and also neatly makes the paintings more his own. It delights him to think of this small, unplanned manipulation. He is becoming more and more deft, more precise each time in the use of his particular weapons. This, he tells himself, is my finest moment. But then his face clouds over—if that's true, he thinks, then the rest of this adventure can only go downhill. So it had better be a lie.

"You really are going to have to finish them soon. After

this, it's going to be impossible to leave this country with a copy of *La Joconde*."

"After what?"

"Don't ask me what you don't want to know, friend," replies Valfierno, and Chaudron looks at him, on the point of pressing it, but decides not to. In a corner of the studio there is a narrow, rickety cot. Valfierno sees it and thinks of his bed during his years as Bonaglia in the shop in San José de Flores, feeling suddenly as if everything has turned around one point. Chaudron has cleaned a paintbrush and is retouching the background of the third *Mona Lisa*. He looks intently at Valfierno, as he usually does, and Valfierno tells him that, one way or another, he'll know everything in a few months.

"If there's something to know, I'd prefer to know it now."

"Be careful, Yves—don't make a mistake here."

"To think that just a few years ago . . ."

"A few years ago what, Yves? A few years ago you told me what it was I needed to do? It seems to me I've shown myself to be quite grateful enough since then. But I'll tell you again, don't make a mistake here. That was a very particular time."

Chaudron concentrates on the painting. It's a good way for him to drop a conversation that he can't resolve anyway. He is pleased to feel the other's admiring gaze on him, but then he rejects it—how stupid! But he needs to ask him something and the best way to do that is to keep his eyes fixed on the painting, on the minute lines in the Florentine girl's forehead.

"You have my trust, I've said that. Anyway, I have no choice. But you have to promise me something," he says. Valfierno looks at him and snorts. His partner has definitely become burdensome. He tells him of course, if he can.

"You can. I know you can. I hope you can. Just promise me one thing. Promise me that we're not going to end up like we did in Buenos Aires."

"Yves, please . . ."

11

HE WAS A MASTER. HE deceived me so completely for all those years. He seemed like just an old man with no secrets, and all the time he was laughing at me. It's easier for old people, they seem harmless to us, always good. But if all old people are really as good as they seem, then where are all the bad people in the world? Weren't there bad people around when they were young? Was it age that smoothed and softened them?

What I never did understand was why he did it, you know? So many times during those years I asked myself if it was his revenge for the death of his daughter, if he thought—God only knows why or how—that I was somehow responsible for Mercedes' death. Whether he came up with some reason why I was responsible and decided to get his revenge, or whether he just decided to take revenge on me without needing any reason to justify it. Or if he just wanted his revenge on a world that had snatched his one great work and I happened to be the person nearest to hand. I'll never know. What I do know is that it was a perfect revenge. The old man had sold me a false future. Day after day, he maintained that falsehood, convincing me that my future would be what he had promised—his false promise. That old man managed to sell me an entire fake life; he was a master.

In the end, it's true that his deceit turned out to be an enormous favor, but of course he could never have known that. For what it's worth, that is my revenge. We all have one, you know? The difficult thing is realizing it.

Don Simón's dying had been so simple. It is the most definitive event in a life, but for all that, it is a small happening. The funeral, on the other hand, is always another story.

In a town like San José de Flores, in the slow beginnings of the twentieth century, no one feels they can afford to waste the opportunities a death presents: its wake, its burial. In those grey lives, each death is a chance to see everyone else and especially to rise above the usual level of everyday chatter. Neighbors can say things at a wake that they can't say normally. They can work themselves up at the burial, feeling shivers at the beyond and the mysteries it holds. In a town like San José de Flores, which is still trying to resist becoming a part of the city with which it will inevitably be joined, someone's death forms one of the town's most vital moments; death serves a purpose.

In those days of transition, Enrique Bonaglia fulfilled all his duties. He was the one who arranged for a service befitting Don Simón, who paid the whole thing out of his meager savings, now that he wasn't ever going to have to worry about money, who paid for the cross and the marble headstone, who ordered the flowers, who received the weeping ladies of the neighborhood, and the men who, for lack of anyone better, extended their solemn condolences to him. He, Enrique Bonaglia, was the one who distributed *aguardientes* and coffees to Don Simón's old card chums, *anís* to the ladies, and *granadinas* to the two or three children who appeared in the shop, presided over by the wooden coffin with iron fittings and the remains inside of a man who had come to Buenos Aires decades before to seek his future.

"Poor old Don Simón. How sad it is to die with no one to survive you!"

"Do you really think things will be different?"

"Doña Puritas! There's no comparison."

"It's just that I . . ."

No one knows what to do at a wake. No one has much experience to draw from. Should you try to put on a brave face, making light of things with laughter and gossip, or instead give yourself over fully to the grief, to the reason for the vigil? As a result, wakes often swing somewhat awkwardly between deepest pain and gratuitous laughter.

"Do you remember the time he got it into his head to buy that old nag?"

"Sure! Poor old guy. He sure didn't know his horses."

The good thing about a wake like that, the wake of a man without any family, is that no one is grieving too much for the dead man. Everyone knows that they will forget this man before long. But they go anyway, and they stay there for a while—his death at least deserves to have those two hours lost to him, for him, deserves to have those things said for him: May God have mercy on his soul. He's not suffering anymore, poor man. Finally he gets to rest. It takes us all, sooner or later. Why is it always the good ones? At least he didn't suffer. His problems are over now. We are nothing. Man proposes; God disposes. When He calls, you go. There aren't many of us left. But he looked so well when I saw him last. Here today, gone tomorrow. We are only flesh and blood. What can you do? That's life. We're the ones who suffer, the ones who are left behind. And with all that said, the mourners continue:

"That old Galician devil! You wouldn't believe how many times he could cheat in a single hand!" says one of his old card mates, and Bonaglia is surprised. He wouldn't have believed it.

"I know! He took it so seriously! Do you remember the time he wanted to bet his whole shop on a craps game?"

"Ugh! If we hadn't stopped him . . ."

Later, he hears two women, customers of the shop, talking about what a flirt he was, what a rascal, and how insistent he could be and just how many girls he went through in his younger years.

"And not just the younger years, Doña Eulalia. I know what I'm talking about!" says an old woman dressed completely in mourning, and Bonaglia takes another look at an older woman sitting away in a corner with a boy not much younger than Mercedes would have been. They say nothing, keeping to themselves and crying softly. And he asks himself: just who was Don Simón? When do you finish writing the story of a life?

And he, Enrique Bonaglia, is the one who leads the funeral procession that follows the cart carrying the polished coffin to the San José de Flores cemetery, and who throws in the first shovelful of dirt, after the priest has finished saying that we return to you, O Lord, a Christian who deserves all good things, his sins never having done anyone any harm.

"Poor old man. That's one thing I bet he does regret."

"Poor man, yes. A whole life of hard work to get to this."

And after the three days of mourning are over, he is also the one who must open the shop. He, Enrique Bonaglia, who for his first time as the owner, prepares to open the shop where he worked as an assistant for so many years. And who, on that morning, the door barely unlocked, finds himself face to face with a man in a long dark coat and a youngish fellow wearing a sort of light cotton riding jacket and a straw hat with a red ribbon. Straw-hat looks as if he's twenty-five, the other one is fifty at the very least. Straw-hat stands back while the older one speaks.

"Excuse me, sir. Are you the one who goes by the name of Enrique Bonaglia?"

"Yes, indeed. That's me. Who's asking?"

"My name is Castellani, Dr. Alfredo Castellani, attorney-at-law. This here is Mr. Augusto Perez Coutiño, nephew of the deceased. At your service."

It takes Enrique a moment to understand what is about to happen. Or rather, he doesn't understand until the lawyer asks to see the papers showing that he is the legal beneficiary of the deceased.

Enrique replies that he has not yet seen to them, due to the mourning, but that everyone knows that he is the one legitimate heir.

"That could be, young man. We only wish—my client and I—to ascertain that this is in fact the case. In the meantime, allow me to present my client's papers, which clearly show, barring any testimony to the contrary, that as the son of the deceased's late sister, he is the true inheritor," declares the attorney, and hands Enrique a sheaf of papers. Enrique looks at them, unable to concentrate, but he does notice amongst the papers a birth certificate in the name of Augusto Perez Coutiño, son of Miguel Perez Perez and Josefa Coutiño Álvarez, and a parish registry entry declaring that the aforementioned Augusto has been adopted by his uncle, Simón Coutiño Álvarez, as well as other similar documents. Enrique's head starts to spin, and he realizes he must think of something quickly.

"A pleasure, gentlemen. I ask only that you give me two or three days to put my hands on what you're requesting. If it's convenient, I will meet you right here next Friday."

"But of course. With pleasure."

Never had I imagined that the existence of a mere piece of paper could be a matter of life and death, but it was. Over the next two days, there wasn't a drawer I didn't search or a book I didn't go through page by page or a notebook I didn't turn inside out, either in the shop or in the house. At first I thought, that damn will must be somewhere, only the understandable distraction of death had caused Don Simón to overlook the detail of actually giving it to me. So that when I finished going through all the logical places, it occurred to me that a document that important would be well hidden, and I turned my attention to the more obscure hiding places I could think of: I tapped on every wall, trying to hear the echo of a hollow, I took up floorboards, unscrewed legs from tables and chairs, poked knitting needles into pillows and cushions—nothing.

There was one moment when I thought I must be going mad.

I was still convinced that the will must be somewhere but thought that it was possible—probable, even—that I would never find it. I imagined I could hear the fates mocking me, watching my entire future slip through my fingers because I couldn't find a single piece of paper. And then I felt it—a blow. Not a figurative blow, but a real, physical blow that no one was there to have delivered. I remained still for a few moments, stunned. It was Thursday evening. Without lighting the kerosene lamp I sat on the armchair I knew to be Mercedes', poured myself a glass of wine, and felt the first dawning of a realization—at first just a suspicion—that I would never find something that had never existed. Then I heard the laughter. Without understanding how or why—a tremendous wave of laughter, coming from me.

I had lost my future.

"Were you sure that he was the rightful heir?"

"Ah, so we're learning, eh, Newspaperman? A question at last. No, of course I wasn't sure. In fact, at some point that night I was convinced that they were conning me. That the supposed attorney had fabricated those papers and—just like Don Simón at his cards—was bluffing."

"And that's when you decided to fight for what was yours."

"That's when I remembered that my name wasn't really Bonaglia, or at least that I didn't have a single document showing that name, and that if they were to find out my real identity . . ."

"Your real identity?"

"There, you're catching on. I mean the identity that they would have considered real. If they did discover it, they would also quickly discover my previous incarceration, and if that were to come out, then I'd be in danger of losing a lot more than just the shop, you see?"

"Yes, I see."

"More progress."

"But I can't believe that, just like that, you would have accepted losing everything you had. Everything you knew was yours."

"It wasn't 'just like that,' Newspaperman."

"But you did accept it."

"Well, at first I thought that even if the will didn't exist, the old man still certainly owed it all to me and that making one wouldn't be too difficult."

"Making one what?"

"A will, Becker. What is it we're talking about? It wouldn't be too much trouble to find someone to reproduce the document, the appropriate signatures, the necessary stamps and seals."

"But you didn't know where to look."

"I didn't, but that wasn't the problem. I could have found that out. What stopped me then was the thought that, if I did go ahead with it, I'd be putting the rest of my life in jeopardy. I would have to stay there, sitting on my little crime for the rest of my life, which would be a mess, and that perhaps that was the revenge that Don Simón had had in mind for me. That's what struck me as Friday morning dawned."

"Of course; I see."

"I doubt it. But you know what? I did feel a great relief."

Day breaks. Into his cardboard suitcase, Enrique Bonaglia puts his three changes of clothes, various books, his other shoes, and a photo of Mercedes. He takes the photo out again and closes the suitcase. He strikes a match, but then puts it out. He walks out of the shop, closes the door behind him, and locks it with the key, which he puts in his pocket. He lights another match, but puts that one out, too, and walks to the train station. There's no doubt: it takes all his will not to look back.

An enormous relief, as if it were possible once again to wake up.

12

"MAYBE SO. HE NEVER DID tell me how he came to be at the brothel, though he did say that he hadn't been there long, not much more than a year."

"Forgive my surprise, Chaudron. I didn't realize that Argentine women ever paid for male prostitutes. I always thought Argentina was more—"

"No, no, Becker, that's not it. That wasn't what he did there. Not that he wouldn't—you know him yourself. He worked there as a sort of bookkeeper or administrator."

"Now I see."

"You do?"

13

YVES CHAUDRON WAS A LOST soul, someone who never knew what to do with that extraordinary ability fate had given him. He didn't deserve it. In his entire life he'd had just one idea. Odd to think that that idea was me.

He feels distant, old. Like a man who has happened but not been, he sometimes thinks. The bitter taste of having been without having been something; the relief of not having to be anything special. The peace of just accepting what one was. The relief. The despair. The humiliation, even.

"Please excuse me, but I really don't understand how you ended up in that place."

"It doesn't surprise me, Becker; I'll try to explain—it wasn't really a place. For me, being there wasn't going somewhere, it was not killing myself. In just a couple of days I'd lost my entire future—again, just like when they blamed my mother for the necklace I stole, I lost everything. This time it wasn't my fault, or at least whether it was or wasn't didn't change anything. I thought seriously about killing myself, but in the end, it seemed excessive."

"Did it frighten you?"

"Perhaps. But mostly I thought that it was just excessive, that it was too much, that I hadn't yet done anything to merit an important death. So I buried myself in that brothel. Old Anunciación offered and I was happy not to think, not to plan anymore."

Later, I was to confirm that there really wasn't any reason for them ever to have spoken to each other. That years and years could have gone by without them ever meeting. They could have spent their lives in different cities, or passed each other on the street without a glance, or even shared a table without exchanging a word. But that night at Doña Anunciación's, the French portraitist suffered a mishap—an excess of alcohol, most likely, though Yves Chaudron didn't seem like the type of person to have any kind of excesses—and the madam had the good grace not to throw him out into the street as soon as he regained consciousness. The situation was tricky—Chaudron was no longer really a client, and it would not have been appropriate for him to return to the lounge in that disheveled state, his thinning hair a mess, a suspicious stain on his shirt, the way he smelled. The madam led him to the one place in that establishment where on a Saturday night in full swing he would not be in the way: the combination office and apartment of Bonaglia, the bookkeeper.

He is working feverishly on the ledgers—one of which keeps track of the sex; it was hard in the beginning to get used to thinking of it as just another unit of measurement—in order to fill out a chart showing, beneath each girl's name or nickname, how much they've earned at the end of each week, after deducting the costs for food, lodging, laundry, medical services, and salaries, his own included, of course.

He barely lifts his head when his boss tells him that Señor Chaudron is going to rest there awhile in the armchair, if that's not inconvenient. It isn't, or at least his position doesn't allow him to say if it is. In the distance, he can hear unusual music, a playful combination of violins and guitars. As soon as she leaves them, Bonaglia returns to working on his charts.

"This looks like great work for a man," says Chaudron.

Bonaglia doesn't respond.

"Yes," presses Chaudron, "a job where a man could have some fun."

"Sure, if you say so," replies Bonaglia, to shut him up, but Chaudron keeps on:

"Yes, sir, all these women around!"

Bonaglia feels it necessary to tell him that the women are only for the clients.

"Surely you don't mean to tell me . . ."

"No," replies Bonaglia, and pointedly resumes working on his accounts. Business is getting better all the time, he thinks. He is responsible for that. He likes the feeling of efficiently dispatching a job that is of no real importance. All the rest is for idiots.

I happened to be there but I could have been anywhere. I wouldn't have cared whether they were selling meat or funerals; it was all the same to me. I didn't care about anything, and Doña Anunciación protected me. One day I made a mistake and confused two accounts, and she told me that I should know that my job there was a gesture of goodwill on the part of a woman who was, above all, always good to others. I remembered then what my mentor in the prison, the Frenchman Daván, had said: that there were two kinds of people, those who like to think of themselves as good and those who choose to believe that they are by nature bad. And that neither group is better than the other, though the people who choose to believe they are good usually hold goodness in higher esteem than evil, since no one would define themselves by what they despise. No one would define themselves as a bad person if they didn't value or admire or envy wickedness even a little. And those who call themselves good probably aren't, though they at least prefer goodness, consider it better for some reason. To me, of course, none of that mattered.

Those were peaceful months. Very peaceful. Time in the present, that's the secret.

"So that's what happened. Who knows what my life would have been like if I hadn't had a couple of drinks that night."

"Probably not that different, Chaudron."

"Now there's a lack of imagination, Mr. Becker. But I would also venture to say, what would his life have been like?"

"Whose?"

"Please, Mr. Becker!"

As soon as I had finished doing the accounts I started over again—revised them, let's say—so that it wouldn't look as if I was doing nothing and so my guest, or refugee, wouldn't pester me. People seem to feel that they're supposed to say all kinds of stupid things out of some misguided notion of good manners. What was strange was that in the end I was the one who started talking to him. I suppose I suffered a moment of vanity, and also, I wanted to see if reading Conan Doyle had served me at all—as I said before, I read a lot.

"You wouldn't by any chance be a painter, would you?"

"Me?"

My silence obliged him to answer the question.

"Yes, I am. Why do you ask?"

I didn't tell him that between the paint stains on his fingers, which he hadn't been able to get rid of completely, and the smell of turpentine that still came through over all the other smells—the undigested alcohol, sweat, cheap perfume, and what might have been vomit—it was fairly clear.

Stranger still, he then began to tell me that he indeed painted portraits, but only from photographs or other portraits, and that if I wanted he could do mine for a reasonable price, and strangest of all, I didn't mind his offer, it piqued my curiosity and we both agreed to meet again. I never did things like that. But I suspect that it was more vanity, and that surprised me—I'd sworn to myself then that I had no vanity. That I, Bonaglia, had none.

"I had never seen myself. It's hard to believe, but I had never had a photograph taken, much less a portrait painted."

"Never, really?"

"I don't think you understand what my life had been like up until then, Newspaperman."

"Believe me, I'm trying."

"I had never really seen myself; it was quite a shock. The face I saw in the painting seemed to be part of a world that was completely different from my own. I wondered, when I saw myself, just how much I didn't know."

He tells him that he doesn't understand why, with that incredible talent for copying, he hasn't put it to better use. He says "better use" so he won't sound too crude. Chaudron just smiles and says, "Who knows?" He learns later that in fact Chaudron has been using his talent for years, but now all he gets is that ambiguous response and the smile, both of which seem to be intended to put him off. But without knowing why, without thinking about it, Bonaglia presses him.

Did he ever think, say, of copying any famous paintings, he asks, and for a moment Chaudron is interested and replies yes, why not, that he's thought of selling reproductions of some paintings before, and he stops talking so Valfierno will reply. And Valfierno looks for a way to say no, I wasn't really talking about reproductions exactly. For a while he searches for a way, hesitating, afraid to cross that line of convention and wondering how it occurred to him to cross it in the first place, and not crossing it until finally Chaudron seems to take pity on him and says, "You know, Bonaglia, that forgery carries some dangers."

It's another invitation. He doesn't use the normal phrase and say that it carries many dangers, which would close off that avenue. No—he says that it carries some dangers, forgery carries some dangers, as if inviting him to weigh these, to take each of them into account in order to think of ways to avoid them. "What dangers, for example, if I might ask?" And Chaudron explains to him that the main danger is in picking the wrong clients. They have to be cultured enough to be able to appreciate and want to own certain paintings. They also have to be harmless enough not to be dangerous if they find out they've been tricked; conceited enough not to want to see anything untoward; and just dishonest enough, he says, smiling, to think that in buying the painting for such a low price they, the buyers, are the ones putting one over on the sellers, and not the other way around. It's important, Bonaglia, for the client to think that he is getting the better of you, even if only a little, says Chaudron, and he seems for a moment like a different person: firm, confident, able to do anything. Not a guy who looks like he's already old and who can't paint anything that hasn't been painted already. Not this Frenchman with the shifting gaze who's all skin and bones, for whom he now pours a glass of wine and looks at in the light from the one bulb that illuminates his office.

Who says to him, "Don't you believe it, don't believe it for a second: no matter what anyone will tell you, it's the seller who makes the rules." Who tells him that he could paint almost anything, but that he could never sell it, that to be able to sell you have to seem as if you don't want to, that you don't need to. That the seller has to be doing the buyer a favor by selling to him—a favor, he repeats, just to sell him the painting; he'll deign to sell it if the buyer insists. He tells him that he couldn't do this, that he wanted to but he couldn't, because he's the sort of person people forget, he leaves no memory. But if he were to find someone who was willing, then he, Chaudron, would also be very willing to set up an arrangement that could be quite fruitful. "Don't you think Bonaglia? What do you say? Just for argument's sake, what do you think?"

"Imagine what I felt. Here I was, in my forties, having decided or at least resigned myself to what I had, little as it was, and to not seek anything more."

"It's a little difficult for me, Valfierno, to recognize you in that sad description."

"No, try to understand, at least this once. I'm not saying this for sympathy; on the contrary, I'm telling you so you can see how far I traveled afterward. So you can understand just how a man can create himself. So you can see the path."

"You mean me?"

"Yes, of course. I mean you. You could do it."

"But tell me, who's going to buy a painting from someone who works for Doña Anunciación?"

"No one. Not from that person, that's what I mean. You'd have to be the kind of person who people would want to buy things from. An amiable fool, easily cheated. A rich man who's come from somewhere else, a wealthy but distant province, something like that. You could be that, Bonaglia, I know you could."

As if that were his mission in life. I took another look at this man, so ardent, so sure. As if he'd been born to create me.

My life was so peaceful. A life in the present.

"No, Chaudron, I'm fine the way I am. If you want to do that, go ahead, but do it yourself. As I said, I'm fine like this."

14

He wanted that calm sea to last forever. If only it would never end, he thinks—so snugly covered by the red blanket, so well secured to the deck of the ship, so definitely not in any one place, so far outside of any laws, so secure—then he wouldn't have to set off down that slippery course waiting for him, down that dangerous path. If only he didn't have to go past this moment now, or at least if he did, if only it could be without the knot squeezing his stomach and his legs shaking. Without the impulse to run, no questions asked.

The drizzle, the noise, the movement, the confusion—he is not bothered by any of these, nor is he intimidated by the arrival in New York. In fact, he tells himself for encouragement, he was there just last summer when he arranged for the sale of the paintings, and everything went smoothly. But he knows that in the next few minutes he will gamble his future. A chain of events is beginning in which he will bet everything on one card not just once but two, three, six times in the next few months. He has been told that this is the easiest part, but he doesn't believe it.

"Eduardo de Valfierno, is that right?"

"Yes, indeed, that's correct."

"Do you have anything to declare?"

"No, I don't, nothing of value," he says in hopelessly bad English as the customs officer begins to go through his bags.

Valfierno wears a suit bought especially for the occasion, sober and very expensive, of an elegance that shows him to be someone for whom none of this is of any interest. With it he wears a short cape of ivory silk and a smart felt hat. The suitcases now being opened by the customs agent are of that kind of fine, light-colored leather so delicate that they can only survive on the better liners, the first-class compartments of trains, and the *grands hôtels*. The investment required for these, along with the cabin on the *Mauritania* and what he will spend in America, will bring him close to the end of his funds. But he is not worried. In a few months, when he has finished, he will never have to think about money again. That will be very strange.

"That's a nice painting."

"Indeed, an excellent copy."

"It looks familiar. What do they call it?"

"The *Mona Lisa*."

"That's it! By an Italian, right?"

"Yes—Leonardo. His name is Leonardo da Vinci. Was Leonardo da Vinci."

The Irish customs agent with the red sideburns stumbles over the pronunciation of "da Vinci" as he continues to lift the paintings out of the big suitcase: two small oils with flamenco themes, an eighteenth-century French landscape.

"Here's another one of those davinchies," he says, placing the second *Mona Lisa* next to the first.

"Yes, I love this painting. It makes a very good gift for the ladies," says Valfierno, giving the man a knowing smile, which comes off as a leer.

The customs agent seems well disposed and not surprised by Valfierno's cargo of reproductions. Valfierno tries to remain impassive. Whoever had told him that it was common for rich tourists to bring back copies of the famous masters was right. That the Americans bought them by the armfuls and that the U.S. Customs didn't pay any attention to them. That they were almost always just reproductions, and—according to the more conspiracy-minded— that the agent would let them pass even if he thought they weren't, as a way to contribute to America's cultural heritage. One way, anyway. This is what Valfierno had been told, and yet he'd had his doubts.

"Is this French cheese?"

"Yes, it's for a friend. Is there a problem?"

"There certainly is. We don't allow foodstuffs into the United States that could be carrying disease or pests," says the customs agent, whose demeanor has in seconds gone from that of a friendly official to a tiger closing in on a kill, all courtesy dispensed with as he smells his prey.

"I'm sorry, but I'll have to confiscate this."

"No, please, it's a gift!"

"I'm sorry, sir, but I have to. I have my job to do."

Valfierno makes a point of his annoyed expression, hoping it will prevent the huge smile he feels from breaking across his face. Later, in his hotel room, he'll take out the two *Mona Lisa*s from the suitcase, as well as another that the agent didn't find, and hide them in the bottom of the clothes closet, wrapped up well in his dirty laundry. The next day, he goes to the offices of a shipping company on the corner of Fulton and Broadway and claims the parcel containing the remaining three paintings. And that evening, he reunites the six of them in his hotel room, leaning them side by side against the wall and staring at them for hours. Strangely, as well as seeing what he expects to see—six times three hundred thousand dollars, his life's fortune, his future security—he sees other things, harder to define, harder to describe. Not only fear, or triumph, or evidence of his own brilliance, or danger. He can't discern it. He wants to know what it is but he can't make it out. He lets sleep overtake him and dreams—of that famous gaze repeated, that reserve, the pleasure of those six smiles.

The next day he buys paper and twine, wraps up all six paintings with great care, and deposits them at a storage company on Houston Street, where they will lie in wait for the moment—in just a few months, if all goes well—when they will meet their destiny.

Valfierno

1

🦋 MY MOTHER, EVERYONE WHO HAS ever changed their country, the girls in the ledgers—at first it was easy. Monsieur Jourdain, who realized he'd been speaking prose all that time and was happy to become that other person. Monte Cristo, who became a count to seek his vengeance. Garay, who went from swineherd to founder of Buenos Aires. Ulysses, who set off as an outcast and a beggar and arrived back where no one expected. Juliet, who asked, "What's in a name?" but whose name killed her.

My mother, everyone who has ever changed their country, Alonso Quijano, of course, Don Quixote. Jupiter himself, who seduced as cow, swan, rain, but not the night, no, not the night, which turns to day to turn back to night, and day, and night again, no. The greatest traitors—who knows?—Merceditas, Don Simón, the Frenchman in prison and far from his home, me—Bollino, poor little Bollino, imprisoned for so little and changed; my mother, the devastation of not knowing, Bollino changed but into what? Going on but without knowing what, changing, changing more, and then Sarmiento, above all Don Domingo Sarmiento; everyone who has ever changed their country.

I had never thrashed about so much in my bed, never turned over so many times. I would think, then turn over again: where did I get the nerve to decide who I was going to be? I thought more. Turned over more. How do you decide who to be? And why? More thinking, more turns, more questions. When I am already me, when I am already this person here.

I had spells of calm toward dawn when I realized that I had already been others in my life, had already done many times what I didn't want to do now. And also that I had not really done it because it had been automatic; I had been others without deciding who to be. I had simply gone from one name to the next, like a leaf blown in the wind, letting fate and certain names carry me along. This time it was different. This time I was deciding who and how to be. This time, a mistake could be disastrous—Juliet with poison, another name. I had made mistakes before, so many times. I kept turning. It wouldn't be easy to keep being who I was, either. I wasn't even who I was. Not easy. Who was I? What would I lose? Domingo Faustino and Monte Cristo. Filthy Ulysses, my mother of the ledgers. I would lose me, as I had before—not a lot to lose, but also everything. Everything is nothing—enough, for God's sake! Garay, Garay. If I sleep then perhaps my dreams will know who it is that's sleeping. Perhaps. Who knows? Who knows anything?

Don Eduardo de Valfierno. I was born on the twenty-ninth of May, 1861, in San Juan, where we owned some land. I am forty-five years old. A little before I turned two, my father moved us to Valparaiso to take over the family business, the principal shipping company there, which his uncle had left him. Of course, his uncle had been born in Genoa. My father was the first generation of Valfiernos to be born in Argentina, and he kept up the customs and traditions of his homeland. Because of this, among other things, when it was time to marry he decided to find a young lady from a good Genovese family, whom he courted by letter and who arrived in Valparaiso when she was barely twenty-one to give herself to this man, who was just a little younger then than I am now.

That girl, my mother, expected the worst. She had few illusions about her future. She knew that her family had sent her to this South American isolation to forge closer bonds with the powerful Valfierno family. She also knew that she would be nothing if she disobeyed. And as this girl, my mother, had expected the worst, I could imagine her relief when she instead found a man who was devoted and respectful, still young, and who tried to make her exile bearable.

In those days, Valparaiso was the busiest port on the South American Pacific coast, and it was there that I grew up. My parents spoke Italian to me, my governess French, and the maid, of course, the peculiar Spanish of that region. I lived there happily, without incident, until I was eighteen. I recall a protected and solitary infancy, my first boyhood games, the jet black hair of that maid, whom we called Nena.

Then that year the war with Bolivia broke out. As all maritime commerce was now interrupted, my father decided to move us to Mendoza, where we waited for over a year for things to change. I saw nothing to attract me in that small, arid settlement, recently rebuilt after its terrible earthquake, and I celebrated when my father, disheartened by the unexpected duration of the war, announced that we would take advantage of this interruption in our lives by going to visit our families in our own land. My mother was delighted; it was the cruelest irony that she died on the Atlantic crossing. My father and I were now alone.

My father refused to return to South America. Over the years, the Genoa family house was the setting for our discussions. He meant for me to continue in the Valfierno tradition of commerce, but I did not honestly feel my heart to be in it, as much as I tried. When I was twenty-five, the death of my mother's father left me with a respectable inheritance, and I wasted little time in deciding that France would be the best place to spend it. I won't tire you by describing those years—you can imagine what it is to be in one's twenties, to have some money, and to take full advantage of what Paris offers. I enjoyed that life until I was thirty-seven; if only it could have gone on forever.

But then my father chose this moment to die. He had

married again, and though they had had no children, his widow managed to get much of what he had, though by then his finances were not in such robust shape. I nonetheless received a fair legacy and of course the title, which I admit I had forgotten about. My father was by rights the Marqués Valfierno but had never liked to flaunt it. On this point I follow his advice: in a republic like this, an aristocrat can be at quite a disadvantage. In Paris, of course, it was different.

I stayed on in Paris for a few years, though in all honesty, my income no longer allowed me the life I had become used to, and on top of that the city was becoming a refuge for decadent bohemians and opportunists without scruples. I no longer considered it a suitable place for a decent man.

People said then that Buenos Aires was the future, though without any contempt for tradition or the old customs. There, they said, a gentleman was still shown the respect he deserved. I have to admit that I had also been thinking of settling down, and that I recalled from my youth the beauty of the women there, and of course the bounty of the land. And that's how I came to return home, and I assure you, I've never regretted it.

"A marqués, Bonaglia? Isn't that a bit much?"
"Who's this Bonaglia, Chaudron?"

His mother, everyone who has ever changed their country, Quixote, Monsieur Jourdain, Sarmiento, the girls in the ledgers, Monte Cristo . . .

It was only later—much later—that he came up with the perfect justification: that he'd always wanted to tackle what was undoubtedly the most difficult of all works of art—a life. And that in order to make a work of art of a life, one had to make it up. That to be the child of one's parents was nature, and that to remain so was simply to resign oneself to nature. That to be a work of art, a life had to be invented.

The justification came much later, though without realizing it, he'd been doing it all along.

"I am Valfierno. I am the Marqués Eduardo de Valfierno."

2

IT HAD IRRITATED HIM AT first, but now the fact that she has delivered Perugia to him has become another of his victories, a prize. It's obvious to everyone, he thinks, that she's not with him for his looks but rather for something else, most likely his money. But he likes the arrangement, it's like wearing a good suit or having a diamond in one's ring—even if people have the wrong idea. And it's not because of that, even if he still doesn't know why it is, even if his attempts to stop seeing her have quietly failed.

And on this day, Valérie is radiant. Her gossamer white dress, a sea of lace, hugs her form. Her necklace sparkles in her cleavage, glinting as it moves with her. She wears a wide-brimmed hat and insouciantly perches a pale pink parasol on her shoulder. Her jet black hair is full and lustrous. Valfierno knows that they envy him, then it suddenly occurs to him that they might instead see him with scorn: another middle-aged man caught in the trap. The idea upsets him.

"Eduardo, listen."

Valfierno looks at her and tries to think of something else. He tells himself he's done a good job with her. He has taught Valérie to hide that vulgar side he finds so exciting so she can be the kind of young lady one can take out occasionally to a place like the Chantilly Hippodrome. Though she still sticks her nose in where it's not wanted:

"Eduardo, I have to ask you a favor."

Valfierno looks around him, imagining all the elegant men and women looking at him. It's occurs to him often, this idea that he is under scrutiny, that he must present himself as if he were on stage. Just in case, he decides to attempt some gallantry.

"Apart from my name and a ring, everything I have is yours."

"Anything real?" she replies, and she smiles with those teeth and everything falls apart. She just doesn't know, can't manage it, and she goes on talking as if she were the same person she was a moment ago, that glorious picture.

"You, I suppose. The only real thing, my dear, is you," he says, playing the fool.

"If that were true we wouldn't keep on seeing each other," she replies, and Valfierno hates her then: she could at least be grateful. It doesn't have to be love, or tenderness, just a little gratitude. Gratitude for supporting her, for taking her out, for playing the fool with her. Why couldn't she play the fool, too? After all, he thinks, that's what arrangements like these are all about—playing the fool together. Valérie passes her tongue slowly across her red lips, pink on red; she knows he can't resist this.

"Really, Eduardo, I want you to keep Perugia out of this whole business. He's too stupid."

At least she doesn't say Vincenzo, he thinks. She's trying to be careful.

"Now you tell me."

"I've always said that, Valfierno."

"What do you mean you've always said that? You've always said the opposite!"

"Never mind, don't complicate things. I want you to leave him out of it. He's a fool, he'll wreck the whole thing."

"I didn't realize you were so in love with that imbecile," says Valfierno, his voice becoming sharp. In contrast, Valérie replies in a throaty whisper:

"Me, in love? Who do you think I am, darling?"

A sea of people advances toward the grandstand as the starting bell rings. Valérie and Valfierno remain by the course, holding on to the rail. The horses' hooves thunder past them on the turf.

"I had a friend who fell in love once. You have no idea what a fool she turned into, or what stupid things she did. I could tell you . . . Make no mistake, I'm serious—if you go ahead with the Italian he'll ruin everything."

"Valérie, you know that without him the whole thing is impossible."

"No, Marqués, I don't know that. Or have you forgotten that you haven't told me a single detail?"

"Why do you want to know details?"

"Because, Marqués, without me none of this could have happened."

"I know that, my dear, and you will be rewarded."

The horses come into the straightaway and the roar of the crowd suddenly swells. Valfierno marvels at how wonderful it must be to have enough money to be able to gamble on something as uncontrollable as some horse's pace. A luxury he will one day allow himself. Perhaps very soon. Yes, very soon.

"Marqués, I insist. That poor guy is a dolt; he'll ruin everything. You have to replace him."

"I don't want us to talk about this anymore, my dear, but take my word for it: without him, this whole thing is impossible. It's that simple. It can't be done without him."

"It can. We just have to find another way."

She speaks to him—she always does this—as if she knew something he didn't. How to handle a man, for example.

"We have to? Valérie, the person who needs to be out of this once and for all is you. All the more so if you don't have faith in your Italian. Think: if he falls, you can fall, too. He knows everything about you: where you live, where you work—everything."

"And not about you?"

"He knows nothing about me. We've met here and there a couple of times. He doesn't know my name, he doesn't know anything. You, on the other hand . . ."

"Yes, of course he knows about me. But don't forget—I know everything about you. Absolutely everything."

Valfierno thinks she might be right, though it doesn't matter. But tells her anyway that there is no way, to forget it.

"Whatever you say. But just remember: if he gets caught, you will, too. I'll make sure of it."

"Who's going to believe a whore?"

"A what?" screams Valérie. He is already regretting it, but it's late for that.

3

I'M SCARED. I DIDN'T WANT to be something I wasn't; I didn't need to. I didn't think I needed anything anymore. And now I'm scared.

"Don't you worry, there's no rush. Let's take our time."
"Our time?"
"Yes, Valfierno, we have to go bit by bit."
"But you said 'our time'?"

I'm pretty sure that at the beginning, he thought he would work on me as if I were a painting. He would find a model, understand its parts, come up with a sketch, color it in, refine every line, and savor the result. I'm quite sure he thought at first that I'd be another of his works.

"That's what I said."

The forger—as I discovered later—is a sort of ascetic, almost a saint. The kind of person who will make big sacrifices, who is willing to renounce all manner of things. There is nothing more dangerous than an ascetic—they think their sacrifice gives them all kinds of authority, all kinds of rights. On the whole, they do the same things as anyone else, just more so. Every creator disappears to some extent behind what he creates. But the forger disappears completely; his existence—and subsistence—depend on his not leaving even the smallest trace. We only know about forgers who have failed. The others—the successful ones—disappear entirely in their works. The one condition of their existence is that they not exist, that they be no one, unidentifiable, having no characteristics: that they pass perfectly as someone else.

I would also have to do this now, to dissolve myself, but into my new life, not a work of art. Though at that moment Chaudron believed that my life was his work of art.

"Our time . . ."

I think—I hope—that there will come a day when I no longer recognize my own face in the mirror. Though the notion is flawed—who would not know who that was in the mirror? For then whose would the face be, and whose the one not recognizing? Of course you'd know the face was yours! Wouldn't you? And me? Would I? Or which one would I be?

Feeling excitement. Still afraid. I'm not a boy anymore.

"Don't you think it was strange to have believed that you could become someone else?"

"Yes, Newspaperman, from this remove it seems like madness."

"And isn't it?"

"Who is it you're talking to now?"

"But where did you get the energy, the confidence to think you could be someone that different?"

"I never had it. I was lucky enough not to know what I was doing."

He asks himself: what will I have to forget? Not: what things will I need to learn or to copy, which gestures or faces or voices will I need to put on, but what things will I have to forget in order to become someone else?

Now, close to being Valfierno, Bonaglia spends his last three months at the brothel preparing, carefully reading about places where he'll say he has lived, studying the lives of the great masters, and poring over reproductions of their most famous paintings. He escapes to the theater whenever he can to learn manners and graces. He spends hours with *Who's Who*, learning about the people who will be his new peers. He listens to Chaudron's stories of Paris, hones his prison French, practices poses and accents in front of the mirror. As if all of this, he thinks—the watching and reading and listening—could be enough to make him another person. As if anything could be.

Many nights I felt like a fool. I feared I wouldn't be able to do this, I wouldn't be able to pull it off.

He takes down the mirror. He unhooks that cracked, badly silvered mirror from the wall of his bedroom-office so that he won't look at himself until he sees someone else. He says this out loud—"until I see someone else"—but in truth he takes it down for fear of seeing no one.

Then one night in that room—where he continues to work for the time being until his transformation is complete and he will finally have to leave it as someone else—he realizes that he's been preparing for this for years, though he didn't know it before. That his early years in the big mansion, all his reading, his days in the shop, his long nights of imaginings, his deciding to stop imagining were all preparation, though he hadn't known it at the time. Seeing now that everything was leading to this, he is overjoyed. He has at last discovered some meaning for all those years. Everything justified at last, he thinks, and he wonders who or what he can thank for this gift.

Everything comes together now, and this coming together fills him with a new energy. Like being born into a new world, he thinks.

"Did you really feel like that, Valfierno?"

"Yes, I really did."

"It must be wonderful to believe that everything has a meaning, a purpose."

"It's humbling. Looking back, I realize that I still had a lot of work to do at that point, a lot of effort before me. For the moment, I was still the same."

"I don't understand."

"It's not surprising, but try. There's nothing more fundamentally human than the satisfaction of following what you believe is your destiny. Can you see how humbling that is?"

"On the contrary. As I said, I envy you."

"Of course, that's why you do what you do; I don't blame you for that. It took me a while to realize that the life I was about to begin was not in fact my destiny at all, but my choice. It was the exact opposite of going along with someone else's decision. It was, ultimately, my own work."

I was going to become someone else because that's what I wanted. All that would be left of my old self would be not wanting to be him.

He grows his beard and tints his few early grey hairs. He has put back the mirror. If he could have remembered the person he'd been before, he'd have said that he no longer looked much like him. He tries to forget all about him, but can't.

"I think it's time now."

"You do? I'm not so sure."

"How much longer?"

"Just a few days?"

He dreams—it's actually a daydream, but he likes to think of it as a dream—that he runs into his mother on a street in Rosario and that she looks at him and is about to say something. Then he dreams—he prefers to think that he dreams it—that he's about to tell her not to say anything, but this makes him sad, and he says nothing and instead listens to his mother talk. But he doesn't understand what she's saying. He can't make out either the words or the gestures.

Sometimes, as practice, to make up new dreams for Valfierno, he imagines that, rich and elegant, he finds Marianita Baltiérrez and marries her and buys the big house for her from her idiot brother Diego—if he owns it—and once again they play in the park, in that little room under the roof, in the big master bedroom. He doesn't dream this, he daydreams. Bonaglia no longer dreams; Valfierno does.

I was afraid.

"Valfierno, come on, it's time to begin."

"What's wrong, Chaudron, are you running out of funds?"

"This can't go on forever, and anyway there's no point. Believe me, when I look at you now I see someone else completely. I never even think of calling you Bonaglia anymore."

"Perhaps, Chaudron, perhaps. I was thinking about how to begin this. I suppose we have to do something, don't we, to start this?"

"Well, of course. First of all, you have to leave this place."

"Of course."

"No, I mean you have to live somewhere else. I'll lend you enough to rent a room somewhere. When we get our first money you can pay me back."

"A room?"

"Sure. Obviously it's not going to be as good as what you should have, but in the beginning we're going to have to adapt. In the beginning, no one should know where you live."

"That's a problem. We'll also have to get me some clothes. But I was thinking more about how I can get to be known. I had the idea of the turtle."

"The idea of what?"

"The turtle. It's simple—I go out dressed well but not too well, no top hat, just a hat, and I walk a turtle along Calle Florida."

"Valfierno . . ."

"No, wait, listen. I go out with this turtle on a leash and I walk it, and the people we're interested in will notice one important thing: that time doesn't matter to me. That I'm an aristocrat, not like those common *porteños* who rush around all day in a frenzy from one place to another. That's what this will say—that I'm not one of them and I don't mind showing it."

"Valfierno . . ."

"No, I'm very serious. We can get in touch with a couple of reporters, maybe the fellow from *Caras y Caretas* or *El Hogar*, and overnight all of Buenos Aires will be talking about me. You see?"

"But Valfierno, don't you see that for the kind of thing we're doing it's very important to be discreet?"

"We still need to get people to know about me, don't we?"

"Yes, but we have to do it bit by bit, without a scene."

"Chaudron, I've spent my whole life living bit by bit, without a scene. That's over for me, you understand? Over."

"But you can't just show up one day out of the blue and be the star of the show. It doesn't work like that."

"Don't tell me how it works, Chaudron."

"Valfierno, please, listen to me."

Without question the easiest thing in the world—to take advantage of death.

4

"THE FUNNY THING IS THAT he says it was you who convinced him to become Valfierno."

"Why is that funny? Because he's some fancy so-and-so and I'm just an old guy stuck in a chair? Because you're such a Newspaperman that you can't imagine anything that you can't see right in front of you? Because you haven't figured out that there was a time when your hero was just a poor sap? Or because you don't want to know?"

"Did he change very much once he started being Valfierno?"

" 'Very much' doesn't begin to describe it, Newspaperman. See if you can understand—when I met him, he was one of those guys who's already given up, who doesn't want to go any further; all he wants to do is to stay where he is and not move."

5

THE FIRST ONE OF US to talk to the widow López del Mazo was Chaudron, if I remember. His partner, the photographer, was making a fortune in a previously untapped part of the market: photographic portraits of people who had just died. Occasionally, someone would also request a painted portrait, depending either on the wealth of the deceased or the guilt of the next-of-kin. Don Indalecio López del Mazo had been an attorney to the great Anchorena dynasty, Vice Minister of Commerce, and above all, through his many memberships in this and that commission or delegation, had organized the Archbishopric of Buenos Aires to protect his various business interests.

His wife had not given him any children. To occupy herself and maintain her devotion free of all tests, she was active in several of the ladies' associations from the better parishes of Buenos Aires society. Her grief on becoming a widow did not prevent her from deciding to commission a portrait of her dear departed that would forever adorn her salon.

When he presented the portrait to her, Chaudron asked if she had decided yet what to give to the Church of San Francisco, where, as Don Indalecio had stipulated, one hundred masses would be said for the eternal rest of his soul. When the widow replied that she hadn't, Chaudron told her that he could recommend the ideal donation and suggested that she contact me, Don Eduardo de Valfierno.

We waited for six days and were finally in despair when I received a note from the widow inviting me to visit her at her house on the Calle Esmeralda. I remember being nervous as I rang the doorbell. A dark young maid opened the door. There was something about the way she lowered her eyes and didn't look at me that calmed me.

The widow raised herself very slightly to greet me and then fell back into an armchair that was much too big for her. I was also relieved at how tiny she was. I offered my condolences and she served me tea in a china cup.

Thankfully the small talk was brief. I had dreaded that part much more than the negotiation itself. But the widow was not one for trivialities, or she may have felt that this was not the moment for them. So as soon as she brought up Chaudron's proposal I told her about the painting that had been in my family for generations and that now, regrettably, I was obliged to part with. A work by the master Murillo, Madam; you can imagine the heartbreak. From what I could tell she could imagine the heartbreak but not a painting by Murillo, the great master of the Spanish baroque, whose name sounded Croatian to her. Of course she didn't want to admit this, and she asked me a few general questions about the painting. I did my best to inform her without wounding her pride: "It is, of course, a painting of San Francisco, Madam, but painted as only a baroque master could, with that richness of detail, and the Christian feeling of such a depth that he seems to be right there, Madam. I can assure you, there has never been a painter closer to the doctrines of our Holy Mother."

The widow López del Mazo listened attentively, sunk in her large armchair, and seemed quite defenseless until I mentioned the price I expected for the painting. At this, she sat up and showed me her teeth. They were a yellow color but all there. She told me that I should not be fooled by appearances.

"Never, Madam," I replied, "but I'm not sure what you're referring to."

"Everything you see around you, Señor de Valfierno, my husband required for his business dealings and social functions; don't for a moment imagine that we are millionaires."

"Please, Doña Socorro—if anyone knows how easily money can come and go, it is I. But what we are discussing is a true work of art."

"Yes, of course."

"A work of art and, moreover, a donation for the eternal repose of your husband's soul."

"Of course, and I realize that it's a different thing to be buying from a gentleman like yourself, rather than from one of those Italian or Galician peddlers."

The widow presented me with another cup of tea and with a smile that was clearly supposed to be meaningful but that I didn't understand. I responded with one of my own. She rose to her feet—a difficult process. While we waited for the maid, she told me she wanted first to consult with the parish priest of San Francisco, and that after that we could speak again—and she asked me to lower the price. I replied that I'd be delighted, but that it was a Murillo.

"A Murillo, yes, of course," she said.

On the way back I passed people but no one gave me a second look. I couldn't believe it, it was working! Ten days later we had concluded the deal, and Chaudron's painting was installed with great ceremony next to the altar in the church of San Francisco. The priest was happy; he must have done some research into the price of a Murillo and had bent over backwards to attend to the generous widow.

It was our first operation. The next two were also successful, and, more than that, they were the confirmation that we could pull this off. The confirmation that I was, finally, Valfierno.

That the world is a place full of things, shining things, and above all, full of other worlds.

"So you made your first big haul."

"Yes. Trite as it is."

"I wouldn't call it trite to have taken ten thousand pesos off a couple of millionaires. Ten thousand pesos is a tidy sum."

"It's very easy to become rich, Mr. Becker. There's nothing easier. All you have to do is to take a look at who they are—the ones who don't have the imagination to want anything else. The ones who want the same as everyone else, only a little more."

Yes, of course. The thing is, I lived in Paris most of my life, that's why, and I no longer care for the city, so I've come back.

Yes, exactly, I'd like to sell a handful of paintings. They're just trifles, really, whims of my late grandfather, and I must confess that the upkeep of my various houses keeps me rather busy.

Yes, why not?

Most certainly. Of course.

In the end, to change—to tell yourself that you are now someone else—is not all that difficult. The problem is to get others to believe it. The problem is not the creation, but the recognition— to be is to be perceived. Lucky that it's Argentina, he thinks.

Argentina was perfect for that.

To look in the mirror and see the traces.

Still

to see

so many traces.

Then he offers me a drink and says, "How is it that we've never met before?" and I explain that I've had such an itinerant life, so many years abroad but now at last I'm back, in the landscape of my childhood, and he says of course, that he'd forgotten that. "A good thing to have met now, Marqués. You know with all the riffraff that's come pouring into our country it's a pleasure when you do meet a decent man, a gentleman, someone like us." And he tells me that we must get together some day soon at his club for lunch, and I say, "Of course, with the greatest of pleasure," and something flashes in his eyes and I find out later that "with the greatest of pleasure" is wrong, that we don't say that, and I don't know that then but I do know that I've made some mistake—the fear of making a mistake always there, always present—but he continues, concluding, I imagine, that my years abroad must be to blame for these small slip-ups. But I have just gone through a difficult moment, another difficult moment, the trap always ahead, always menacing.

I was right on the edge. Always right on the edge.

She isn't thinking what all the others have thought. She sighs heavily when I lift my champagne glass and tell her that her eyes have cast a spell on me. Her smile is an invitation I pretend not to accept yet so that she'll have to insist. She fixes my eyes with the most provocative gaze and slips the strap off her left shoulder like a dare, challenging me to keep my eyes on hers as she undresses, and I do, of course, being a man of the world, with lots of experience. This is what she is thinking about me—not about whether I am who I say I am—as she lowers the other strap and her slip slides off her shoulders and barely catches on her breasts, in such a fortuitous and precarious way, threatening to fall with every breath. And, breathing fast now, she looks up at me and smiles awkwardly, nervously, afraid of how my eyes are judging her, and my hands, and of my years of carousing; afraid of not measuring up. To cover this, she lets herself fall onto the couch with a little pout and I pretend not to notice that now, mischievously, the slip has fallen down to her waist, barely around her waist, no longer covering anything, and finally she says, "Marqués, please! Can't you see that I'm crazy about you? Please, Marqués, I can't pretend, don't be so cruel, Marqués," and then at that moment I know that I wasn't mistaken.

Yes—on the very edge, crossing back and forth over it constantly. Inventing myself, creating myself.

The important thing is to appear indifferent. Everyone there believes that to betray any hint of wonder would be vulgar, a sign of poor breeding. There are more than nine hundred guests present, as if to prove that Buenos Aires is one of the cities with the greatest number of the great and the rich, and they eye one another knowing that apart from the occasional oversight, they can be safe in the knowledge that they are the best, or as they say, "the right sort," which is to say, the ones who held on to their lands and their retinues. They are comfortable—it's so good to be in such a privileged setting, surrounded by friends, family, and colleagues, not out of fear, thinks Aliaga, but just for the comfort of knowing one is understood.

While the guests project a certain indifference, they look around surreptitiously, impressed by the display: the Limoges china monogrammed with a gilt *G*. The solid sterling cutlery by Christofle, the handles capped with a cattle-head crown. The Baccarat crystal smashing periodically in a constant tinkle of money. The fine Andalusian needlework of the table linens. The enormous arrangements of flowers. An orchestra made up of twenty-four music professors, which can barely be heard. The commemorative medal every guest has received, inscribed: Guerrico Family—Golden Wedding—By the Grace of God.

It isn't too difficult—certainly less difficult than it looks—to maneuver the partridge stuffed with foie gras without spilling it on himself. Valfierno is wearing tails; between sips of the French champagne he dabs his lips with a napkin.

"So you are Eduardo de Valfierno? My aunt Amelia has told me a great deal about you."

"Marqués Eduardo de Valfierno, at your service."

"Ah, yes, of course—Marqués. I am Mariano de Aliaga. How do you do."

"You told him you were a marqués?"

"Yes—I am a marqués. If you're going to make it up, my

dear Chaudron, you mustn't be timid. You must exaggerate if you want them to believe you!"

"Be careful, Valfierno. Make sure you don't ruin everything now."

The servants who approach with the *rôti de veau truffé* and the Château Latour are English and German. Valfierno, too, is feigning indifference, but he is afraid to speak. In spite of all the preparation of the past few months, he is afraid of getting his words wrong, of just missing the accent. By contrast Aliaga, his neighbor at the dinner table, has no such problem. It's stupid, thinks Valfierno, that what takes so much effort for him is so natural for the rest of them. They don't even notice his effort: they have no way to appreciate it. He does it better than they do, he thinks, and he'd like them to realize it, but he knows he must be satisfied with simply parting them from their money.

Aliaga is ranting. He tells Valfierno that he won't put up with these European servants who for God knows what reason believe they are superior.

"They steal from us, they sneer at us, and they live off us! They're only here because they were dying of hunger in their own country and now they act as if they're doing us a favor, those good-for-nothings! There was a time when we had our faithful Negroes, who had been with us sometimes for two generations."

The woman across from him nods vigorously in agreement and says, "Don't worry, Mariano, in ten or fifteen years this lot will also have learned their place."

"You're right, my dear, it doesn't usually take longer than that, but right now it's very annoying. We've had enough of these foreigners coming in and watering down our traditions, don't you agree, Marqués?" and the Marqués agrees, of course. And he tells some Bavarian to bring him more wine—yes, Latour.

"Did we manage to get any clients?"

"Let's not get ahead of ourselves, Chaudron. Just to be there was itself a real triumph."

"In other words—no."

"You need to show a little patience, Chaudron."

Mariano de Aliaga tells him he mustn't pass up the Château d'Yquem, that though he himself prefers it as an aperitif, it has to be said that it's delicious with the *marrons glacés*. Valfierno, who has never had it but has read about it somewhere, replies that no, he considers it a dessert wine, and the two begin a debate. Aliaga is about the same age as Valfierno but is at least a head taller, even sitting down, and he shows the signs of having lived, with greyish skin and small veins around his eyes.

By contrast, Doña Inés Ezcurra, a distant cousin of the hosts, is a woman of more than seventy years, imperious and wealthy. She says excuse me, that she happened to hear his name and wanted to know if he was the one who had sold Doña Soledad that nice painting. Valfierno can't decide if this is lucky or a disaster, but he has no choice but to respond.

"Yes, Señora, I was the one; delighted to make your acquaintance. My grandfather, you know, was an incurable collector. Unfortunately, these are different times."

"I think I understand," says Doña Inés, and she attempts to exchange a knowing look with Aliaga, but he doesn't respond. The first waltz begins to play—the "Blue Danube"—and the honored pair, bearing their fifty years of union, dance heavily while a thousand people applaud.

Soon more people follow, their pristine soles moving on the floor of English oak, dancing beneath an enormous chandelier, its three thousand crystals sparkling under a cupola painted with seven buxom nymphs escaping from Apollo, three plump sirens driving men mad, three curvy maidens bathing the blood from their bodies, and two even plumper Hesperides watching over their mythical garden. And in the middle of it all, up on that ceiling, was Jupiter, as a bull, ready to take a voluptuous Europa, half naked, her skin white.

Below, turning in time to the waltz, were women such as Valfierno had never imagined, women who don't exist outside of that realm. Women from the society magazines but who in those photographs didn't smell like this, whose hair and skin didn't shine like this, who didn't move like this, who weren't graced with such majesty. These women are clearly of another world, one that smells of roses and gardenias, and Valfierno tries not to be too affected by it, knowing that whatever else, they are not his. Women, he thinks, who work on themselves even more than I do. Who make themselves more beautiful, into superior works of art, to be seen.

"So, my friend," says Aliaga, "you are something like an art dealer," and he raises his champagne glass in a toast.

"I'm not sure that's it exactly, but yes, I have sold the occasional painting here and there," replies Valfierno. "Only classics, mind you."

"That's what we're missing, dear fellow—classics," says Aliaga. "We're a young country. And powerful. We are the future; what we don't have at the moment is a past," he says, and Valfierno takes a chance.

"That, too, can be purchased," he says, and surprises himself for having said it. But Aliaga is with him.

"Very true, dear fellow. There's nothing easier to buy than a past," he says and smiles to himself. Valfierno hopes that the sound of the waltz has covered up his sigh of relief. "Soon, my friend, Europe won't even have that left. *Quelle décadence, mon ami, quelle décadence.* They created it, but we'll have it," says Aliaga. "And then soon, we'll begin to make our own."

"Perhaps we're already making it," says Valfierno. *"Peut-être, Aliaga, ne croyez-vous pas?"*

"Perhaps, Marqués, perhaps. I'll drink to that."

"The smugness of some Argentines knows no limits!"

"You should be grateful. If it weren't for that we wouldn't be able to make our deals."

"You're right, Valfierno. That's what we're living off now."

"Not just living, Chaudron. This is more than that."

There's a moment where many people finally let themselves go. They have eaten like the kings in their fantasies and drunk rivers of silver. They have exchanged the highest compliments, valuable nuggets of information, thrilling gossip, jokes that are subtle and jokes that are coarser, and then even eternal promises of friendship. They have danced with bodies they know and with new bodies, rejected the temptation to respond to the pressure of that hand on their back, accepted that temptation, imagined futures with that hand, rejected those futures. Grateful for their luck and to their God for having put them where they are, for bestowing on them that country, that moment, that surname, that grace. For being allowed to be one of them, offered the chance to decide for so many others, to help so many others.

And then more champagne, more toasts, more smiles, more satisfied faces, promises, greetings, the stifling of a belch, some gentler dances, then exhausted, they rest briefly, feeling a pang that the end of the party is approaching. They sit—many of them—on chairs and in softer armchairs, and they loosen—some of them—their ties, or a button on their dress, and they let their bodies relax, their minds relax; they tell themselves they deserve this last rest before declaring the party dead. It's at that moment, tucked away on his chair, that Valfierno notices the hands.

He discovers—has just discovered and been surprised, then amazed, then finally alarmed—what hands can do when their owner isn't paying attention. He had been looking around for a while at people's hands, and suddenly he sees his own hands and is startled. Unattended, his hands lie with their palms up as if beseeching, the fingers slightly bent, an air of flaccid disarray that discredits them and, he fears, discredits him also.

He looks back at the hands around him, the perfectly poised hands of the wealthy partygoers, delicately posed—the hands themselves both delicate and posed—their jeweled rings glittering along the edge of a tablecloth like a miniature, sparkling shoreline. One hand on the other, resting delicately on the thigh, on the black evening dress. One hand resting delicately on the other with the white gloves held in between them to prevent sweat from making them moist and slippery. The fingers of one hand laced with those of the other and held in front of the midriff, or the chest, not touching, just in front, intertwined in midair. An ancient learning, years of work that allows their hands to be controlled even when they are not controlling them. Valfierno looks at his own hands, which are now sweating, and sees that he has no control over them, that everyone can see them, can see him. That he still has so far to go.

Then, to signal that the party is over, the orchestra begins to play the overture to Ponchielli's *La Gioconda*. The sound is sad. Valfierno is not listening.

"The most complicated thing was to have to keep making up my history. To have to do it all the time."

"What do you mean?"

"If someone asks you about your family, Newspaperman, I'm sure you don't have to think too much. All you have to do is remember, right?"

"Sure. Though I do forget some things."

"That doesn't matter. I, on the other hand, had to be ready all the time to put aside my own memories and replace them with Valfierno's. Doesn't that seem to you like a fascinating exercise?"

"No, it sounds terrible."

"Well, Newspaperman, it was and it wasn't. Until the day that it wasn't anything: the day I realized that I no longer had any memories of my own. Then I knew I had truly become Valfierno. But you have no idea what it cost me later to get those memories back."

6

"So do you have a buyer yet, Boss?"

"Why would that be any business of yours?"

"No, I'm just saying . . ."

"Well don't say, Perugia, don't say anything. Let's get things straight from now on: you stick to the plan and you'll get lots of dough and you'll live like a king for the rest of your life. I'll take care of everything else, and the less you know about it the better things will go for you in that new life of yours, understand?"

"Yeah, I get it, Boss, you don't need to be so—"

"I'm not so anything, Perugia. I just want to make sure you know that if there's any slip-up I'm not going to be the one in deep water."

"Okay, sure."

"I'm not the one who was in jail three years ago over some story about broken locks. Or two years ago over a jackknife."

"What?"

"You heard."

"No, Signore, I don't understand . . ."

Valfierno realizes that subtlety will not work with him and decides on brutality. Sometimes, he thinks, there is no other choice.

"See if you understand this—the police know you very well. You make any mistake and I'll make sure they know exactly where to find you."

Perugia looks at him, startled. Valfierno wonders if he's overdoing it, if he's got the tone right.

"Easy, Boss, calm down."

"Do I look nervous to you?"

Valfierno is wearing a checked cap pulled low over his eyes. His Panama hat would have stood out in this Les Halles workers' bar, and it amuses him to think that he now has to disguise himself to go to a place where he wouldn't even have been noticed just a few years ago. Perugia, bareheaded, raises his glass of red wine in a toast; Valfierno touches his glass half-heartedly. The air in the bistro is a fog of tobacco smoke, stew, and sweat.

"Starting now, you've got to watch yourself with the drinking, Vincenzo. Wine makes even the dead speak up."

"Don't worry, Boss, I know how to be careful," says Perugia and, superstitious, he makes the sign of horns with his right hand. He doesn't like people to mention the dead. He also doesn't like that his boss has his hat on inside—everybody knows it's bad luck. Some people just can't stop playing with fire, he thinks. And then they're surprised when they get burnt.

"Let's go over the plan again, Perugia."

"Again, Doctor?"

"Like I said: we're going over it again. Now, next Sunday you and your two friends will meet up in the Duchâtel Room. You know which one that is, Perugia?"

"Sure, Doctor, of course."

"Let me repeat: you are not to go in together. You're to meet up once you're in there. You go in one side and your friends can go in the other, all right? And dress decently so you don't attract attention. And don't forget the tools . . ."

Perugia carefully follows what his boss is saying. His mouth hangs open slightly in concentration.

". . . very important to have the white coats. You know this better than I do—any guy in a white coat can do what he likes in that museum and no one will ask him any questions. The French are big on uniforms, aren't they?"

From the next table over, two very mature whores try to get their attention with pouts and subtle signs. One runs a dry tongue across her lips. The other grabs her crotch with her thick, rough hand. The two men pay no attention.

". . . and as soon as you get the painting out onto the street, go right to the woman's house. I might show up then."

"Yes, Boss. We need you to—"

"I'll be the one to say what we need. If I don't show up, leave the painting there and then each of you go back to where you were, you understand, Perugia? Don't change any of your regular habits, keep doing everything like you always do. That Monday, go to work like nothing happened; don't change anything, you hear me? Don't change anything."

"No, Signore. Why would I change?"

"Because I'm about to give you quite a bit of money. But if you know what's good for you, you'll leave it alone for a few months . . ."

"You'll give me half, like we said?"

Perugia's eyes light up—small, black, close together, they grip his wide, hooked nose over an unkempt mustache. His features look as if they've been hewn with an ax, reflects Valfierno, and he asks himself what Valérie could see in him. Those large cheekbones, the thick fingers drumming on the table. He tries to thinks about something else, but he can't. What the hell does Valérie see in this hick, he asks himself, and for a moment his indignation turns into hatred, and he wonders if he could take advantage of this whole plan to get rid of him—a tidy little scheme. Valfierno tries to calm down. It would not be easy to do without risking the whole operation; enough of that! He has to calm himself, to keep talking, to show Perugia that he's in charge. His reward for now is showing Perugia that he's the boss—showing Valérie, too, though she can't see them.

"Yes, half, your half. But I'm serious—don't change anything. Nothing has happened. The police will probably come by in the first few days."

"The police? Why the police?"

Perugia is startled, and Valfierno thinks he might have found a way—and this idea both comforts and worries him.

"Don't worry, man. They're bound to visit everyone who works at the museum or who used to work there. Don't worry, don't be frightened—they have nothing on you. It'll be a routine visit, and that's how you should treat it. As soon as they've been to see you, you go get the painting and bring it back to your pension. Take good care of it there and send me the message we talked about. I'll come by, pay you the rest, and take the painting."

"Sounds like that's everything, Boss. You think there's going to be a lot of excitement?"

"There's going to be more excitement than you can imagine, Perugia, but don't worry; it won't be about you. But there is going to be a huge fuss. You see how proud the French are? Stealing *La Joconde* is going to seem to them like an insult to the whole country."

"Shit! And when they find out it was an Italian carpenter!" says Perugia and immediately regrets it. Nothing is worse luck than to say something that could come true. Making sure Valfierno can't see him he touches his left testicle for good luck as he suffers a brief wave of fear. Why does he keep doing things that are bad luck? How many things has he already done? The world is too complicated for him.

"They're never going to know that, Perugia!"

"No, I know, Doctor. I was just thinking out loud."

"You're not supposed to think, I already told you."

"I know, Boss, I know. But think about it—the French took her from us and now we're going to get her back!"

Valfierno and Perugia speak Italian to each other, Perugia with a Tuscan accent, Valfierno with an accent that's impossible to define. The Marqués thinks about his mother. What would she say if she could see him—a marqués now? If she knew that soon all the world's newspapers would be talking about him—even if they didn't know who he was.

"All right, then, Perugia—is everything clear?"

"Everything's clear, Boss."

"Next Sunday."

"Next Sunday."

Valfierno thinks he ought to feel some fear—he's just set in motion the robbery of the century. He ought to feel something; how odd that he doesn't. Perhaps it's a bad sign.

7

WE HAD AGREED TO SEE each other again, but it was another three weeks before I presented myself at the house of Mariano de Aliaga. I excused myself and told him that I'd had to take care of some things at the Mendoza ranch. He asked if we made wine there, and I told him that we did but not much, just for friends, though I'd be delighted to send over a cask for him.

His house was modest when you compared it to the great Guerrico mansion—just two floors by the Plaza San Martín with a French mansard roof and Italian Carrara marble. But I had done some research. Aliaga had fifty thousand acres of lush pampa there.

My new friend received me warmly. He led me to his study, offered me some fine cognac, and we spent a couple of hours there talking about everything and nothing, and especially about art. I couldn't get over the fact that we could just sit there, chatting, sharing those peaceful moments—me, there, so close and so far away.

Above his fireplace he had a small painting in a newly gilded frame that was done very much in the style of Delacroix. I told him that it looked like the work of a serious disciple of his.

"No, please, look closely. It's Delacroix *lui-même*," he said.

"Ah, yes, of course."

"And most of all, you can't deny the influence he had on the eighteenth-century French painters."

"I'm sorry—who is that?"

"Vermeer, Valfierno."

"Yes, of course—Johannes Vermeer. His *View of Delft* is so beautiful, Aliaga. Have you seen it?"

"Beyond words. And it shows how wrong the world can be.

How do you explain that it took two hundred years before he finally got the recognition he deserved?"

"It does make you wonder—how can the real genius of the man have been overlooked? And I don't mean by the masses—by enlightened people!"

"Yes, a genius—a real genius. And his interiors! His *Dentellière*, his *Girl Reading a Letter by an Open Window*, his *Milkmaid*."

"Ah, yes, the *Milkmaid*. I can't tell you how much that affected me when I saw it."

"In the Louvre?"

"Yes, of course."

"Yes, in the Louvre. A delight. I'd even say a real masterpiece."

He lives on the Calle Laprida, near the Calle Santa Fe, in an apartment with two bedrooms and a small living room which are nicely—almost fussily—furnished. It's the first time in his forty-odd years that he's lived anywhere like this, though of course he can't give out his address, as it's still not appropriate for a marqués.

His wardrobe consists of six suits, one evening suit, a top hat, three homburgs, four pairs of the finest Grimoldi shoes, two walking sticks that he doesn't like to use, and a dozen shirts. Everything is of the finest quality. He has spent more money on clothing than he has, and Chaudron had protested, but Valfierno had told him that these were the necessary tools of his trade, though he knows it's only partly true. He likes the elegant clothes and knows that without them he could not continue to be Valfierno. Sometimes, furtively, when no one is looking, he'll feel the softness of a sleeve's fine English cloth, or the fit of a collar, and it seems to him as if he's feeling his own history.

His circle of acquaintances is growing; it is no longer unusual for him to be invited to social events, and the bad taste left over from his first, clumsy appearances is now gone. He is sure now that in a few months, or perhaps a year or two, he will have become a full member of Buenos Aires high society, though he knows that he will never be able to let down his guard. He has noticed this happening occasionally, and it worries him.

He has recently met a young widow, not very wealthy but quite respectable, from a very good family, who has given him clear signals that his attentions would be welcomed. He has taken her on walks near Palermo and is considering inviting her to the Colón Theater and perhaps out for dinner afterwards at Charpentier. But he does not want to move things along with Amelia because he considers her a good woman and the relationship potentially serious. He supposes that she is attracted by his title, but he can hardly fault her for that—him, of all people.

He has also met a laundress who doesn't know how to wash clothes—a young Milanesa, ambitious and blond—who sleeps with him on Tuesdays and Fridays, accepts his gifts with a suitable pout, and produces in him a strange disquiet—he is afraid that this might be an error that could cost him dearly, knowing as he does that these extras are never free. But he feels wonder at the fact that on the following Tuesday, the next Friday, that voluptuous body will tumble with him in his bed. It's clear that she is attracted by his apparent fortune, but he can hardly fault her for that—him, of all people.

He tells her that he knows what it's like not to know how one's life will turn out, that he understands her. When he says this she looks at him with a strange expression that he can't make out. It could be that she simply doesn't believe him: "How could you know, Eduardo, you, a marqués, what it's like to be a poor laundress like me just starting out." Or it could be that she's never actually felt what he's attributing to her. That it's never occurred to her to think of her life as something to consider in advance, as something to think about at all. Or it could be that she simply doesn't understand him. He tells her she's right—that he doesn't know, that he knows absolutely nothing.

But she laughs and thinks he must be lying.

"If you could be something else, Giannina, what would you be?"

"Ay, Eduardo—the things you think of!"

"You know what, Newspaperman? I was content. I'd venture to say that for the first time in my life I'd found my place. And I'd learned that anyone who blamed circumstances for not reaching his goals was just lying. That anyone with enough will can get what he wants, and that those who don't are the weak, the ones who don't measure up. That those who only get part of the way deserve it. That if you're poor it's because you don't know how not to be, or because you want to be. And that there's nothing worse than those who call themselves Socialists, who believe it's good to be poor. Just like the priests, who comfort them and convince them that wretchedness is a blessing."

"Did you ever think about that, Eduardo?"

"Well, sure I have, sometimes."

"And what did you think?"

"Oh, nothing; I barely remember."

But neither did he feel like a great man. He thought that there might have been a moment when he was almost there, but that was much later, after the moment had passed. That's how those moments are, he thought. Who could ever recognize them when they were right there in front of you, and not long after they'd gone? Who could ever really know them, savor them, grab hold of them?

He thought that he'd become accustomed now to being who he was, and that you could only feel great in those rare, short moments when you passed from one state to another, those moments in which you grow, the way a river appears, he thought, or a word comes into being. And that now he would never feel that. He had let his one chance slip away. If only he could start everything again and be right at the beginning of it all.

Now that he'd achieved it, he'd lost that chance.

He is proud to have learned so much about art and paintings. He can now unfailingly tell the difference between a Murillo and a Zurbarán, for example, though he still cannot differentiate between a Murillo by Murillo and a Murillo by Chaudron. This comforts him.

He is also proud of his library: all of Mercedes' books, along with the books he bought during all those years and the books about art that he buys now under the pretext of needing them for his work. He only wished he had more time to read them; building his life is a project that takes a great amount of energy.

And he is proud because, from time to time, he realizes he has recovered an idea that he had had before, and hated then—the idea that things would go on being the way they were now. Unlike then, he now finds this a most comforting thought.

There are times when he forgets just how new his life is, or that some would not consider it his.

Once in a while he gets the idea—if you can call it an idea—that there might still be time for him to have a child. At one point he'd wondered about Amelia, but worries—whose child would this be? Eduardo de Valfierno? A false child. Then he tells himself that everyone is like that: the child of someone, but who can always say of whom?

But most of all, how strange to think of this now, to want it. That more has changed than he expected. He thinks he likes it but he can't be sure.

No, not sure.

Sometimes he thinks that in spite of everything, Valfierno can never be sure.

"I have a great many friends, you see? That's what makes all the difference—having or not having friends. Being a part of things, or not. And I have many friends; we've all known each other forever. We can't even remember when we met since we've just always been friends. These are the kind of friends you can ask for almost anything. They are decent people, these friends of mine—most of them."

"Of course. I, too, have some friends, but as I lived so many years abroad . . ."

"Exactly. As I was saying, my friends are decent people, though in fact some of them are not. You have to have friends like that, too."

"I know what you mean."

"No. I don't think you do. The thing is, I had some of these friends find out about you. I know all about you, Bonaglia."

"What? What are you talking about?"

"Don't play the fool, Bonaglia. And above all don't take me for a fool. You don't get to where I am by being a fool. You must have thought we were all idiots, that you could just appear out of nowhere and say that you were a marqués and that you'd come from Paris—without even knowing where to find the paintings that you claimed you had seen, Bonaglia. *The Milkmaid* in the Louvre? You have a long way to go. If you'll excuse my saying so, Bonaglia, the only idiot here is you."

"But—"

"No, Bonaglia, no buts. I've already listened to you too much—now you listen to me. I would, if I were you, if I wanted to survive. If you care about surviving, if it matters to you. Very simply—either you give me all the paintings or you'll go to jail for false identity, and that's just the beginning. That'll get you a few years in prison. After that, if you're lucky, you'll be deported. And we've got more in store, you can bet we have more in store for you."

"Excuse me, but I don't know what you are saying to me."

"You know very well, Bonaglia. Far too well."

I was sweating. A few days earlier, Mariano de Aliaga had said that he was interested in a Ribera I'd mentioned and we'd left it that I would bring it over to his house. I noticed that he'd tried to insist on coming to my house instead, and I had some difficulty persuading him that I should come to his house. Finally, he assented, and that afternoon, I appeared with the painting under my arm. It was a painting of a Franciscan friar done in chiaroscuro, his cheeks rosy with wine, an almost degenerate smile on his face. Chaudron had done an extraordinary job. He had outdone himself; the friar's portrait was not a copy of an existing painting but an original—an original José de Ribera by Chaudron.

And Aliaga had been elated, thought it incredible—or so he had said. Ribera could paint the decadence of man like no one else, perhaps he did it to emphasize the glory of our Lord, but there really was no one like him for being able to bring degradation and loss to life in a painting. He was the painter this world deserved—if he'd been alive and painting today, he'd have been condemned for being too dangerous, too corrosive, too much of a wild element. Aliaga was exultant—he examined the painting carefully, an expression of joy on his face, the way a stallion looks at a filly. His eyes shone.

"As I say, it's very simple: either you give me the paintings or you go to jail."

"What are you talking about, Aliaga? What paintings?"

"This one, to begin with."

Chaudron had told me that to copy a painting was a stupid idea, that what interested him more and more was to create a painting. Not to forge a painting but to reproduce the actions, the process of its creator, he said. And to reproduce certain days from his life—the days that he'd spent thinking about the painting's themes, doing sketches for it, finishing it. That what he wanted was to recreate a painter's painting, to do everything the painter would have had to do in painting it. Not what he did, not what he could have done—what he had to have done. "To create paintings of his that were better than his own paintings because I now know," Chaudron told me, "I now know what he could have done but never did." He frightened me sometimes. His pride would be his downfall.

"I know there are others, Bonaglia. You'll leave me this one for now."

"But why would you want it if it's a fake?"

"You still think I'm an idiot? I want this painting and all the others. I'm not going to let a fraud like you continue to wreak havoc on decent folk."

"But—"

"No buts. It's your life. I won't ask where they come from, where you steal them. Right now I don't care; it's not my problem. You're going to give them all to me. I want them all here in one week; every one right here. I'll make sure they go where they need to."

He has walked for hours, all over the city. He comes to Chaudron's house at one in the morning and wakes him by shouting outside his window.

"They've found us out! We've got to leave!"

"What? How? What happened? Tell me what happened. What are you saying?"

"There's no time, we have to leave now!" says Valfierno, extremely agitated. Later, as he calms down, he tells him: "If we don't leave Buenos Aires now we'll end up in jail."

"Aliaga?"

"Yes, Aliaga."

Chaudron tells Valfierno that he'd always given him a bad feeling, that prig, that he'd never wanted to say anything before, but that he'd never liked him. He tells Valfierno to calm down, to wait, to sit and have a glass of wine and think it through. But Valfierno tells him there's nothing to think about, that they have to disappear as soon as possible, it's the only way out. Perhaps they can go to Mendoza, he says, and see what they can do there. Perhaps to Chile, who knows; the main thing is to get far away from here. Chaudron remains silent for a few minutes. Valfierno has his eyes closed, trying not to look at all the canvases piled up against the wall, his treasures, now rapidly becoming his accusers, the collapse of his new life, just as it was beginning.

"There's a ship leaving for Le Havre in three days."

"What good does that do us?"

"What do you mean, 'what good'? We can be on it. We can escape to France."

"France?"

"Sure. Isn't France where you lived for all those years?"

"Not now, Chaudron."

"Seriously, Enrique. I don't think we have a lot of choice. And with the money we have now we can get by for a few months in Paris. We should be able to figure something out in that time, don't you think?"

"What I think, Chaudron, is that you don't understand anything. What the hell are we going to do in Paris? What in God's name am I going to do in Paris?"

8

ANYONE WHO SEES HIM IS going to know that it's not his jacket, he thinks, and see how out of place he is in the straw hat, black jacket, and blue tie. And even though the suit he has on is old and slightly rumpled, it still doesn't look as if it's his, and he imagines that everyone going by is looking at him, and noticing, and that one of them is bound to suspect.

In that short walk, Vincenzo Perugia has to tell himself several times that it's not true, that no one is looking, that luckily—for once it is lucky—he's the kind of guy no one looks at twice, and that Valérie was right to say she didn't want to see him anymore; what had been unexpected was that she'd fallen for him like that in the first place. What happened afterward—well, that wasn't unexpected. But she had looked at him twice, and for that she was special. Sweat drips from his hat.

"Tickets! Buy your tickets here! Line up over there to go inside!"

It's three in the afternoon on Sunday, and it's punishingly hot, even for August, though all the papers had said that this summer of 1911 would make history. Vincenzo Perugia crosses the Louvre's main courtyard and slips through the Denon entrance into the cool interior air. He is surprised to see so many people there—it still amazes him that there are so many people in the world, all of them so different, and he's even gone so far as to ask himself why.

This afternoon he is surprised by the hundreds of people entering the museum through the main door on either side of him. They must all be seeking the cool of those enormous dark galleries, he thinks, but then he changes his mind: that young couple there—him in a white shirt and her in a white dress—look like they've come to grope each other. And that group of Germans in their seventies, who are listening intently to what their guide is reading them, must love art and paintings. And that mustachioed father with his four children probably just had to get out of the house. And those two American ladies in their forties must be looking for men.

So many people, and all of them out without a care, thinks Perugia. They are at the museum just as they could be anywhere, knowing that in an hour the museum will close and they will all go home—all except for him. Rather than envy, he feels a kind of solitude, a strangeness. It doesn't occur to Perugia that to anyone looking at him, he, too, looks like he's just out for the afternoon, and that any one of them, like him, could also be hiding any number of things, secret desires.

Later—that same night—he'll think that if he hadn't been such an idiot, if he'd only had a little more imagination that afternoon it could have occurred to him to go right back to his pension, and he might still have done it. But there, on that hot afternoon, it does not occur to him, and he keeps walking.

As he walks he is jostled by the crowd, and he realizes suddenly that the crush of people is lucky for him. Everyone is talking. Perugia thinks it strange how the whispers of so many people, saying of course-tomorrow-boat-painting-oh Paris-my sister-no question, can converge to become such a roar. He thinks that it's strange, and that in itself is strange, for he never usually thinks about such things. He hopes this will not last long, for now the noise is bothering him; he is a little nervous. No, he tells himself, I am not nervous, but he's not sure. Perhaps he should be—he does not know which is better.

Then he is standing by the enormous, sweeping staircase. Once again—it is months now since he's been here—he tells himself how magnificent it is: the staircase, the ceiling, the columns, the marble, and the mirrors, most of all the mirrors. Perugia looks around him and imagines the impression this must be having on those people. Not so much on him, for he has seen it before, but certainly on all those people: "They must be amazed. Luckily I've seen it, and even so I'm impressed—me, an Italian from the land of emperors and painted churches, and I'm impressed. I hope the brothers don't get scared," he thinks. He is sure that they never come here. "I hope they show up."

"Excuse me, sir, could you tell me where to find the Venus de Milo?"

"How should I know? Why don't you ask one of the guards."

Perugia turns to the staircase that leads up to the second floor and as he does so he has the impression that one of the guards is looking at him. He is worried, not because the guard might recognize him but because he notices that the guard is wearing a yellow badge in his lapel, and he knows only too well that yellow is the most unlucky color of all, and he slips his left hand into his pocket to touch his left testicle without anyone seeing. He exhales, slightly calmer, though it's true that the guard could recognize him. Even though Perugia doesn't recognize him, the guard might know him from when he worked there the year before. It's unlikely, and would be terrible luck, he thinks, deciding to reject the notion.

It had happened purely by chance: his boss at the time had been hired to install panes of glass over the museum's more famous paintings. It was pure luck, and this surprised him, for he was never lucky. He knows this. He doesn't like to think of it but it's true: he's never been lucky in his life, that's why he has to try to pay attention to everything. If only he could have just a little of the Signore's luck; he clearly has enough to go around.

But it really had been pure good luck that his boss had got the job of installing the glass, except—but he doesn't want to finish the thought. Just in case. It's better not to think of these things, especially on a day like today. Pure luck that just then, alarmed by a gang of lunatics who were going around vandalizing paintings, as if there were nothing else to vandalize, the museum directors had decided to protect their most famous paintings behind panes of glass.

What Perugia didn't know, had no reason to know, was that the directors' decision had caused a huge scandal. There was outrage in the elegant salons and letters to the newspapers over this unspeakable attack on classical art, and a young novelist had come with his brush and razor and shaved himself in the reflection of one of the panes.

But Perugia is not aware of this. He knows only that his boss had told him to build the large wooden box frames for the paintings to be protected, and that every day for months he had gone to the museum to install them.

He'd had plenty of time then to learn all about how that great palace operated, which is obviously why the Signore chose him for this job, and why Perugia has dressed in his Sunday best, as the Signore instructed, though the jacket is uncomfortable. Perugia wonders briefly if it was a mistake to tell him to wear a jacket, and if perhaps the Signore has made other mistakes. Who really knows who he is, after all, this guy who has told him to do all these things, this man he's trusting enough to take part in this charade with who knows what consequences? But then he looks around him and sees a number of people in jackets and realizes that the Signore was right, that if he'd shown up at the museum without a jacket he'd have attracted attention, and he adjusts his blue tie. The Signore was right.

"Holy Mary, Mother of God, pray for us sinners . . . ," whispers Perugia, trying not to move his lips, and he is comforted by this as he enters the Duchâtel Room. "Now and at the hour of our d—," he says and he stops short. Everybody knows you can't say the word "death" in a situation like this; it's better not to tempt fate.

There are never many people in the Duchâtel Room, which is why Perugia and the Signore chose it—that, and because of the little room. As Perugia walks in he sees no guards, just another pair of youths, indifferent to their surroundings, three distinguished-looking older women, and, down at the end, by an enormous painting, the two Lancelotti brothers. Perugia breaths a sigh of relief and then immediately starts to worry again. The brothers have to remember that they are not to greet him or speak to him or make any sign of acknowledgment, just as he told them at the Bistro Berthe the previous night. He can't be sure—the brothers are both thick as planks, but he had told them so many times that they may just have understood.

"What if something happens?" they'd asked him.

"Like what?"

"I don't know, something might happen—anything. Like if they ask us what we're doing, or if they grab you, or if there's a guard there the whole time."

"Nothing's going to happen! You're both being idiots," he'd snapped and immediately regretted it, though they'd said nothing. He had stressed that they were not to acknowledge him and that they were to stay in the room until he gave them the signal.

It is now 3:25, thirty-five minutes until closing. They have to pass the time. Perugia walks over and stands behind the brothers, who are pretending to look at the big painting. He looks at their shabby, threadbare suits and thinks to himself that everyone will know that they don't belong here. Then he realizes he must look the same, and he worries again. On top of everything, his jacket is too big, so it can hide the bundle of tools he carries.

But there is no one else in the Duchâtel Room now except for the three ladies, and Perugia pretends to look closely at the details in the large painting before him. As he does so he gets a shock. The painting is enormous, painted in dark tones with a lot of brown and red, showing Jesus suffering on the cross with the two thieves near him. Perugia crosses himself; exactly the same—with two thieves near him! He looks at the two brothers and tries to stay calm, cursing the moment he agreed to get involved in this mess. He looks up at Jesus and asks his forgiveness for these insults.

"O Mary, conceived without sin," he murmurs and looks

again at his watch. It's 3:27, and the women are leaving the gallery. Now he and the two others are alone in the Duchâtel Room.

"Now! Let's go," hisses Perugia, and the three of them walk silently—as if their mere footsteps would give them away—toward the northeast corner of the gallery. There, hidden by the moldings, is a door barely the size of a man. Perugia fumbles with the hidden catch, working it with his penknife. An endless minute. Then the catch gives.

"Quick! Inside, now," says Perugia, and the three of them shuffle into a small dark room, filled with things that they can't make out. They close the little door. Perugia leans back against the wall and the sound of his breath escaping is like thunder.

9

"THE FUNNY THING IS THAT he says it was you who convinced him to become Valfierno," I said to Chaudron, and immediately realized my mistake.

Before my eyes, Chaudron's face was becoming a storm of bitterness.

"I'm sorry, I shouldn't have told you that. But I have to admit it got my attention when I heard it."

"Why? Because he's some fancy so-and-so and I'm just an old guy stuck in a chair?"

Chaudron was shouting. This man who normally seemed as if he could barely get his words out was shouting at me, in his own way—almost without raising his voice, his fists pressed against the flowered arms of the chair, pushing each syllable out. As he shouted, his eyes and the rest of his face became sad, as if by having resorted to this he was already defeated.

"Because you're such a Newspaperman that you can't imagine anything that you can't see right in front of you? Because you haven't figured out that there was a time when your hero was just a poor sap? Or because you don't want to know?"

Ivanka was watching us from the kitchen door and looking at me with hatred. Her thick legs were planted wide apart as if in defiance. The closeness we'd achieved over hours of interviewing was dissolving in front of me, just when I needed to ask him my most delicate questions. To try to get back in his good graces, I asked him how he'd thought up the name Valfierno.

"Do you really think that crazy name was my idea?"

Again I'd made a mistake, but for some reason I didn't understand, Chaudron was starting to calm down.

"No, that was his idea—who knows where he got the name. I even argued with him about it, like I did about him wanting to be a marqués. But that's what the man wanted. He said that with Argentines, you couldn't leave anything to their imagination; they were too stupid. He said that if you wanted them to understand anything you had to spell it out. We did agree on that."

Chaudron stopped talking, but only momentarily. He seemed to decide something.

"Sorry about what I said before, Becker. I want to believe I don't care anymore, but there are things about all of this that I've never been able to swallow."

"Did he change very much once he started being Valfierno?"

" 'Very much' doesn't begin to describe it, Newspaperman. See if you can understand—when I met him, he was one of those guys who's already given up, who doesn't want to go any further; all he wants to do is to stay where he is and not move."

I'd sworn I wouldn't let my face show what I was thinking but he must have seen it anyway because he answered me, though his fury had now passed. Now he just sounded tired, almost condescending. He'd gone from anger to despondency.

"Now don't get the wrong idea—it's not the same. I'm old now, and sick. I have this house and some money in the bank and a wife who says she loves me. Back then he was just in his forties, counting fucks in a whorehouse and living like a dog, Becker, like a dog. Maybe I wasn't clear."

He'd been quite clear, but he went on. He started to explain to me how a person makes plans and still believes they'll change as long as they don't yet have stories written on their face. That's how he put it: "when their face isn't full of stories yet."

"I mean, when your face is just one story with a nose attached. Haven't you seen how, later, your face starts to break up into different stories? Two fault lines separate your cheeks from your mouth, your chin becomes its own entity, your forehead looks like a wrinkled potato? Well, when your face gets filled with all those stories you begin to think you're done with plans, right?"

I said yes, of course, and asked him as carefully as I could if he knew why Valfierno wanted to stay in the brothel, why he didn't want to move on with his life. Chaudron said that he was trying to convince himself that he'd attained a certain wisdom.

"He would say what I told you before: that he was satisfied with his dreams, his imagination. That only fools tried to make their dreams into reality. He said he knew that and didn't need anything else."

"He didn't need it or he was afraid to try for it? From this distance he sounds like someone who was terrified, and I'd like to know why."

"Excuse me, did you come all the way here just so we could talk about him?"

"No, of course not. I came to hear about you and about the things you did together."

" 'Doing things together' is one way of putting it. There was a point where he just started doing things and all I could do was follow him."

Chaudron summoned his wife in a whisper—the kind of sound only a spouse can hear through a kitchen door—and asked her to bring us two coffees. Ivanka told him not to take advantage of the visit, that he knew he couldn't have coffee this late at night.

"I didn't ask you if I could have coffee, woman, I asked you to bring it," said Chaudron in a surprisingly mild tone, and then he began to tell me how he and Valfierno had arrived in Paris with almost no money. They hadn't dared to bring any paintings out of a fear of French Customs, and they barely had enough to find a small apartment and for Chaudron to buy canvases and oils and to set up his studio there. But Valfierno had got in touch with certain Argentines in the city and very quickly found a couple of buyers for Chaudron's Murillos and Riberas.

"Paris was very tough for me. I don't know if you've ever had this feeling, Becker, of coming back to where you started without having achieved a single thing. I was back where I had been almost twenty years before, when I'd had to leave, and everything was the same. That was tough, very tough for me. You know how I figured out that something was badly wrong?" Chaudron asked me, and then he stopped, as Ivanka had come in with the tray and the two coffees. Something had happened between them, too; he no longer wanted her to hear what he was going to say. There was an uncomfortable silence as she served the coffee. After she'd gone back into the kitchen he told me that everything went wrong once he stopped trying to find things.

"Yes, don't make that face, Becker. We lived in that studio and it was chaos—two of us in that small space with all my painting tools and materials. I used to lose things a lot, and I'd look for them. When things were all right, I'd find them, no problem. I'd lose something and then I'd find it, I mean I'd look everywhere, and it would turn up. Until one day, I don't know what happened, I suddenly thought that I shouldn't look anymore—I should think. And for a while everything seemed to go better. I didn't look for things anymore. If I couldn't find a particular color, I wouldn't go through dozens and dozens of tubes trying to find it—no, I'd try to remember when I last used it and what I'd moved since then, and right away I'd find it. This'll seem crazy to you, Newspaperman, but that's when everything started to go wrong."

Chaudron fell silent; he was far away. I had the impression that he was staring at his painting of the Virgin with the baby Jesus as if there were some clue hidden there, but perhaps I was wrong— the idea of finding clues in everything was just too French for me.

"As soon as we sold a few paintings and made some money, he moved out and got his own place. I don't think he could stand me anymore then, even though the fact that Valfierno was my idea was something I never threw in his face. I'm not one of those guys who goes around all the time boasting about what they've done."

"But you kept on working together?"

"Sure, or you wouldn't be here, Newspaperman. You would never have come to see me if all we'd done was to sell a couple of pretty good copies of Spanish baroque painters. You came here to see me because he had that one brilliant idea. But I tell you, that only happened because in Paris he finished changing himself into Valfierno." Chaudron told me that it was a process that had begun in Buenos Aires but that Valfierno had always seemed to be looking behind himself there, he was always afraid that someone was going to find him out.

"But when we got to Paris all his fears went away. In Paris he really was his new self, he believed that he was that person I'd invented: the Marqués de Valfierno. Isn't that ridiculous? And isn't it even more ridiculous that because of that, the whole world remembers us now, even if it doesn't know who we are?"

I had the impression that his patience was running out, but there were still things he wanted to tell me. He said that in the middle of all his unease, he had begun to feel that the copy occupied a more and more important place. He didn't want to tell me any more stories now, he wanted to recount his theories. But I still needed answers to some important questions.

"I don't know if you've noticed this, Becker. What's happening now is that progress and all our modern advances are bringing the world closer and closer to the copy. Think about it: before, if you wanted to draw the plan of a city you had to imagine it. Nowadays, you just go up in a balloon and you look and you copy it down. You can see everything, and in the future you'll be able to see more. My trade is full of people who compete with me who've had no training, there's a whole gang of cheap imitators. I noticed this a while ago, Becker, and I also realized that the copy does not have the reputation it deserves. The copy is the basis for civilization; I don't know if you realize that."

"Well, no, but—"

"Please—don't interrupt me. I'm telling you that if it weren't for the copy, the world wouldn't exist. Everything would be disappearing all the time. We are ephemeral. Originals don't last; someone has to make a copy of them for them to keep existing. Sons of their fathers, the blacksmith of the blacksmith before him, the hammer of another hammer, chickens of their hens—everyone copies. Sons—copied by nature's art—are imperfect reproductions of their fathers, with the mother meddling more or less. Without the copy there wouldn't be any culture, there'd be no society or traditions, just animals. Just a din of individuals with no history."

Chaudron was getting excited; he was transformed. I had the uneasy feeling that he'd spent years working on this speech without ever before finding anyone to listen to it.

"If we didn't have the copy we'd have to invent everything over and over again all the time. A revolution worse than all the other revolutions. If it weren't for the copy, I'm telling you, the revolution would never stop. Imagine—if we think the world is already a mess the way it is, with the Russians, the Germans, all of that. The copy is order, it's the only guarantee we have that order will be maintained."

"I'm sorry, Chaudron. You were telling me about when you decided to go ahead with the plan of *La Joconde* . . ."

"I wasn't telling you anything about that, Newspaperman. Don't treat me like an idiot. What I was telling you is that there's terrible injustice in all of this. You know, an artist who makes a copy is more skilled that the one who is being copied. All the copied artist has done is to free his instincts, he just lets it come out, does what he can. But the artist who copies him works hard, twists himself around to make what the other man made without even trying. What's nature for one is art for the other. And art is what we were talking about, if I understand right."

Defiantly, Chaudron stopped talking. He didn't look at me—didn't look at anything—but he was seeing something. Then he told me to come close, that he was going to tell me something very important, a secret, he said, which could be worth a lot of money. He told me that times were very hard when he painted his *Jocondes*, that he had felt diminished; he couldn't stand what he was doing.

"This was what I'd done my whole life, you know? And then suddenly I couldn't bear it anymore. I don't know if that's ever happened to you, Becker, but there's nothing worse."

He told me he couldn't stand the idea that his work was so overlooked, and that he'd had a moment of vanity, which he sometimes regretted. He also told me that he'd left a mark on all of his *Jocondes*.

"Anyone who knows it could easily pick them out. All you have to do is look underneath the smile—that famous smile. There are two small, red eyeteeth just beneath the smile, Newspaperman. Just look for those—you'll see them," he said, and he let out a laugh, though it was hurt and harsh, the bitter sound of someone laughing at himself. I didn't know what to say. He was giving me an incredible scoop—the proof I'd been seeking for so long.

"No, Newspaperman, don't listen to me. This is stupid— don't pay any attention. Sometimes I can't help getting caught in these things that have been eating at me all this time. You want to know the truth? I have a satisfaction that very few people have. I didn't let myself get consumed by this work. I told my wife once what she should put as the epitaph on my grave, what Stendhal wrote about Saint Paul: 'He was a true artist—a man surpassed by his work.' My work has left me completely forgotten. And I could never stand it if I were better than my work. Can you imagine anything worse, Newspaperman? Anything more humiliating?"

He looked at his hands, which were perched on the lace that covered the arms of his chair. They were tense, and looked like two large spiders.

"I told him so many times, Newspaperman, but he never understood. He couldn't understand."

Yves Chaudron fell silent, and this time it seemed that he had told me everything he was going to tell me. And yet I had to try anyway.

"How did you think up the business of the six *Mona Lisa*s? How was that supposed to work?"

"Please, don't bore me with details now, I beg you. It's gotten late."

Ivanka was standing by the door again, regarding me in a mixture of surprise and fear. Or perhaps it was him she was looking at. I cleared my throat and thanked her, and said I wouldn't disturb them any further, that they'd been very kind. I wondered once more whether to tell him that Valfierno was now dead. He looked fragile, but it occurred to me that the news might give him a lift. I didn't know. I got up quietly and told them both again how grateful I was for their time.

10

He hears footsteps and holds his breath. They come closer. Vincenzo Perugia listens, trying to decipher them. It sounds like only one person, and the footsteps are not very firm, as if whoever was out there was dragging his feet; it could be someone old. The footsteps keep approaching; the more he thinks the closer they get and they are now very close. Perugia remembers the guard's yellow badge and thinks that nothing in this life is free. And that he knew he should never have gotten mixed up in—another step.

Perugia thinks back to the time he saw a shooting star. He hears the footsteps and is amazed at the number of things you can think about in such a short space of time. Perugia would have been about fourteen or fifteen when he saw the star—who knows? Every year was the same in his village. Perugia was still living there. His father used to take him along every day to work in the fields. The girls used to tease him because of his voice, and that night in summer he saw the shooting star.

The next day, he told his grandmother, his father's mother, who was still alive then, and she asked him if he'd made his wishes. She was already scrawny by then, but she spoke the way she had when she was still large—arrogant, always talking.

"So, Piccolino, what did you wish for?" she asked him.

"Wish?" he replied, and the grandmother let loose a huge bray of laughter.

"How can you be so dumb you don't know that when you see a shooting star you're supposed to make three wishes?"

His grandmother laughed and laughed, smacking her thighs with her hands. She was sitting on a little straw chair in front of the house, underneath the vine, and she slapped her hands down on her thighs.

"How did you get to be so stupid?" she says to him, and she tells him she can't believe that a grandson of hers would have missed his big chance by not knowing that.

"You don't see a shooting star every day, Piccolino, not even every year; you just never know, maybe once in your life, and you missed your chance, Vincenzo. How can you be so dumb?"

So dumb, he remembers. The footsteps keep getting closer. So dumb—the chance of his life, he thinks, like always. So dumb, so lost, and now here, shut up in this dark room with footsteps coming closer and closer. So dumb, always so dumb, the noise of the footsteps, now here, lost, dark—he holds his breath.

The footsteps move away, get fainter, and for a few minutes—no one can tell how many—-no one moves or makes a sound.

"That was very close," says Perugia, when he finally dares to speak.

"I thought the guards didn't come at night," says Michele Lancelotti reproachfully.

"They're not supposed to. Maybe they do now. Don't worry, they're gone. They won't come back."

"How do you know they won't come back?"

"I don't know. I think—yeah, I'm sure."

"They better not," says Vincenzo Lancelotti, and Perugia hates him. Who does he think he is, these idiots can't even tie their own shoes. He only got them because he had no choice, they're the only ones he knew he could handle. Anyone else would have asked too many questions and wanted too much money and might even have bossed him around. Not the Lancelotti brothers. He had worked with them before on a couple of building sites and jobs, and while they might complain some, in the end they always did what they were told. They knew their place.

It's hot. A few weeks earlier, in the Bistro Berthe, Perugia had asked the Signore if he could do the job alone; he didn't like the idea of having to take on two more, or having to share the money with them. The Signore had smiled and asked—perfectly friendly— if he didn't think he needed any help, and Perugia had replied no, that he could do this on his own and that those two would just be a burden. The Signore had said that there was no chance, that he gave the orders, and that Perugia was to do as he was told. Perugia had looked away and agreed, but now he was having his doubts.

"Try to get some sleep; it's going to be a long night."

"Sleep? Here? You're nuts, Vincenzo, you can't sleep in here! How could anyone sleep in here?"

You can tell that the Lancelottis are from the south—they can't say anything without a torrent of words coming out, he thinks, and half closes his eyes. The room smells of oils, clay, turpentine—it's a storeroom where painters who come to the museum to copy its paintings can keep their materials, and it's crammed and dirty. He opens his eyes; he is not going to be able to sleep either, it's too uncomfortable. His eyes are now used to the darkness, and next to the door he sees two brooms with their handles crossed. He knows this means something bad but he doesn't remember what. If only his grandmother were here she would tell him. He snorts. The world is full of signs he doesn't understand—if only he'd taken the time to learn them. If only he'd paid attention! His hands are sweating. His hands never sweat, he thinks, it must be the heat. He wipes them on his pants but they keep sweating. It's as hot as an oven in the room and his legs are stiff. He'd pay money to be able to stretch them but there isn't any room. Michele Lancelotti keeps fidgeting, driving him crazy.

"Vincenzo."

"What?"

"You said everything was going to be easy."

"Yeah."

"Are you sure?"

"Yeah."

"Doesn't look like it."

"Yeah, you'll see. Or are you scared?"

"Scared? Me?"

There are still hours to go, many hours. Perugia lights a match and looks at his watch: nine fifteen. It should just be getting dark outside, and they have to wait until just after dawn.

"Vincenzo."

"Now what?"

"Nothing," says Michele. The other one, Vincenzo—why the hell did he have to be Vincenzo, too, thinks Perugia, like him? At one point it had brought them closer, but now it annoys him. He didn't think Vincenzos were like that. Vincenzo Lancelotti's thoughts are on a point too far in the future.

"What do you think they'll do when they figure out it's gone?"

Perugia doesn't answer. The Signore said it was going to be a huge scandal, and he thinks so, too. When he worked at the museum he noticed how everyone treated that painting with more respect than the others—they looked after it better, they'd handle it differently. To him, it doesn't look all that different from a lot of the other paintings, but for some reason he doesn't understand, he knows that it is. One time in the bistro he had spoken up and asked, "Signore, can you please tell me why that painting is so important?" But the Signore had just looked at him the way his grandmother used to, with that look of disdain he knows so well, and said nothing.

But Perugia knows he's not stupid. It's everyone else who's going to be stupid, he thinks. He and his friends are going to be the ones who steal this painting that's so important—he and his two friends—he, the stupid one. Let's see all their faces when they find out! Tomorrow, when they figure out it's not there anymore. Tomorrow, when we'll have it. After we're out of this hole.

The Marqués
de Valfierno

1

THERE ARE PLACES WHERE TO be a marqués is nothing special. Places where, oddly enough, that's just what I can be.

"You cannot imagine what that was like, Becker."

"I'm sorry—what was like?"

"To flee from Buenos Aires. Just when everything looked as if it was starting to work out, I suddenly had to get out of there in four days."

"I or we? I thought you didn't leave by yourself?"

"That's not the point. The point is that it was so sudden, so unexpected."

"I can imagine. It must have been very difficult."

"It was. But the strangest thing about it is that if it hadn't happened, I would have lived out my days as a small-time provincial swindler in that country of braggarts. See how things can happen, Newspaperman?"

At last I was a foreigner. It's so easy, so comfortable to be a foreigner.

He'd only been in Paris a short while and already his face had changed. Not just because of the dummy monocle he wore in his right eye, not just because of the carefully trimmed salt-and-pepper beard, or the hair worn slightly longer than usual to show that he wouldn't be told what to do. Not just for the surprising ease with which he'd picked up the local language or the pleasure he took in using it. Not just because his height was no longer a disadvantage, nor for the casual disdain in his look, nor how easily he now closed some of his deals, nor how natural he now found it to handle women who years before would have terrified him. And not just because it meant something to be Argentine now—it was a passport he used judiciously but tirelessly, a way to open almost any door, because being an Argentine in Paris in those days was a guarantee of extravagant wealth. And not just because any mistake he made now was forgiven because he was Argentine, because to be Argentine now meant something and the French knew it and treated them with a new respect. No, the most surprising thing was that his face in the mirror now showed the calm that had recently come over him. "Calm"—there was no doubt that was the word. He had thought about it and concluded that this was the right word.

There was also fear, of course, and the thrill of launching what he rightly or wrongly considered to be great ventures, but that same thrill produced in him the calm of knowing that for once, for the first time, he was doing something worthy of notice. That he—Bollino, Juan María, Perrone, Bonaglia—was finally someone with a story worth telling, finally the person he was always meant to be: himself, though he was now so different. And it amazed him, above all, to be at the center of a story that no one would believe in its entirety—but perhaps that was the way of any story really worth telling.

I was amazed to be the hero of my own story.

Though there was nothing quite so dizzying as not knowing what would happen to me in the next year, two years, five years.

"At last, here I am, back in my own city."
"But Valfierno, this is the first time you've ever been in Paris!"
"Oh, really, Chaudron? How can you be so sure?"

Sebastián de Anchorena is a master—he takes a fish knife and, very discreetly, he places one of those ridged swirls of butter one gets in the finer restaurants onto the sharp end of the knife and, with a lighter, gently melts the top of it. Then, carefully balancing the knob of butter on the knife, he takes the handle of the knife between the thumb and forefinger of his right hand and the sharp point of the blade between the thumb and forefinger of his left hand and holds the knife just in front of his middle, parallel to the floor. With an almost imperceptible movement that is nonetheless both swift and sure, he pushes the tip of the blade down and releases it suddenly so that the butter is propelled up to the ceiling with some force. I have seen him perform this feat various times and today is no different: the top of the butter, lightly melted, sticks to the ceiling and the butter hangs there menacingly until the room's heat eventually melts it enough so that big drops of warm butter begin to rain down on whomever has the misfortune to find themselves below. Some of the other Argentine boys also do this, but as I've said, Sebastián is the master. Though I no longer envy him.

"See," I say to him, "what an Argentino I am."
"Of course, indeed, Señor Marqués. *Bien sûr.*"

And I know that this would just have killed me before. The antics of Sebastián and his friends are the essence of art for art's sake, symbolic of those lives, completely free of concern, in which all that is important is to assert that the needs of common mortals don't affect them, do not touch them. That people like them have no need of what either time or money can offer; the only truly elegant thing being to spend these and ask for nothing in return, without aims, without regrets. People who can devote their efforts and their whole futures to perfecting a completely unnecessary skill. Pure art.

They are aristocrats by an accident of birth, no more—just nature. I, on the other hand, built myself piece by piece. I, on the other hand, am indeed human.

But there were nights when he couldn't sleep. Though he washed his face and undressed and got into bed and closed his eyes, resting his head against the pillow, always a little cool, his head sinking into the pillow, he would realize, as he sought sleep, that he wasn't going to find it.

No, there were those nights when he knew long before trying that he would not sleep, that if on one of those nights he were to try, he would unleash an overwhelming torrent. He risked again being Bollino, Juan María, Perrone, Quique—any one of the dead. He risked the terror of getting up and going to stand in front of the mirror to see his own face, to convince himself of his face and his name, to tell himself that death could not reach him while he was still intoning each letter of his name, that as long as he was Valfierno nothing bad could happen to him, to tell himself that at last he was who he was but that he had to keep repeating it, sweating, in front of the mirror. This was what he risked.

And so on those nights he wouldn't even try. He would comb his hair and wax his mustache, he would put on a good felt hat and go out to lose himself in cabarets and cafés where he would be just another gentleman on the prowl, where everyone would look at him with envy and respect, and where he could seek out a girl who could give him a few hours without sleep. Where he could be no one.

Sometimes my weakness frightened me. In my worst moments, it was my strength that I feared.

Feigning nonchalance, Sebastián launches the little swirl of butter. The knife is left quivering in his hands, the butter on the ceiling. Santiago and Ramón smirk quietly and bring their napkins up to their mouths, and we go on talking about the new show at the Opèra-Comique, the girls in the chorus, and their weekend at Château Longueville. The skill of Sebastián's little trick has delighted me, too, but I no longer envy it. I have to pretend that I am one of them. For the moment I still have to pretend, although I know that now I am also doing something important, that I am going to give the world something to talk about. That if these boys knew—if I could tell them—they would envy me. Tomorrow night, if everything goes well, I'll go and see that little cocotte I used to know from the Faux Chien, Valérie. Nothing special—she's just one of many—but if all goes well and she gives me the information about her Italian friend, then I can get something big going. Finally, I'm going to do something important.

"In the end it wasn't that difficult. It turns out there's nothing easier than convincing someone who wants to be convinced. Look at you, for example—you accept my story without question."

"You're talking about me?"

"Who else, my Newspaperman, my indispensable Newspaperman."

2

VINCENZO PERUGIA AWAKES WITH A start and realizes he's been asleep. Opening his eyes, he is surprised that he can't see anything, then remembers where he is, in the darkness of the little room. He is startled by his leg touching something—the leg of one of the Lancelotti brothers. Confused, he looks over at them in the darkness and can just make out that they, too, are sleeping, and he thinks suddenly that it must be too late, that the hour is past, and that, like idiots, they have missed the biggest opportunity of their lives. The shooting star, that cursed shooting star! He is filled with a deep unease, his eyes burn, and his forehead weighs on him like a tombstone. He struggles to find a match in his pocket and lights it: it's 5:20 in the morning. Now what he dreads is the time still left to wait.

"Vincenzo."

"What?"

"Are you awake?"

"What do you think?"

"I can't sleep."

"Looks to me like you just were."

"Yeah, but I can't. I'm asleep, but not really."

"Just wait. Not long now."

The hour is interminable. Perugia tries to imagine himself arriving back in his village in a luxurious car, like a Bugatti, or a Mercedes, but still the time drags. He imagines all the girls who will want him to take them out, who will look at him and say, "Yes, whatever you want"; they are all the same, completely shameless. He thinks about how difficult it will be to find a decent woman he can marry. Then he tries to imagine the house he'll buy in the village, and about the life he'll have as a rich and respected craftsman, but the pictures won't come. And the time seems to stand still.

"Vincenzo."

"What?"

"How long now?"

"I don't know; not long."

"Will you tell me when it's time?"

"What do you think?"

Perugia fights drowsiness; he must not sleep now. Now all his fear is focused on the danger of falling asleep, which helps him. His visions of his village aren't enough to keep him awake; he might have dozed off, he can't be sure. Then it occurs to him that he should think about Valérie, her neck, her tits. Valérie's tits are worth all the *Jocondes* in the world, he thinks, and he gets nervous. Now he tries not to think of her, but that doesn't work. He spends a long while thinking about Valérie, going back and forth, round and round, as if he were trapped on a merry-go-round: her tits, her neck, her ass, tits neck ass, nick tets ass tits tits tits . . . At last his head gives a little shake and he lets out a sort of cough, or snort. A whore, like all the rest. Michele Lancelotti wakes up.

"What is it? What happened?"

"Nothing. Nothing happened."

Perugia lights another match and looks at his watch: twenty to seven in the morning on that famous Monday.

"Okay, guys, get up. It's time."

The three of them try to get to their feet without bumping themselves. They pull out their white aprons and put them on. On Mondays the museum is closed, and the only ones allowed in are the employees, the guards, and the maintenance staff. They all wear white aprons. The workday begins at seven. Vincenzo and Michele Lancelotti grab cloths; Perugia picks up a broom. It occurs to him for a moment to wonder what this means, but there isn't time.

"Okay, you know what you have to do."

"No."

"Sure you do—what do you mean, no?"

"Yeah, okay—follow you."

"Yeah, and keep your mouths shut, don't forget," says Perugia, and he opens the door very slowly.

3

"IF IT WASN'T FOR THAT whole business I'd be Mr. Nobody now, Mr. Becker. But look at how they greet me, see? Look, look at the respect."

It's true that they're looking at us. At the tables around us everything stopped when Perugia and I walked in. The tiles of the domino players froze in midair, people who were talking stopped in mid-sentence. Even the birds quieted down. The domino players inclined their heads slightly, in deference; some of them touched a finger to their hats. Two or three said, "Ciao, Vincenzo, how are you?" Now everyone has gone back to what they were doing, and Perugia takes a swig from his glass of wine. He wipes his mouth on the back of his hand, his hand on his pants under the table.

"You're not a Jew, by any chance?"

"Well, yes. Why?"

"Nothing, just asking. It doesn't matter to me; everyone respects me here. But some others would have problems if they were seen talking to a Jew, you know?"

"No, why?"

"Come on, Boss—don't pretend like you don't know."

Vincenzo Perugia is wearing a straw hat that used to be white with a new red ribbon, a cotton shirt with the sleeves rolled up, and black suspenders. He looks around him and doesn't seem as calm as he says he is. He speaks in a low voice:

"With a Jew, of course, but it would happen with other foreigners, too. You said you were American?"

The café in the main square of Dumenza is a perfect oasis: six mismatched tables under the heavens between the Roman door of the small church and the whitewashed façade of the town hall with its little Italian flags. There is a fountain, abandoned by water and time, paving stones, and the smell of tobacco and lavender.

Perugia goes on in a loud voice, speaking for everyone there:

"We're not the same as before, when we were embarrassed by what we were. Il Duce has made us proud to be Italians again! Now other countries look at us with respect, especially those queers, the French, who treated us like we were their slaves!"

Perugia is about fifty but looks older. He takes off his hat and mops the sweat on his head with a dirty kerchief. He has a very narrow forehead, his hairline low and close to his eyebrows, which are thick and tangled. At last I have him in front of me and I don't know how to begin to talk to him. I had put in months of effort, telegrams, unanswered letters, before finally deciding to travel here to his village in Lombardy. Vincenzo Perugia was the best known of all the people involved in the theft of the *Mona Lisa*—the only one to have been in the public eye—and he had also turned out to be the most difficult.

"That's why they respect me here, because I was one of the first ones to give those Frenchies what they deserve."

I had taken the train from Turin that morning, getting off at Dumenza and asking at the post office where I could find him. They told me to go to his shop, a paint and building supplies store, and pointed out the way, which led to a new house at the edge of the village. It looked like many others there. His shop took up the ground floor, and Perugia and his wife lived above. They hadn't had any children, I was told—"No, you know, they married late, for company."

The shop didn't look very well outfitted or cared for. "He says he started it with the money he got from the war," a woman from the market told me, "from his soldier's pay. I guess he made sergeant. He was at Caporetto. But who knows where the money came from. Now I'm not judging him, mind you; I don't like to judge anyone. To me he's a good Italian, a patriot."

Perugia was yawning as he came out to attend to me. I asked him in French how business was.

"Fine, why not?" he said and then was silent. His nose was red.

"I'm Charles Becker, a reporter from America—"

"How did you find me?" he interrupted. He was clearly very tense.

"It's easy, Perugia. You live in the same village you were born in, and your name used to be in all the papers. I need to talk to you. Is that possible?"

"It's possible, but I don't think I want to. I don't talk to reporters now."

"You get a lot of them?"

"No, they don't really come now. But there was a time when everyone wanted to talk to me."

"I'm sure. That was a while ago."

"Twenty years; nineteen—who knows? I can tell you I don't miss them—no, sir!"

When I told him I'd come all the way from America to see him he took another look at me. It was more or less true, and it seemed to impress him.

"From America? New York?"

Only the Italians say "New York" like that—with that mixture of admiration and scorn. I told him yes, and that I'd spent a lot of money to come and see him and I didn't mind if I spent a little more.

"How much more?"

"Why don't you tell me?"

The negotiation took only a few minutes. In the end—I'm ashamed to say it—the amount in dollars was a pittance. He told me to wait for him in the café at six that evening. He arrived at 6:30 and began his patriotic sermonizing. I let him go on, to get him comfortable.

Now, having calmed down somewhat, he asks me if it's true that I'm writing a book about *La Joconde*. I tell him it is.

"And you want me to tell you what really happened—the truth."

I look at him in silence. Perugia corrects himself:

"I mean, to tell you different things, new things."

"Well, sure—the truth, as you said."

"Yeah, sure, of course. But I mean, you've read all the papers from then, right?"

"Yes, of course."

"Well, it's all there, mister. How I returned the painting to Italy, how I was betrayed. It was all politics, you know. With Il Duce now that wouldn't happen."

Perugia takes another swig of wine and looks around him. In the doorway, the local priest is talking to a woman dressed in mourning. Beyond them, five young men in black shirts surround a peasant who is leading a heavily loaded donkey. The sun is going down behind the hills.

"It's all there, you know. There's not much more I can tell you."

"Perugia, please. You're the main character in this story, you can tell me a lot."

"The main character? Yeah, I suppose, but it's been a long time."

Perugia wavers some more and I tell him that I'd be willing to double my offer. The amount still seems pitifully low. He tells me he'll think about it, that maybe we'll meet here again the next day. He gets up, drinks down the rest of his wine, and puts his hat on at a slight angle. He spends longer adjusting it than I would have expected. I'm on my way out when he grabs my arm:

"Do you know who the Signore was?"

His hand is squeezing me too hard.

"Yes, but I'm not supposed to tell you yet."

"You want me to tell you everything and you're going to tell me nothing?"

"No—I said not yet."

"Look, mister, think it over till tomorrow. I'll answer all your questions if you tell me who the Signore was."

4

🦋   IN HIS SUITE, WRAPPED IN a dressing gown, Valfierno smokes. He looks at his watch: five past seven. He has been up all night, smoking, waiting for this moment, and now that it's here he realizes that he has waited for nothing. There's nothing he can do but wait and smoke and knead his hands.

"Jesus Christ Almighty," he whispers, and his voice surprises him. The words surprise him. He puts his Turkish cigarette out in an overflowing ashtray and thinks about emptying it.

"Jesus, Jesus. Christ, Jesus!"

Perugia grabs his broom and the Lancelotti brothers take their old dust cloths and the three of them set to cleaning a corner of the Duchâtel Gallery. It's ten minutes past seven in the morning. Perugia realizes that everything will have to be resolved in the next fifteen minutes and tries not to think about how those fifteen minutes could change his life.

Clutching his broom, he walks toward the arcade that gives out onto the Salon Carré. Just before he leans out he hears voices coming from below. He tries to keep calm and finds a place from where he can see what's happening without being seen.

"This is the most valuable painting we have in the museum, the one all our patrons want to see. It is said to be worth millions, if it were ever to be sold, which of course will never happen," intones an old man whom Perugia knows—Georges Picquet, the head of staff for the museum. He is accompanied by eight or ten museum employees wearing new smocks.

"Needless to say, I expect this part of the museum to be kept extra clean," Picquet instructs the recruits. Perugia cannot believe his bad luck. Once again the star has evaded him. He begins sweeping again and looks over at the brothers, across the Duchâtel Gallery, dusting frames with their cloths. Thanks to the sweat on his hands, his broom is on the verge of slipping from his grip. He listens to the voices below. If they are not gone within ten minutes, he will have to admit defeat. Please God, he thinks, make them go somewhere else!

". . . of the museum. I also want to show you this area over here, where . . ."

He hears footsteps. The procession moves toward the Apollo Gallery. The white smocks drift out, and the Salon Carré is empty. This is it, he says to himself, and, not really believing it, has to repeat it: This is it!

He finishes sweeping some tiles, telling himself not to rush. He thinks about the star, his grandmother, and, finally, about the fact that he cannot wait a moment longer. He looks over at the Lancelottis and makes a sign to them to follow him.

The night before, he had dined with Valérie at Ledoyen. The Marqués Eduardo de Valfierno had wanted to be seen in public, and he couldn't think of a better place than that elegant restaurant where *le tout* Paris ate. He ordered champagne and oysters. He felt far away and close at the same time, both appraised and protected by that distinguished clientele. Valérie was in a chatty mood, and they passed the meal talking—about the Comtesse de Noailles at a nearby table, the dress she had on, the oppressive heat, the possibility of going to Deauville for a weekend. The horses Sebastián de Anchorena had imported. Then, over the coffee and cognac, Valfierno looked into Valérie's eyes and reached across the crisp tablecloth for her hand.

"Valérie, I can now tell you what I'm sure you already know."

She smiled at him and said, "Yes, Marqués, I know. You don't need to tell me anything."

He thought that she probably didn't know everything, but

he wasn't going to stoop to asking exactly what she did know. Keeping silent would punish her for her arrogance. She didn't say any more, and it occurred to him that he really had to find a way to neutralize her once and for all.

They finished their liqueurs in silence. As they rose from the table, he said, "No, not tonight," that she should go home, and he returned to his suite. There he has spent the entire night awake, recalling foolish memories, trying to imagine his future, or rather, trying not to imagine the future this night could bring him, though as much as he tries, he doesn't succeed. He is assailed ceaselessly by images of wealth and splendor, and each time he pushes these from his mind with a shudder—you mustn't sell the bearskin before you've killed the bear, he reminds himself.

"Perhaps the bear is already dead," he says to the room at large. "I'd give anything to know . . ."

It is now a quarter to eight, and he is about to light another cigarette but stops himself. He walks to the bathroom, looks at himself in the mirror, seizes his toothbrush and his box of tooth powder. He spreads the thick powder onto his toothbrush and goes to work scrubbing his teeth like a lunatic. People believe in you if your teeth are white, he tells himself, and brushes harder. I can't afford yellow teeth now!

He cannot believe that she is up there, alone, hanging on the wall, just that easy, helpless—like a woman who no longer knows what to ask for in exchange for herself, who knows she can't ask for anything. Perugia can't believe that it's this simple, that all he has to do is to reach up and take her down from the wall for the blessed *Mona Lisa* to be in his hands, but there is no one in the Salon Carré, Vincenzo Lancelotti is beside him, Michele is in the gallery keeping watch, and she is hanging right there, ripe for picking. For the first time in all those hours, Perugia smiles: whores, all of them whores, he thinks, and a wave of heat rolls up his face, reddening it. For the last time, he looks to either side. Then the yellow badge comes into his head and he is furious that he had to think of it just then. He again brushes his left testicle lightly, for luck. Then, slowly, as if he still cannot believe it, his hands reach up.

Yves Chaudron has awakened early, which is nothing un- usual—he has been waking up at this time for months. Today he is up at quarter to seven. He feels clearheaded and almost optimistic; he has washed and shaved and even applied a few drops of cologne. Sitting now with his unsugared tea, he thinks that he might have found the way out.

Since he finished the last of the *Joconde*s he has found it very difficult to paint. He has finished a couple of small Zurbaráns to pay the bills, but he knows that he did these indifferently, with small mistakes, though none that anyone will notice. They held no interest for him. Compared to the accomplishment of those six per- fect *Joconde*s, any other work seems like a joke.

For months now he has felt adrift, without a future or the desire to do anything. But this morning, it is still cool, his tea has a slight smoky flavor which for once he likes, the sun is a festival of color in his window, and a painting occurs to Chaudron. Having been Leonardo all that time, having been able to be, and then hav- ing felt the shock of being Chaudron again—surely the solution is to go back? He knows what he will do, he thinks: he will paint a Virgin of the Rocks, but not the one he has seen so many times in the Louvre, with Jesus and John the Baptist and the Angel Uriel; the great Leonardo Virgin—no, he will paint the one Leonardo did not paint. The one he should have painted.

It takes an enormous effort to walk slowly. He fights the impulse to run out of the building, and each step seems to last a year. One foot is raised and describes an interminable arc in the air before it is again placed on the tile just in time for the other foot to begin. Time seems hardly to move. Somehow Perugia manages to keep his pace calm. The gallery is full of mirrors, and while Perugia thinks this is a good sign, he is not sure. Then, in one of them, he sees two museum employees in white aprons, one of them carrying a wooden box under his arm that looks like it must contain a painting. It takes him a moment to realize that he is seeing himself and Vincenzo Lancelotti; Michele follows behind.

Perugia knows that, in theory, no one will ask them any questions. It is normal for museum employees to take works back and forth for an inspection, or a photograph, or some restoration. They cross the Grande Galerie. About a dozen other workers are preoccupied with their own tasks and pay them no attention. For a moment, Perugia imagines he is carrying the star under his arm, and that it's burning him. Then he doesn't think anymore, and that is a relief.

"This way, this way," he says, opening a door concealed in the molding, and he and the two brothers find themselves on the landing of a service stairway. They close the door, take a deep breath, and pause. The light is poor. Perugia selects a couple of screwdrivers and quickly takes apart the wooden box, sets the covering glass aside on the floor, and wraps the *Joconde* in a large cloth without looking at her. She is painted on poplar board measuring approximately thirty inches by twenty, and she is light; she is so light.

"Okay, let's go—downstairs and out!"

"Just like that?"

"I don't know—yes, I think so."

Without making a sound, the three of them descend the stairway to the ground floor. Perugia grasps the latch of the door leading to the Cour du Sphinx, but the door doesn't move; it's locked. He is not worried; he simply takes out the copy of the key the Signore gave him and slides it into the lock. This doesn't move either. He tries to force it and almost breaks the key.

"Mother of God," he says, and he notices that his voice

sounds high and tight. The two brothers look at him but do not dare ask him what comes next. To go back up to the second floor to find another way out would be crazy—he can't keep on walking around with the *Joconde* under his arm. If they can't get out on the ground floor they're going to have to leave their prize. Perugia tries again, but the key remains firmly stuck in place.

"We've got to do something, and now!"

Perugia thinks, but nothing comes to him.

The night before, when she got home from the restaurant, she thought she might not sleep and had two more drinks. Now, Valérie Larbin lies on her bed asleep, face down, head to one side, the sheets on the floor beside her, her left arm under her head, her right arm flung out and her legs slightly bent. She has on the white cotton nightshirt she wears when she is alone, and her dark curls spill down her back. A little thread of spittle connects her upper and lower lips. Her grey cat peers at her as she always does.

He is suddenly surprised by an idea—the pleasure of having an idea! He feels magnificent, unstoppable. He tells Michele Lancelotti to go up to the first-floor landing and keep watch at the door there. He has decided to remove the lock, and he begins by unscrewing the door handle. It comes away easily, and he stows it in his pocket.

"A little lock isn't going to beat us," he says to Vincenzo, who is watching him. Then they hear Michele hiss and they freeze.

"Watch out! Someone's coming!"

"Get down here, quickly," whispers Perugia, and he slips the painting under his arm, covered by the smock. Michele is down with them now, and together they listen, frozen, to the steps coming closer and closer. There is no time to put back the handle. Perugia closes his eyes. Once again, that blankness. When he opens them he sees Sauvet, the plumber, who is hurrying down the stairs with his bag of tools.

"Some idiot has stolen the door handle," cries Perugia, almost shouting. "How are we supposed to get out of here, through the keyhole?" He is now genuinely angry.

"Hey there, don't worry. Take it easy, brother," says the plumber, opening the door with his key. "Leave it open, then it won't be a problem," he tells them before he goes on his way. All they have to do now is to cross the Salle d'Afrique and the Cour Visconti to get to the vestibule and then walk out of the door onto the street. Thirty or forty yards at the most.

"Come on, come on, we're almost out!"

They are crossing the Cour Visconti when Perugia sees a uniformed guard up ahead. Vincenzo Lancelotti stops dead, and the others with him.

"What do we do?"

"I don't know, I don't know; wait a minute!"

Perugia looks over to the door on the other side of the Cour Visconti, but it is padlocked. Now they are really sunk.

Valfierno is admiring himself in the mirror. He smiles at himself—such whiteness—and looks at his watch: almost eight o'clock. He tries to concentrate on the races at Longchamps and how he is going to spend his day of glory without anyone realizing, mingling with the elegant crowd to secure his alibi, but he can't stop conjuring up the image of Perugia. That idiot, he thinks. That idiot Italian! He resigns himself to thinking about Perugia, and it is a black hole. He imagines him walking through the Louvre with the painting in his hands, following each of his instructions, having to make decisions in the face of unexpected events, and he cannot fathom what, if anything, must be going through Perugia's head. He tells himself that this is always how it is. That the perfect plan often ends up depending on a moron for its success. It's the same thing the general faces on the battlefield: all his brilliant planning and preparation relies on a bunch of imbeciles who are not worthy of cleaning his boots. He tries his smile again in the mirror, and this time it doesn't come. He feels so superior, and so helpless. The danger of other people, he reflects, ruefully.

It occurs to him then that it is precisely in this that he is an artist—that he, too, is an artist and that this is his art. His particular talent is in arranging things so that everything depends on one moron. So that you could also say that this is how he gives chance a role in the equation, that he plays fairly. This is how he shows the world that we are all toys in the hands of an imbecile—this is his art.

He is now extremely nervous, frightened. Not that he could be implicated in the affair, for Perugia knows nothing about who he is, much less his friends. Only Valérie could ultimately make things very difficult for him, and he will take care of her later. But if they are caught, all his plans will disintegrate—everything he has spent more than a year putting together, his plans to secure his future. Most of all, the act that would have defined him forever, the one that would have declared once and for all who he was: Valfierno.

The three Italians hide in the Cour Visconti behind four big wooden boxes containing recently arrived works of art. Perugia knows they cannot stay there; dozens of windows give onto the Cour Visconti and anyone could see them. It's a question now of seconds, perhaps a minute. Two minutes if he were very lucky, he thinks, but luck is something he has never had; that star.

"Look, he's leaving," whispers Michele, and Perugia sees that the guard has picked up a bucket and is going through a side door that leads to the vestibule. He must be going to get water or soap; he won't be long. Just the thought that he might be lucky in spite of everything causes him to lose a few seconds, and he loses a few more crossing his fingers.

"Okay! Let's go!"

The three of them move quickly across to the vestibule, then across to the door and out into the street. They are on the street! They had taken off their aprons as they went, and now they are walking along the Quai du Louvre in the sunshine. In seconds they have become just three more ordinary guys, walking.

Valérie Larbin turns over in her bed, and the movement wakes her. She is startled, her head jerks, and she sees that it is light. In a fog, she reconstructs what happened: it's the morning of the day on which maybe . . . She remembers the words Valfierno didn't say, the drinks she had to get to sleep, something she dreamed that left her neck tight. She closes her eyes and tries to go back to sleep. The best choice.

Vincenzo Perugia is sure you can see it on him. It's just not possible that you can't see it, he thinks, that I look the same now as I did yesterday, that it was all nothing. He sidesteps a puddle. The Lancelotti brothers walk beside him. He's told them to flank him, just in case; the Rue Saint-Merri is dangerous, a refuge for petty criminals, and he has to be careful, though he doesn't believe any- one's going to think to steal the piece of wood he carries under his arm, wrapped in a white cloth. I can't believe no one can tell I've got millions of francs here under my arm! he laughs to himself. I'm lucky they're all so stupid.

"Here we are," says Vincenzo Lancelotti, and the three men look to either side before opening a narrow door with peeling paint. They go down a dark passageway, climb two flights of a dilapidated staircase, and bang on a small door.

"Vovonne! We're here," says Vincenzo Lancelotti, and a woman with meaty arms and sagging breasts opens the door for them without saying anything. Yvonne Séguenot is his girlfriend; he has offered her some money in exchange for storing an object for them for a few days. "Don't tell me it's the first time," he had said. "Or the last, I bet," she had replied. Now, in her soot-blackened kitchen, she serves the men a pastis.

"The Signore's health," Perugia declares, and the four glasses clink together. The woman reaches for the panel of wood, still wrapped in its apron.

"Don't touch that, woman," says Perugia, and Michele takes it from her and begins to unwrap it.

"Leave it, Michele, don't take it out."

"Come on, I want to see it."

"The Signore told us to leave it wrapped, to wait for him before we took it out."

"Come on, Vincenzo, he'll never know."

"You never know. Don't risk it."

Perugia takes it from him and hands it back to the woman, telling her to keep it under her bed until he asks for it, to go on with her normal life and not to worry about anything.

"I got to go. I'll be back at seven," he says, and leaves. The Signore had been very clear: they were not even to think about not going to work. But spending the whole day at his boss Perrotti's workshop was going to be almost as hard as the robbery itself. He was going to have to act as if nothing had happened, he thinks, and that kind of acting is what he is no good at.

Sir Galahad has just won the third race at Longchamps, and Valfierno reproaches himself for not having bet on him—his friend Sebastián had pointed him out as a hot tip. Then he thinks how stupid it all is.

It is three in the afternoon. The sun is beating down, the men are sweating, the women open their parasols, and Valfierno is cold. He is trembling—fear of the cell, he thinks. Right about now they'll be telling the police about him, he says to himself. They'll have been caught and they'll be giving me up. Everything is lost. I am lost. They're coming to get me. Even though they don't know who I am or what my name is, they'll tell the police every last detail about me: what I look like, my accent—anything they can remember. If they get tough with the Italian he'll remember a lot, thinks Valfierno, and he tries to calm himself by reminding himself how little Perugia knows, but it doesn't work. Everything is lost; I am lost—or maybe not, he thinks, but now he cannot bear not knowing. It's obvious that when he planned this whole thing he overestimated the strength of his nerves. How could he possibly have thought that he could spend this whole day not knowing what had happened? But in order to know he would have had to give them a telephone number or an address—far too big a risk. But he'd been mistaken to think he could last the whole day in this state.

"Marqués."

He is greeted by an acquaintance and he touches the brim of his top hat in salutation; the other smiles. Not all is lost, maybe the plan worked—soon I'll know, he thinks, and he knows, too, that he will manage to wait out the next three hours because in any case he has no choice, and because he is the Marqués Eduardo de Valfierno, with his walking stick and his top hat and his acquaintances who so deferentially greet him—greet him, the Marqués de Valfierno.

But perhaps he no longer exists, he thinks, and he can't be sure. Right now, at this very moment they are singing like birds, telling them everything, and they'll get me and put me back in jail, in a French jail, in prison with Frenchmen, and in the middle of his panic he has a memory: in prison with a Frenchman—they were together for so long. To go back to all that! he thinks with a start: Perrone, Juan María.

They're going to put me in jail; they're going to find out everything, who I really am, my name. They're not just going to put me in jail, they're going to put an end to me, to the Marqués Eduardo de Valfierno, to all of that, and for a moment he feels relief. I won't have to act anymore, he tells himself, I won't have to keep up this theater; but right away he sobers. In that case, he really would become nobody, he would have to start the whole thing over again, and he smiles at another gentleman who greets him amiably as he walks past.

There is no light he likes more than the light you get at six or seven in the evening, when the rays of the sun enter the studio almost horizontally and turn the air inside into something thick. Chaudron has a sip of wine from a broken cup and takes two steps back. There on the easel in front of him is a canvas with a charcoal sketch of the figure of a woman sitting with a child in her arms before a background of rocks and waterfalls. Lifting the broken cup to the canvas in a toast, he smiles to himself and leans forward to make an adjustment to the Virgin's left arm.

"Perugia!"

"Signore?"

"Yes, it's me, open up, open the door!"

The door opens on a small, poorly lit kitchen. There is enough light, however, to see the enormous smile on Perugia's face.

"Do you have it?"

"What do you think, Signore?"

It takes a huge effort for Valfierno to maintain his composure. To hug the Italian would be a stupid mistake.

With a short piece of charcoal pencil, Valérie extends the line of her eyebrow. Her face is stretched tight, tilted upward, eyes wide open, mouth in a small O. She finishes and rummages for the copper mascara and her brush. Before applying it, she takes a step back and assesses herself in the mirror: she is radiant. Yesterday Valfierno had told her that he didn't want to see her tonight, and so she is going to the Faux Chien. Screw him, she says to herself, if he thinks he can toss me aside that easily he is very much mistaken.

There she is: those thin, slightly cold lips in that indecipherable expression, that famous expression in which you can see a smile or disapproval or resignation or sadness or much more. Those lips like a mirror, in which each man sees what he wants, or what he fears, or what he can, thinks Valfierno. And those eyes that follow you whether you move to the right or the left, or raise or lower your head, or move away. And the chubby hands that hint at the hidden volume of the breasts behind them, and everything around them that leads you back to the eyes, the smile, the face that never stops telling you what you think it's telling you. Now I'll make you open your mouth, he thinks, and is surprised; for that moment, he is so far from being Valfierno. He smiles to himself and looks back at her. There she is, exactly as he has seen her so many times at the museum, so many times in copies and photographs and reproductions, except that now she is his, she is his the way everything else is his: without anyone else knowing or able to find out.

"Congratulations, Perugia."

"No, on the contrary, congratulations to you, Signore. Your plan worked perfectly."

"Now then, tell me everything . . ."

The two men are sitting in the kitchen with glasses of wine. At the end of the table, leaning against the wall, *La Joconde* looks at them distractedly. Valfierno is surprised by her size—now that he has her, she is so small! In the museum she seems imposing, but then that's true of everything there. And she looks too much like Chaudron's copies; for a moment he wonders if she is one.

". . . and then, just in time, we spotted a guard at the door, imagine! Right when we were almost out! But . . ."

Perugia recounts the day's events in a torrent of detail, with the occasional exaggeration for heroic effect. Valfierno listens as if it scarcely matters to him; he cannot stop listening to his own thoughts, the sheer excitement of knowing that he has finally gotten what he wanted, that he finally has what everyone wants, and now that it's his, he will do with it what no one could guess: this is his masterpiece.

"Tell the others to come in, Perugia."

"Yes, Signore."

Yvonne Séguenot and the two Lancelotti brothers file into the kitchen with their eyes lowered. The room is crammed and smells of garbage and stale sweat. Valfierno takes out a bulging wallet and counts out several large bills: some for the woman, some more for the brothers, more still for Perugia.

"I don't need to tell you that you must not say a word to anyone. If anyone talks, it will be all of you who get hurt, and only you. So keep your mouths shut and wait for my instructions. If you keep doing what you're told, there'll be plenty more of this," he says, and he takes Perugia's arm and leads him into the other room.

"So—leave the painting here until the police have finished asking you their questions—" Valfierno stops talking as he sees the expression on Perugia's face. "Now, don't worry, Perugia, I told you already, it will just be routine procedure. They will come to interview you; they might search your room, but you don't know anything, you have nothing to tell them, they won't find anything. You were working that day, so don't worry, and try to stay calm. That's the most important thing, Perugia—to stay calm. Do what you normally do, and don't spend any of that money until I tell you. And most of all, don't breathe a word of this to Valérie."

"Who?"

"Don't pretend, Perugia. Don't treat me like a fool. I know everything about you, what did you think?"

Vincenzo Perugia says nothing, surprised. He wonders how this man could know what no one knows; now he feels completely under his control. Valfierno also remains quiet, perhaps for a moment too long. He might have said too much. Above all, he thinks that he used a phrase that is not his, that sounds as if it came from someone else. He clears his throat and wipes his mouth with a handkerchief. Once the police have finished the interrogation, Perugia is to take the painting to his house and wait for instructions, he tells him: under no circumstances should he decide anything on his own.

"I will be going on a trip now for a few days. When I return, I will come by and give you the rest of the money and take the painting with me, understood?"

"Yes, Signore, of course," replies Perugia, wondering why the Signore doesn't just take the painting now and be done with it. He tries to think of a reason, but he can't. Still, he tells himself, the Signore knows what he's doing. Everything so far has gone well, the Signore knows exactly what he's doing, and if that is his decision then there must be a reason.

5

🌸 "You don't know how many times I've asked myself who he was, what happened, why he never came back. So many times in twenty years."

Back in the café in Dumenza's main square, nothing has changed from the previous day, nor, in all likelihood, in the past several decades. Perugia is wearing the same cotton shirt, or one just like it, equally worn, under his suspenders. We have ordered a jug of the local red wine with two glasses, some cheese and some olives. The other patrons are no longer paying any attention to us. Perugia pushes his hair back with his hands. His fingers are stubby, his nails bitten down.

"And you never mentioned him?"

"Who?"

"Who are we talking about? The Signore. The man you called the Signore."

"What do you mean I never mentioned him?"

"To the police, to the prosecutors, to the newspapers."

"What was I going to tell them? That some man I didn't know told me to do it? For what? They wouldn't have believed me, they would have called me a liar. I may be a lot of things, but I'm no liar."

I had been told that for an Italian, to be a thief was not a serious dishonor, whereas to be thought a liar—this was truly terrible.

"And anyway, you'd prefer people to think that you'd done the whole thing on your own. You were a hero, right, Perugia? The lone crusader?"

Perugia gives me a hostile look and I decide to watch what I say. We have already talked about the theft itself—about that night and that incredible morning—and I am trying not to ask him questions that could sound hostile or accusing; it's a complicated balance. Now I try to bring him back by recalling his memories of triumph.

"That must have been a great moment."

"Which one?"

"The one where you return with the painting under your arm, knowing that you did it, that you have what everybody wants," I say admiringly. I learned a long time ago that to make someone talk, nothing works better than a little flattery. To show that they're truly worthy of the praise, they end up saying things they didn't intend to.

"Yeah, sure. I was nervous but very happy."

He lifts his glass and silently we toast, I suppose, the success of the robbery. Then he tells me how they left the painting in the house of that French washerwoman—"that cow, Lancelotti's girl," he says—for a few days, waiting for the police to come to his room to ask him their questions. Finally they did come. It took them two months, but they came.

"They were a couple of idiots," he tells me, "French idiots. They asked me if I'd ever worked in the Louvre and I said, sure, and they asked a few other things, I don't remember what."

"Weren't you nervous?"

"Why should I be nervous? I hadn't done anything," he says, and though I can't explain it, he seems quite serious. He tells me the only thing that spooked him was when they asked him why he'd arrived at work late on that Monday, the twenty-first of August. He tells me that they knew he hadn't got in until nine o'clock. "I said, 'How should I know?' and that it was a Monday, and you know how you often sleep late on a Monday, what difference does that make? And I smiled at them," he says, "not too much, and they smiled, too, and nodded, and agreed with me. Then they looked around a bit but of course they didn't find anything. Then they went."

"And you thought that you had convinced them?"

"Sure, what else was I supposed to think? I didn't even think about it; they believed me."

"And then you took the painting back to your room."

"No, no, I'm not that stupid, mister. No, I waited a few days, a couple of weeks. When they didn't come back, then I took it home."

"How did you carry it?"

"How was I supposed to take it? I wrapped it up in a cloth again and stuck it under my arm and took it, just like that. I just walked with it, no problem, through the Marais."

Perugia pours more wine and chooses an olive. I try to imagine myself in the same situation—how terrifying that walk would be—and I consider the advantages of a limited imagination. It takes a certain intelligence to be able to imagine potential dangers. Perugia had other strengths. He decided to build himself a wooden toolbox with a false compartment in which he could hide the painting.

"Then I read in the papers that the top policemen from France, England, and America had been searching for the painting. That they'd sent people to Germany, Belgium, Greece, Spain, Russia . . . Think of that! And I had it! What morons! All they had to do was find me," he says, and again he is quite serious. More time went by. Perugia was getting anxious at the lack of news from the Signore, but he continued to wait.

"When he left, he said he was going to send me instructions and more money. He said he was going to come back to get the painting and take care of everything. I believed him; why shouldn't I? Think about it—why would he go to all this trouble and then not come back for the painting? But then months went by, he didn't come, and I started wondering."

He tells me that occasionally, he would take *La Joconde* out of her secret hiding place and prop her up on the table in his room, with a candle on either side of her.

"Yeah, you know sometimes I'd spend hours just looking at her. Did you ever see her, mister, close up?"

"Not as close as you."

"Yeah, that's right. And I bet you saw her in the museum. It's real different to see her in the museum and to have her at home, to know that she's yours, that you could do whatever you wanted to her."

"Like what, for example?"

"I don't know—nothing. Can I tell you one little thing?" he asks me, tilting his head in a very odd way.

"Sure, go ahead."

Suddenly Perugia seems very shy. He doesn't look at me while he's talking.

"You know what I would do? Sometimes, I'd take out my mandolin and sing to her."

"Your mandolin?"

"Yeah, didn't you know? I play the mandolin real well," he tells me with a flash of pride. I ask him then what he used to sing to her, but he doesn't answer. He is silent, looking at something far away.

"And did you talk to her?"

"To who?"

"To La Joconde."

"Why would I do that?" he snaps, now irritated. I suspect that he did but that he'd never tell me. Then I ask him what he thought about the Signore, who he imagined him to be, and he tells me he thought different things. He tells me that he tried not to think about who he was or where he came from, but that he couldn't avoid it. He says he had imagined lots of things, but that he didn't want to tell me what they were, just in case. And he says that, at the beginning, he waited calmly.

"He didn't tell me what he was going to do, but that didn't worry me 'cause he never told me anything. I don't know, first I thought that he was looking for someone to buy the thing and that he needed to wait until things calmed down, so I wasn't surprised that it was taking so long. He wrote to me a few times, you know . . ."

"Where did he write to you from?"

"Phew, incredible places—New York, Cairo . . . Once he wrote to me from Tangier. I thought he was looking for someone to buy her. It was going to be hard to sell her with all those police. I was sure he was just looking for a buyer," he says, and at that moment our table is hit squarely with birdshit, white, green, and brownish. Perugia smiles and says it's good luck.

"Especially for you," he says. He tells me that it's good for him as well, but that he has no need of luck now, that his life now is all set. But that in those days he sure had needed it.

"Why?"

"I don't know, it was tough. I waited, I'd get nervous; I couldn't keep any job. I couldn't stick to a schedule or put up with my bosses."

"I can imagine."

"I don't know if you can. I had *La Joconde* under my bed—you think I was going to let some nobody yell at me?" he says, smiling. "And I still had money left, even if I was starting to run out."

"So you bet with the money you had left."

"Why do you say that?"

"Well, that's what happens, isn't it?"

"What do you mean by that—did you check up on me?"

It had only been a guess, but his reaction told me I'd been right. His face especially.

"Did you lose all of it?"

"Yeah, you're right, almost all of it. I thought my luck had changed, you know? If I could steal the most valuable painting in the world, how come I couldn't win betting on soccer or boxing, or playing goddamn cards? But of course I was wrong; my luck hadn't changed."

Perugia was running out of money, but he wasn't that worried. He still thought Valfierno would appear with a pile of cash to pay him what he owed him.

"See what my life was like, mister? I was sleeping on a gold mine and I didn't have a penny. Later, when I looked at her I thought the bitch was laughing at me. You know that smile—she was laughing at me! Because I was going hungry with her under my bed. What was I supposed to do? Hold on to her for that guy? I would have waited as long as it took, but for that he had to say something, at least ask me. I started to hate him, that stuck-up bastard. I waited two years. You know how long that is—two years?"

Perugia is getting worked up, waving his hands in all directions. I try not to look alarmed, but I'm beginning to understand one thing—Valfierno's mistake. What had seemed like a perfect plan had one critical flaw: it abandoned its principal actor. And it could have been much worse if Perugia had not waited so long to act—his lack of imagination once again. He was penniless, he had the painting, and he had his new hatred, but it didn't occur to him to put those things together. About a year after the theft, Perugia started to think about what to do with the Madonna he was sharing a bed with.

"See how it was? Look, since I'm telling you everything, I might as well tell you this: it occurred to me that he must have died. I thought he must have died out there someplace and he couldn't tell me. One night when I was with the candles, looking at the painting, I suddenly thought, What an idiot! He's dead; the guy is dead! I was even a little sorry, I'm not kidding. Who knows where it happened? And if he was dead, that explained everything, and then the painting was mine, you understand?"

"Sure, of course."

"Was he dead?"

"No, Perugia, he was quite alive," I tell him, and it's true; it was true then.

"Shit!" he says, and again: "Shit! He wasn't dead!"

Then he's looking into space again, his hands on his hair, on his glass, the sound of him drinking. It's a tough moment—once again the story he'd built about what had happened is coming apart. I feel sorry for him. I'm tempted to tell him the truth, but I need to hear the rest of the story first. Then I ask him what he decided to do with the painting, but he doesn't answer.

"I suppose you tried to find someone to buy it?" I venture, to see what he will say.

"No, no, I wasn't interested in that. I don't know anybody like that, who buys paintings in that way. Anyway, I didn't think of selling it."

"Come on, Perugia. When you were arrested in Florence, they found a list of well-known collectors in your room in Paris. You even had the addresses of people like Carnegie, J. P. Morgan, Rockefeller."

"Yeah, that's what they said."

"And it was true."

"It might be true. But I don't know how to get to people like that, and anyway, I wasn't selling anything. I wanted to give the painting back to my country."

This had been his claim throughout the trial, though it just wasn't believable. At least it wasn't what he was thinking at first, when he was trying to figure out a way to sell it.

The ants on our table are attracting the attention of the sparrows. Perugia scares them off by banging his hand on the table—too hard, almost knocking over a glass.

"Who gave you the idea of bringing it to Italy?"

"No one gave me the idea. I thought of it myself, once I thought he was dead."

"Come on, Perugia, I know how it is. There you are one night, someone says something, a man, a woman . . ."

"No, it was a man, a man," he says without thinking. Suddenly, he scrambles to his feet. It's late now; Perugia knows it. He takes another gulp of wine and then tells me how one morning, out of work, he was in the bistro with a fellow Italian, talking about how badly they were treated by the French; who did they think they were? And his compatriot said that the French treated them like thieves, when in fact it was the French who had stolen lots of things from the Italians: statues, paintings, even some words. And Perugia asked him what paintings, for example? And his companion told him that the most famous one was the *Mona Lisa*, and that Napoleon was the one who had taken it when he invaded Italy, and brought it back to France, and that now they were making all this fuss about the painting being stolen, and wouldn't it be funny if an Italian had taken it, what did he think? And he said yes, that would be funny.

"So then I knew what I had to do, you know? I had to give my country back what that Italian turncoat Bonaparte had stolen from it. Now that sure was good—a carpenter defending his country better than any generals or kings, isn't that a good one?"

"But Napoleon didn't take that painting."

"Who says?"

"Come on, Perugia, you know this now: Leonardo sold that painting to the king of France, François I."

"That's what some people say. You know how it is—everyone lies."

Perugia is uncomfortable again and falls silent. The sun is going down and the birds are getting raucous. Two girls on bicycles pass along the cobbled street in front of the church. They are wearing flowered dresses, their hair loose. The blackshirts whistle and call out offers of love. The girls keep riding without turning around, playing their role.

"You know what? There's something not a lot of people know, but I'll tell you. The Signore told me, and he was right: The *Mona Lisa* is cursed."

"What?"

"She's cursed, she brings bad luck. The Signore explained it all to me when we were going over the plans. He told me the whole story. It's long; I don't want to go into all of it. The point is that she gets everyone who tries to keep her. What you have to do is give her to someone else, keep her moving."

"And you were brave enough to steal her, knowing this?"

"I was just stealing her, not keeping her. Sure, it was a risk, but fortune favors the bold, didn't anyone ever tell you that? I took a risk stealing her, but keeping her . . . ," says Perugia, and he touches his left hand to his crotch, making no attempt to be discreet.

The wind has come up. The domino players are already gathering up their wooden pieces. Valfierno must have told Perugia this gypsy curse story to discourage his henchman from betraying him or making off with the painting. But his invention had ended up working against him. Perugia got more and more anxious. Many nights he would take *La Joconde* out from her hiding place in the box beneath his bed, and he would look at her, touch her, talk to her in his own dialect, and try to understand where she kept her curse.

"Two years with that witch under my bed, Signore, two damned years! I know you won't believe this, but a lot of times I thought about just burning her."

"Burning her?" I say, barely able to speak. Perugia smiles to himself.

"Sounds strange, doesn't it? It isn't that strange. But I didn't do it, I was scared that if I did burn her all the bad luck could stick to me forever. In the end, that's why I didn't. What a joke! As if you could avoid it . . . ," he says, almost in a whisper. I suddenly understand that it's been years since he's spoken about any of this. That he needs to tell it all again to someone, to revisit who he is and what his story is.

"So you decided to bring the painting here."

"Yeah, that's what I'm trying to tell you."

"You took it to your own country knowing that it would bring it bad luck?"

"No, no, it's not bad luck for countries. Look at France—they should be completely sunk, but they're doing pretty well. No, it's only for people," he says, with unassailable logic. He tells me that this is why he brought the painting here. That and because finally he would be someone—the hero who returned the *Mona Lisa* to Italy.

"Think about it—I had everything working in my favor. I didn't count on the politicians doing what they usually do. Thank God Il Duce has got rid of them all."

"And what did Matilda say when you decided to take the painting home?"

"What?"

Perugia stands up again, puts on his hat, and looks at me as if seeing me for the first time: a judge, a policeman, an enemy. I touch his arm to calm him; his sleeve is greasy. He sits down. I can't go back now:

"Yes, Matilda. Don't pretend, Perugia, you know exactly who I'm talking about."

"Look—don't bring Matilda into this," he says fiercely. Now he's defending a girl's honor—a girl who must be fifty by now. He had known her in the months after the theft, a peasant girl from Alsace, a maid in a house of bourgeoises. Blond, no doubt.

"You've got no right! She had nothing to do with it! She was a good girl—simple, loving; not like the other."

Perugia had lost control. The journalist had a duty to take advantage of it.

"What other one? What do you mean, 'the other'?"

"Nothing! It doesn't matter. Matilda never knew anything about the painting. In all that time I never said a word to anyone about it. I know how to keep a secret; not like some people . . ."

"Who are you talking about?"

"No one, it doesn't matter."

"Tell me, please."

"No. I can keep a secret."

I don't push; it's a good idea to let him have the occasional small victory.

"And Valérie never knew anything?"

"How should I know what she knew? Don't even say her name to me. That woman thinks Italians are dogs, that Italian men aren't real men—I don't even know what she thinks. Don't even say her name out loud!"

I need to know what became of her, but it's obviously something I won't be able to get from Perugia, who is agitated and twisting around in his wooden chair, glancing all around him. We are alone now. Standing by the door to the café, the owner waits for us to leave once and for all.

"Didn't it remind you of Valérie?"

"What?"

"I mean the painting, *La Joconde*. Didn't it ever make you think of Valérie?"

"I don't understand."

"It's all right. It's just that the Signore told me that it reminded him a lot of her."

"The Signore?"

Perugia pours himself what's left of the wine, drinks it down in one gulp, and tells me that he's never been able to decide whether or not he still owed the Signore anything.

"In the end, I don't know whether he ruined my life or saved it," he says, and for a moment it occurs to me that I have misjudged him, that he is much more astute than I've given him credit for. Then he tells me it's time for me to pay him. I reach for the wallet in my jacket pocket.

"No, Mr. Becker—I mean really pay. The Signore's name.

Maybe if I know it I'll be able to figure out if I owe him anything or not."

He's right—I had promised him much more than money.

"His name was Valfierno—the Marqués Eduardo de Valfierno."

"Marqués? And why did you say 'was'?"

That second question seems to me to be the important one.

"Because the Marqués de Valfierno is no longer," I tell him, and he asks me where he came from, and before I can answer him he also tells me that he had noticed that the Signore spoke good Italian but that he had also noticed an accent, and he couldn't figure out where it was from. Maybe Calabrese, he tells me, or Sicilian.

"He was Argentine."

"Argentine? Where from?"

"From Argentina, Perugia. From South America."

"Really? And he's dead?"

"Yes. That's why I'm talking to you now."

"Dead? He's really dead?"

"Are you surprised?"

"It's funny, I don't even know. When did he die? Where? What happened?"

The
Jocondes

1

He opens the newspaper and scans for the story. It's not there. He must be an idiot, he thinks—if the story is in here it's got to be on the front page. With mounting concern, he opens another paper, and another, and another. There is no story. The Parisians publish so many newspapers, and not one of them has the story. The afternoon editions say that the heat will continue but not the rains; that Nijinsky is dancing Stravinsky with Diaghilev's Ballets Russes; that the Germans have sent torpedo boats to the Moroccan coast; that the train workers are preparing to strike; and that those cheap new cigarettes, Gauloises, are too strong for French tastes. Nothing of any interest to him—all garbage. The story is not there.

In that arbitrary moment in history, the father of that man is a man who does not define himself that way. He is not yet convinced that to be that man's father—to be anyone's father, for that matter—is the way to define a person. And as it happens, he does not have much time left to find that definition—or any other. A man can go through his whole life without discovering what truly defines him; he can go through his entire life without even bothering to look for it. He can quite sensibly suppose that it isn't possible or necessary to define himself in terms that words can encompass. But it often happens, in this story and in others, that a man is identified as the father of another. Then the rest of his life, apart from the four, or five, or twenty minutes of excitement spent on a woman, will count for nothing before the force of that jet of life, of the blood essence in that jet. It can take a man years to learn that this is what will define him in the end. Most men will never learn it.

The man walks along that street and does not think of himself as a father.

"And is it true that you hate Italy? That you hate everything Italian?"

"Why would I hate Italy, Newspaperman?"

"Because of what happened to your father; your father's death."

"Who told you anything about my father? Didn't I tell you a million times that I don't have a father?"

He had read when he was in Buenos Aires that there have always been forgeries. That the Egyptians made precious stones with pieces of colored glass. That the Romans kept on carving Greek statues, and that the first Christians made fortunes selling pieces of the cross, the bones of martyrs, the spikes that had held Jesus up. That anything worth anything gets forged, and that nothing worth nothing does. That to forge something is an act of homage. That to reproduce nature itself was a sign of man's greatness, a way of showing nature that its power could be matched. And that to forge art is a form of humility, of showing that the value of a human creation is an illusion—one convention among infinite possibilities.

And that everything that man does is either a copy or a forgery—that man's only original invention has been the right angle, something nature never came up with. In other words, he tells himself, the only thing that is definitely not fake, the only thing you can know to be genuine, is the right angle, a rectangle, any corner. Which really doesn't get you very far.

The man walks along that street very differently from the way he's walked down the same street so many times before. On this walk, important things could be decided.

Despite the fact that he is facing a moment that could prove to be critical for him, an act whose consequences would be irreversible, we imagine that this man—GianFelice Bonaglia, born in Pescara, on the twenty-fourth of June, 1844, a Monday, the feast of St. John, a textile dyer by profession, married to Annunziata Perrone and with a son named GianMaria—does not seem fully convinced of what he is about to do.

He asks himself why he is doing it but does not come up with an answer that satisfies him. Let us say that in spite of this, he cannot think of a way out—he thinks it would be even more difficult to find a satisfactory answer to the question of why or how not to go ahead, and so he keeps walking.

Or let us say that he does not think that what is about to happen is of such great consequence; that if he could anticipate what was about to happen he would find—would certainly find—a way to retreat.

We can say then that he is about to become the victim, as much as anything, of a poor imagination. We can postulate that bravery is often more than anything a failure of the imagination. Or a surfeit of reality—a confidence in the insistence of reality. Men who tell themselves that since fearsome things do not usually occur, there is therefore no reason to fear that they will occur now.

Valfierno does not want to see anyone that night. He goes to his room and tells himself that he must come up with some alternatives. He has always told himself that the most important thing is to anticipate the various possibilities, all the potential developments, at the beginning of any endeavor. But tonight he has had enough. The situation seems incredible to him, and he concludes that if he were to think about it he would understand it less and it would disturb him more.

Today, he—his men—stole the *Mona Lisa*. He has finally achieved something he's been contemplating for years. He's done what no one else has been able to do, he has stolen the most famous painting in the world, and the story is not in the newspapers. He pours himself a generous cognac and tries not to think but cannot help himself. He wants to get dressed and go and see Chaudron, who is the only one he can tell about this, but he can't. It would be a mistake, he warns himself.

He makes himself another drink. He knows that *La Joconde* is no longer in the Louvre, he knows they took her, he's quite sure that he has just seen her, and yet there is nothing in the papers. Without the story in the papers, his plan is worth nothing; the paintings—nothing. Without the news, his own story crumbles. If those poor guys knew that he had sent them to steal the *Mona Lisa* just so that the story would be in the papers!

He tries not to think, then tries to guess what could be happening. The museum does not want the story to come out. The police don't want the story out yet—they know something that he doesn't know, something they don't want anyone else to know; they're about to figure everything out and they don't want the story to come out until they've wrapped it all up. They're on their way to pick him up now. They have no clues, there is no way they can know anything. The painting was a copy that they had on display in case it was ever stolen.

He had stolen a copy.

Valfierno breathes deeply and gets very still, his eyes staring at the closed window, his neck tight: he has stolen a copy. He's fallen right in the trap. They've given him a taste of his own medicine. He has fallen into their trap.

He tries to console himself, telling himself that if he'd been sure everything was going to work out perfectly there would never have been any point in doing it. He considers this for a moment, as if he'd just found a way out, then: Utter stupidity! he thinks, annoyed. Just the Marqués's sophistry!

Now he thinks that it isn't possible, the Louvre could never put a false painting on display, they couldn't bring themselves to do it, they have patrons who would notice, and he smiles bitterly to himself, the small consolation of disdain in the midst of his downfall. He knows better than anyone that there are few, if any, who would know. He has stolen a fake, he thinks, and in the face of this theory all the others fade. He fell for his own trick. He has just begun to relax—to turn his head, to reach for a cigarette, to look around the room—when it occurs to him that he can bring down many others in his fall—he is going to tell everything. The newspapers are going to hear that the painting hanging in the Salon Carré was a copy, that the Louvre lies to the public, that everything is a fake.

He walks. GianFelice Bonaglia is not yet thirty—between twenty and thirty—broad and almost tall, with bulging legs, his rough head crowned with a mass of black hair that tumbles beyond control. Trying to tame that hair has always seemed to him like a waste of time, a prissy concern for rich young men. His face would certainly be a concern for such a young gentleman: a square jaw, a nose that looked as if it had been hacked out, the thick eyebrows sitting above dark sunken eyes like narrow slits, the mouth without flesh, more like a puncture.

It is summer. GianFelice Bonaglia is wearing a dirty white shirt open at the chest, and black corduroy breeches—his only pants—which go down only as far as his midcalf. The modest clothing of a humble textile dyer. It is summer, and GianFelice Bonaglia does not think of his wife or his son, he just walks on, sweating. Walking beside him are hundreds more men of similar description. It doesn't occur to Bonaglia—or at least it wouldn't occur to him, were he to think about it—to consider those hundreds around him similar. Not a man among them would think such a thing. Not even walking all together along the Roman streets, under the Roman sun, with others who have come out because they believe they are all the same and believe, or think they believe, in the same things.

That to copy a work of art is to recognize its value, whereas to forge it is to recognize its price. That a forger is an easy bastard, a whore, high-priced or otherwise, who doesn't do what he thinks he should do, what he has no choice but to do, or what he ought to do, but rather what someone else has done, and what he thinks others want and will buy.

That he was an idiot. That he deserved what he got.

These are the final days of something that has been building for a long time. The men march, having come out of their factories that afternoon, they march, lured by the rumor that the great Garibaldi is arriving to put an end once and for all to the papists' power. They walk along the narrow, shady streets of the outlying districts toward the wall. Some of them carry knives, one or two even a musket, but you couldn't really say that they are armed; they are unwilling to believe that it will be necessary to raise arms to defeat those who are already defeated.

Every now and then a shout rings out—a man bolstering his courage, the courage of those around him. They shout out "Viva Garibaldi, Viva Italia," "Death to the Papists," and several shutters swing closed as they pass. They might begin to wonder if they are not mistaken in believing that this march will be just that, with a peaceful triumph awaiting them at the end. Perhaps, in the face of those closing shutters and the women who cross themselves and that silence, they might begin to suspect that it won't be like that, that they are mistaken. But those men are not marching because they believe they are mistaken.

In the morning they brought him all the newspapers he had requested and the story wasn't in any of them, only the same trivialities, and so he has stayed in his room until two in the afternoon. In certain moments he savors his anticipated revenge of telling everyone the truth; in others, the idea seems stupid. Sometimes he delights in it and savors the details—which newspaper, which reporter, what he'll say, what he won't say—but then he realizes that his life is ruined, and that it's all just a way of trying to forget that he has lost his one big bet.

So it has taken a tremendous effort for him to bathe, to shave, to comb and dress himself and to prepare to go out. He doesn't know what to do. As deeply as he remembers feeling anything, Valfierno does not know what to do next. There have been many times in his life when he hasn't known what to do next, even in important situations that were to define his life. These were moments in which he faltered, and he remembers them as experiences at the edge: when he decided to join the anarchists' group in Rosario; when, unable to make any decision, he had ended up in the shop in San José de Flores; when he decided that only by leaving Buenos Aires might he have a chance to make it. He remembers these as moments of extreme stress, the most difficult, but realizes now that they weren't; there was something about them that was kinder. Then, he had only the pressure of having to choose among a few options, whereas now there were no such options, only pure discomfort, perfect incomprehension, the despair of realizing that events that had been counted on to go a certain way had not. The feeling of not understanding what is happening, or what to do, or even what not to do. He wants to surrender himself to something, to God, to some kind of fate, but he finds none, and he doesn't know what to do. It has taken all his will to bathe and dress and go down to the lobby and into the street.

"*La Joconde!* Read all about it! The *Mona Lisa* has disappeared!" shouts a paper boy. And another yells:

"Ladies and gentlemen, *La Joconde* has escaped!"

Others, too, are running with front pages that declare in mammoth letters: "Inexplicable!" "Incredible!" "Shocking!" and many more. Valfierno rushes to buy one of each of them before he realizes that he is doing what he has dreamed of thousands of times, that the wondering and the faltering are over, that these newspapers—that all the world's newspapers—were talking about him.

The men pour out into a wide piazza, in which there are two oak trees, flaking ocher walls, and a battalion of Swiss Guards in two rows. The first row is down on one knee holding rifles up to their shoulders and the second row stands behind them at the ready. Seeing the Swiss Guards, the men at the head of the great mass of men slow their pace. They turn for a moment, looking to either side for a way out, or at least a way to stall their advance. The men behind, who have not yet seen the Swiss Guards, push forward. The men at the front yell out. Bonaglia is among them. They look to either side, raise their arms, and shout two words before turning once more to face forward, where the standing guards are lifting their rifles to their shoulders.

"And would you say that this really happened?"

"That? I wouldn't even call that a story. Much later, I understood that all of it had happened, and then, even later, I also understood that none of it mattered in the least."

"So why did you tell me?"

"At last, Newspaperman—a question!"

The guards open fire. The man—the father—flees.

He finds it exceedingly strange to be reading these stories that, without their knowing it, are about him. He is sitting in a café, next to the window, and watches as more and more excited newspaper vendors go by with late editions, the breaking story, and customers pull the papers out of their hands, the heat no longer important, Nijinsky sliding—the world now just a manifestation of his idea.

"What audacious criminal, what magician, what maniacal

collector, what hysterical fan has committed this act of outrageous thievery?" he reads. "Leonardo da Vinci's *Mona Lisa* has disappeared! An event that overwhelms our own imaginations," he reads, and he sits up taller, proud now, and cocky.

He reads on, learning that on that morning, Tuesday morning, an amateur painter who wanted to paint a copy of the painting had asked a guard why the *Mona Lisa* wasn't in her usual place. The guard had told the painter to wait, that they'd probably taken her to be photographed, or some such thing. The painter had waited until eleven and then returned to ask again, whereupon finally they had spread the alarm and begun to search through the various departments—photography, restoration, cleaning—and that, still not having found her, there had been complete confusion as they had tried to determine where she might be.

Finally, just before noon, they had realized that she was not to be found and had called the Chief of Police, who called the Minister of the Interior, who called the President of the Republic. And that then panic had given way to scandal. That they did not know when the painting had been taken. That since yesterday—Monday—the museum had been closed, no one had noticed anything. A museum employee had said that he had noticed on Monday morning that *La Joconde* was not hanging in her usual place, but that since she was always being taken away for one thing or another, he said, he hadn't given it any thought. And that this was why it had taken thirty hours for the theft to be discovered, reads Valfierno, and he cannot believe it. Such idiots! Pure incompetence. If he'd only known.

"Clearly the thief or thieves had all the time they needed to complete their task, the details of which, at the moment, are a mystery to us as well," the Chief of Police told one reporter. "But we will catch him. The thief always makes a false move."

"A false move," reads Valfierno, wondering what his might be.

2

I WAS NOW, WITHOUT DOUBT, the Marqués de Valfierno. I had won my title in battle, like the medieval knights who were made noblemen by the king as the sounds of battle died away.

I had won it doing what no one had ever been able to do, and what many had wanted to. Or perhaps I had really won it doing what no one had wanted to do, since no one had ever been able to imagine it. I was finally the person I had wanted to be—though I didn't notice much of a difference.

The world was changing even more than I had. War threatened. This threat can in some ways be worse than the war itself: days in free fall when it seems to makes sense to believe that anything could happen, including what makes no sense. There is nothing more terrifying than that feeling that there are no longer any limits. Though when what we fear begins to happen, what actually happens—while momentous—is always less than it could be. I know that when the event finally happens, including catastrophes, terrible things, it can be a relief.

We expected a war; the world had changed a great deal. The looming threat put men in strange moods, and everything seemed to be moving toward crisis without any particular course. In spite of this, the general instability did not prevent me from concluding the sale of the paintings.

I could say that it was no more than a simple transaction, but that wouldn't be quite accurate. What I can say with certainty is that I saw six people who thought they already owned virtually everything achieve the joy of acquiring something so rare that no one can or should possess it. They had taken the art of possession to an extraordinary level, to the height of absurdity. That autumn after the theft I dedicated myself to distributing the six copies of *La Joconde* around the United States.

It was cold on that afternoon in November when I presented myself—at five o'clock on the dot, as we had agreed—at Colonel Gladstone Burton's Fifth Avenue mansion. The butler, having sized me up in the doorway, seemed to approve of what he saw. He took my mink coat and the tan leather case with gold fittings that I was carrying and led me through a series of grand rooms. Standing in his study, the Colonel appeared far too anxious to waste any time on greetings or formalities.

"Let's see. Do you have it there?"

I replied that of course I did, and then kept quiet. It was amusing to watch his embarrassment. This man, who had inspired fear in entire regiments and in legions of workers, didn't know how to conduct a transaction which, after all, should have been simple for him.

I looked at him. The colonel frowned and appeared to remember something.

"Oh, excuse me: here is your money."

He pointed to a black leather case resting on his Imperial-style mahogany desk. Asking his permission, I opened it and saw that it was filled with one-hundred-dollar bills. To count it, I thought, would be in very poor taste. Looking it over, I calculated that it was right: the agreed-upon three hundred and fifty thousand dollars appeared to be there. I said that I assumed he'd read the newspapers. The casual tone came out perfectly.

"Of course! I've been waiting since I saw it," he said, without taking his eyes from the tan case.

"It was not easy, though it might have sounded it."

I was enjoying the moment. Though the poor old man was dying of impatience, he had to listen to me allude to the source of his new pleasure, to the fact that he was an accomplice in a huge theft. It was important for him not to forget this.

"I know, Marqués, I can imagine. I have to say, you've done an extraordinary job. To tell you the truth, I didn't believe you'd be able to pull it off."

It might have been true, or he might just have been sugaring the pill—it made no difference. Either way, I enjoyed it.

" 'Extraordinary' is the word. My congratulations, Marqués," he said, and then a shadow passed across his face. Perhaps it was dawning on him that he was alone with the world's most wanted thief. Or perhaps that he was one of the very few people who knew his identity. The shadow was not fear, I supposed—it was more likely being reminded of his own complicity. I took advantage of this to press a point:

"You will remember, Colonel, the terms of our agreement."

"What do you mean?"

He was getting exasperated. I reminded him that he had promised never to show *La Joconde* to anyone, ever.

"Remember that if you do, the biggest risk is to yourself."

"Please—I know."

He had lost almost all patience, but he was swallowing his pride. There was no point in continuing to torment him. I took the leather case and flung it open with a gesture that, for the first time, I found too showy. Colonel Burton was speechless, his mouth hung open, his hands were clutched to his head like someone watching a disaster unfold.

"You have no idea what this means."

"Indeed, Colonel?"

"No, you don't know. You simply don't know."

I thought of saying that if I didn't know, his constant repetition would be sure to teach me, but I don't think I did. The Colonel gazed at the *Mona Lisa* without yet really being able to believe it. He stretched a hand out to touch it and then pulled it back quickly, almost scared.

"Now I have her. She is all mine."

He believed this, as would, in the next weeks, the banker I paid a visit to in his country house, the oilman in his office, the steel magnate in his suite at the Waldorf, the Philadelphia aristocrat, and the big Chicago slaughterhouse baron. Each one of them took enormous pleasure in the belief that no one else could have what he now had. They thought they were unique, and my job was to make sure that they could think this. Not one of them doubted the authenticity of the painting I had delivered to him. No one wanted to ask me for too many details. They had all seen—there was no way not to—the story of the theft in the newspapers. They all admired my skill and sangfroid. Each of them was grateful to me—though not without some confused feelings—for having chosen him as the beneficiary of my scheme. They were all dying to tell someone what they had, but felt—and still feel, I hope—the virtue of resisting that temptation.

What was certain was that I had won: I now had almost two million dollars. It was more than I could ever have dreamed. I entertained myself by thinking up things to do with such an unlikely fortune. I could buy two thousand five hundred of those new cars of Mr. Ford's, a Swiss heiress, a castle with land in Lazio, in Italy, and a spotless reputation anywhere in the world. I was very rich. I had won. I was Valfierno.

"And no one suspected anything? Really?"
"Would you have suspected, Newspaperman?"

He told me that Michelangelo's own fame began with a fake, that he sculpted a statue in the classical style—a sleeping Cupid of extraordinary beauty—and buried it to give it the appearance of being ancient, and that he then sold the fake to Cardinal San Giorgio in Rome for two hundred ducats. The Cardinal was delighted by the statue until someone revealed the truth about it, whereupon he was mortally offended, humiliated for not having been able to distinguish between the supposedly real and the supposedly false, and threatened Michelangelo and forced him to return his money. He returned the statue, and because of his pride, lost the chance to own a Michelangelo Buonarotti that in time would prove to be much more valuable than an ancient Cupid and was a great deal more beautiful.

After this, Michelangelo renounced all artifice and decided that true art lay in discovering what was natural and innate—in wresting from marble its very essence. But his Cupid secured him the reputation of being able to do what before only the ancients had achieved, and he had done it more for that glory than for the ducats.

Valfierno told me that he, too, had done it for the glory—as well as the money. And that the problem—his problem—will be how to achieve that glory. How to have his secret glory recognized and yet still be secret, so that his creation is not ruined and all his glory lost.

"No, I guess not. What about you?"
"Never. I've already told you—I am completely gullible."

Valérie was the one loose part in his otherwise perfect machine. The security of his scheme rested on the fact that each one of his pawns knew only him and none of the others. In the case of Perugia and his friends, they didn't even know his name.

Valérie, on the other hand, knew quite a few things about him and also knew Perugia well. And while he hadn't told her the details of his plan—while she didn't know that the whole goal of the scheme had been the sale of the copies—she knew that he, the Marqués, had masterminded what Perugia and the two brothers had carried out.

After the theft, Valérie had become insufferable. He had tried to avoid her, but even so, during the few times they had seen each other before he had left Paris she had demanded her share, saying that without her none of it would have been possible: "What did you think, Marqués" —this last word ringing with sarcasm— "that you could just push me aside so easily?"

"It's hard to believe, Marqués, that after all this time you really don't know who you're playing with."

"What are you saying?"

"Nothing I haven't already said. If you don't pay me what you owe me I'll break this whole thing wide open."

Valfierno offered her a considerable sum of money with two conditions: that she leave Paris and that she never—"and I mean never in your miserable life, you understand?" —see Vincenzo Perugia again. It really was a lot of money.

"Are you jealous, my love?"

"Don't be ridiculous."

"Am I being ridiculous?"

In the end, Valérie accepted. She told him that all things considered it had been a good deal, and she proposed that they wrap it up with one last night together:

"Don't you worry, my love, there are no strings. It would be to seal our new alliance."

Valfierno refused her, and in so doing, believed that he had shown her something.

Several days later, he received a postcard from Marseille. Valérie was writing to let him know that she had set up in an apartment in Canebière and that she was devoting herself to her little sailors. "I can't tell you, Marqués, how far ahead I am now." Valfierno wrote back to say that she should do whatever took her fancy, but that she was never under any circumstances to communicate with him again; that to her, he was now dead. He felt a little foolish on rereading this.

"I can't tell you, Marqués, how far ahead I am now." Valfierno returned to that phrase over and over. Valérie was the key to his vulnerability; in some obscure way, he felt himself still to be in her hands. He tried to console himself, telling himself that she was what had prevented the whole operation from being simply a common robbery; that she was the element of risk that transformed the whole adventure into a work of art. But he was not convinced.

Becker

"Is THIS CHARLES BECKER?"

"Yes, Becker here."

"I am the Marqués de Valfierno. I'd like to talk to you."

"What is this about?"

"I have a story to tell you."

At first, I didn't understand. He telephoned me at my office at the *Chronicle* and told me his name was Marquez and that he had a story to tell me that might interest me. The war had just ended, and San Francisco was teeming with soldiers, recently demobilized and out of work, looking to sell whatever they could, including the most unlikely tales. I got six or seven calls like this every day and rejected most of them outright. But something in the way this man spoke made me pause; his voice wasn't so much asking as commanding. He didn't ask me if we could meet, like most of the other unfortunates, nor did he tell me he had the biggest scoop for me that I'd ever heard, as the typical smoke-and-mirror guys used to do. No, he simply told me that he had a story to tell me, and I asked him where and when would be convenient. As I hung up, it occurred to me that he also had a strange accent.

"Marquez?"

"That'll do for now, but it's Marqués, a title, not a name. I am Marqués Eduardo de Valfierno. How do you do?"

It was impossible not to spot him. The bar at the Fillmore Hotel was humming with excitement, alcohol, girls in short hair and skirts, and men on the prowl dressed in garish ties. The piano was playing, but no one could hear it. The men and women flirted, yelled, shot each other looks, touched—all of them intent on making up for the years lost to fear and the trenches.

At the end of the lounge, sitting in a black leather armchair as if none of this had anything to do with him, sheathed in an impeccable suit of cream-colored linen, was the slight figure of a man in his fifties with the majestic head of a statue, the mane silvering, an aquiline nose, graying, pointed beard, and very lively eyes.

"You telephoned me."

"You are Charles Becker?"

"I am."

"What will you have to drink?"

"What have you got to tell me?"

"Whiskey? Two ice cubes? Three?"

The Marqués's eyes never stopped moving. As if he wanted to be sure to see everything going on around him, or perhaps, as I was not to think until much later, as if he knew what was coming.

"I can wonder about what I did, but not about what I'm going to do. Not because what I did is more important than what I might do, but because the past is infinitely malleable, whereas the future can only be what it is going to be."

"What?"

"You understand perfectly well, Newspaperman."

He spent a while traveling. For him, those first months of 1912 would always be his happiest, if by happiness we mean the peace that comes from knowing you have done what you set out to do and have nothing else pressing. Or, to immerse yourself only in the present.

Every so often he would read news accounts about Paris and the hunt for *La Joconde*; he took great pleasure in these. The police were baffled, and though they consulted all of the city's psychics and witches and fortune-tellers, they were getting nowhere.

The museum's director was fired, the security procedures were changed. These were the gropings of the blind, and there were several. Embarrassment over the affair reached up as far as the government. Finally, they managed to apprehend a suspect. The press supplied the details: he was a poet of vaguely modern style, perhaps homosexual, by the name of Guillaume Apollinaire, who aroused suspicion when a friend of his who worked at the Louvre either sold him or gave him as a present a small Iberian statue, which he in turn had stolen from the museum. His accomplice—this word would sometimes appear in quotes—was a young Spanish painter by the name of Pablo Picasso. He was interrogated and then let go. The poet, Apollinaire, was held for a week; in the end he was released without charges.

The newspapers kept on printing nonsense. What the reporters wanted to know more than anything was how the thief would be able to sell such a famous painting. Valfierno was like a child in his glee: he would enjoy these accounts hugely at first and then suddenly be irritated by their stupidity.

And then the story stopped appearing in the newspapers. Sometime in the middle of 1912, the Louvre's management gave up and filled in the space on the wall with a portrait by Raphael. Valfierno understood, even as they did not, that they were trying to forget.

He traveled. All of his destinations seemed to him to merge into one: the Carlton Hotel on the Côte d'Azur, the María Cristina in the north of Spain, the baths at Marienbad or Baden-Baden, the Select—or was it the Excelsior?—in Alexandria. The scenery changed, and the climate, and the language spoken by the staff, but the people were always more or less the same. The meals, the conversations, the occasional trysts, the gossip. In the end, he thought, we do not amount to much.

He meandered. For the moment, he preferred not to return to America, and the thought of Argentina also still made him uneasy. But the rest of the world was his.

He had no obligations and had never before fully realized

the significance of that state, having heard the phrase repeated in error so often by others. He had no obligations. No home, no country, no family. Just a name and a mountain of cash; he was free to follow any whim at all. The sheer possibility was infinite; sometimes, in the middle of his pleasure, it seemed almost terrifying. There were too many possibilities, and above all they were unpredictable.

He told himself there were certain things he had to decide. He had, for example, to come up with a place to live. But in order to decide that, he would also have to decide who to be. This he avoided, as he avoided reminding himself it was something he had to think about.

For the time being, he pretended that the only question was to choose what it was he wanted to do. He wanted to do nothing but didn't know how to go about it. After a few months, the usual ways of doing nothing were proving repetitive and rather boring. And whenever he thought of doing anything, it seemed so trivial compared to what he had just done. Trivial and unnecessary.

The only thing that interested him was to entertain certain additions to his recent, perfect feat. "Something that is perfect"— he was told by an educated Russian woman whom he encountered at more than one spa—"is something that can't be improved, something finished and perfectly complete."

"In that case, Madame, nothing is really perfect."

"No, Marqués, but sometimes we ought to pretend."

He still had *La Joconde*, or rather, Perugia still had her. He had known from the beginning that he didn't want to keep her; he had only arranged her theft so that he could sell the copies, and any contact he had with her now could only complicate things. At some point, though he had no desire to do so, he knew that he had to come to a decision about what to do. From time to time he would write a brief note to the Italian telling him not to despair, that he had not forgotten him, that he would be back to see him. He knew that he would eventually have to see Perugia and do something—he couldn't just leave the world's most famous painting under some peasant's bed, though there were nights when the absurdity of it seemed perfectly appropriate to him.

He considered different options. The simplest, without doubt, was to get rid of her entirely: to destroy her. He had recently read Stefan Zweig's account of Herostratus, who, wanting his name to endure at any cost, burned down one of the Seven Wonders of the ancient world, the Temple of Artemis at Ephesus, in 356 BC. The city elders condemned him to death and above all decreed that his name be forgotten forever. Yet now, in the twentieth century, Herostratus's name was known while no one remembered who had been on that council of elders.

But Herostratus had not been able to think of a better way to ensure his everlasting fame, whereas he—Valfierno—had already found a way to ensure his, though nobody knew it yet.

He continued to think that burning the painting was indeed the best choice, and also the simplest. It would put an end to the whole affair: the Louvre's painting would never reappear, his buyers would be happy, and eventually the theft would be forgotten. By burning *La Joconde* he would be destroying the only proof that the others were Chaudron's copies.

He liked to imagine that some day—decades, perhaps centuries in the future—the originals would start to appear: two, three, eventually six identical originals. Then this most celebrated painting would become a collection of identical paintings, indistinguishable one from another.

But he thought the idea of just setting fire to the painting seemed a bit weak, a little gratuitous. Then he was struck by a brilliant idea. He would collect the painting from Perugia and take it to a safe place. There, he would get a moving picture camera, which he would teach Chaudron to use. Together they would film a true work of art: the destruction by fire of the great painting. He imagined that old wood resisting the fire at first and then slowly catching, the colors changing, dripping, the smell of scorched oil paint, the wood now in flames, that gently smiling face dissolving into ashes, the eyes dissolving, that myth and all those centuries of nonsense dissolving, just because he, Eduardo de Valfierno, had known enough to show that they were nothing.

They'd be able to sell that film for thousands, millions. Then they'd return one of the copies to the museum—that would be the real coup! True art: to present the copy as the original, cause them to put that lie on display, and know that millions of people would gape in sacred awe at a painting that wasn't. Fools, believing in their foolishness! On, flock! To your trough! Sometimes he liked to tell himself that this is what he had actually done.

But he didn't do it, either this or anything else. His leisure was becoming unbearable, and the morning's brandy was no longer able to liven him up enough in the face of another day like all the others. His breakfast brandy became two, sometimes three. One night he woke up sweating: he was terrified of ending up as Bonaglia again. He got up, lit a long, fat cigar, and sat with a drink in his hand. The real problem was not that he might go back to being him, he knew; it was the suspicion that he had never stopped being Quique Bonaglia.

That night he thought of a thousand ways he might leave that man behind. As the dawn came, in the dim light, his guard down, he thought he would go back to Argentina one day to find Mariana de Baltiérrez; she was still so blond in his memories.

He says—wonders, tells himself—that he is grown up now.

The Marqués said nothing while the waiter put my whiskey beside me on the low table. Then he lifted his glass and murmured something in French. I returned his toast and asked him if we could start.

"By all means."

"What is it you want to tell me?"

"To put it discreetly: the story of the greatest theft of the century."

"In other words?"

"The disappearance of *La Joconde*—the *Mona Lisa*—you'll no doubt remember it," he said, and of course I did. She had been stolen from the Louvre seven or eight years earlier, and the story had been on the front page of every newspaper on earth. But it was an old story, filed away now. In the midst of my disappointment, I tried to be polite:

"Forgive me, but that whole business was resolved a long time ago."

"Was it, indeed?" he replied, with a mischievous smile, and I remembered the way it had ended, in another story that all the newspapers had carried on their front pages, when the thief, Vincenzo Perugia, had shown up with the painting at the Uffizi Gallery in Florence claiming he had stolen her in order to return her to her native land. Then his arrest, the initial widespread call to release him as a reward for his patriotic gesture, the trial, the gradual fading of interest after a few weeks of nitpicking legal arguments, and finally his sentence of seven months in jail, which by then he had served. Finally, his liberation, neither in glory nor disgrace.

"Well, I'd say it was resolved. They caught the thief, recovered the painting—everyone saw the story."

"And you believed all that?"

"I beg your pardon?"

"You believed that that illiterate peasant was capable of pulling off an operation of that magnitude?"

He spoke without either gestures or inflections of his voice, as if what he was saying didn't particularly matter to him. I learned later that this was one of his favorite tricks, but at the time it impressed me: it made him seem quite invulnerable.

"Look, actually, I haven't really kept up with it."

"Then it would behoove you to catch up. If, when you're done, you would like me to tell you the truth about what happened, I'll be staying here in the hotel for another three or four days. But don't be too complacent—you could just miss the story of a lifetime."

He doesn't want to think of himself as old already, but he's almost fifty now. If all goes well, he could have another ten or fifteen good years.

The news of Vincenzo Perugia's bolt reached him in the villa he'd rented in Tuscany, not far from San Gimignano. It struck him as a cosmic joke that the Neanderthal had gone to Florence to surrender the painting not a hundred kilometers from where he was. His first thought was to flee; it took him a couple of hours to convince himself that no one would be able to connect him with the news that was now shaking the country. Only then could he begin to consider the situation.

Clearly he had been wrong: he'd overestimated Perugia's intelligence. He understood now that he should have acted sooner—he had known this before—but he'd thought he had more time, not because Perugia seemed particularly patient, but rather because he didn't think Perugia would come up with any kind of plan. He could imagine that the pressure of sleeping night after night with the *La Joconde* under his bed might have gotten to him and caused him to commit the worst kind of foolishness.

It was not particularly dangerous for him, not in terms of the law or the police, since no one could connect him to the theft, but it was possible that one of his buyers would start to get nervous upon seeing all the newspapers talking about the sudden appearance of the painting. This was not a good time for him to be in America, but perhaps if he were to go he would be able to convince them of what they themselves wanted to believe—that the painting that had just appeared was itself a forgery. That the French, no longer able to bear the humiliation of having lost the *Mona Lisa*, had come up with this plan to show the world that they had recovered her. But that, just to be clear, the one and only original was the one that they kept hidden in their deepest safe or in their private vault. And that if they had any doubts they should call in an expert. And by all means, if they should have the opportunity, they were to go to the Louvre itself and look carefully at the copy that had been hung there. A true art connoisseur such as yourself, one who knows the original, after all, would see it right away. The thing is, the world is full of idiots. But we, we know the truth, you and me: we know.

He often remembers something that Don Simón, that unlikely con man, had said to him, so long ago now. Don Simón had told him that after a certain age, it no longer paid to boast: the truth would either disprove you and make your boasts look pathetic or it would bear you out, and they would be unnecessary. And that this was called maturity and could be quite pleasant.

I bet it is, thinks the Marqués. I bet it really is.

"But don't be too complacent—you could just miss the story of a lifetime."

It sounded like a serious threat. I picked up my whiskey and took a last gulp.

"And why do you want to tell me this?"

"Haven't you guessed?"

"I'm afraid not."

Valfierno gave a condescending smile. Around us, the men and women continued their pursuit, though to us it felt as if they had disappeared.

"Be patient; you'll understand soon enough. If I were to ask you for money for my story, what would you say?"

"That you don't look as if you need it."

"Perhaps not. Perhaps you don't see the significance of that."

I tried to think fast. If what he was saying was true, then I was looking at the opportunity of my career. But it was all very, very strange.

"Again, excuse me. I'm inclined to hear your story, to work with you. But how can I be sure that you really were involved in the theft?"

"Involved?"

"Whatever you want to call it."

From the inside pocket of his linen jacket Valfierno took out a wallet of Russian leather, and from it a photograph, its edges curled. He handed it to me. It was a picture of him, a few years younger, his hair less white, in a dark suit, holding the *Mona Lisa* up for the camera. To me, the photograph seemed like conclusive proof.

"I never did the very best I could in my life, but you know, in the end, that was the best thing I could have done. Others fake paintings, tickets, feelings. As far as I know, I was the first one to fake a theft."

I did not yet know that, with Valfierno, the whole notion of a conclusive proof was a mistake. I looked at the photo for a moment and then turned it over. There was nothing on the other side.

"Satisfied?" he asked, sarcastically.

I proposed that he come to my office the next morning, after breakfast. We would have room to talk there without any noise or interruption. He said no, that he would wait for me in his room at the hotel—room 712—at 8:35 in the morning.

"Be punctual," he told me. "It will be the most exciting day of your life."

I was ready to believe him.

Though he knows he created something that no one else could, that no one could have imagined: his life. He knows—tells himself—that he has created art.

It was then—with Perugia in jail, when there was no more point in wondering what to do with *La Joconde*, when the most important phase of his life appeared to be over, and with the war looming—that he received news of Valérie Larbin.

She had sent him a letter via Chaudron, which itself was unnerving—a way of letting him know that she knew more. But that was not the worst part: "I just heard what happened to our carpenter friend. He might still have some reason for not talking, but I don't." And she went on to explain that the reason she had kept quiet until now was not the money he'd given her, but her wish to safeguard the Italian. Now, she could talk without worrying about that.

The Marqués de Valfierno received the letter in Marienbad; it took him less than a day to get to Marseille. When he finally found her, in a tavern on the port, he had to hide his shock. She could only have been twenty-two or twenty-three by then, but she looked like an old woman. She had lost that freshness that had made her so appealing before; she had become fat, and something in her face had gone dull.

"You don't seem very happy to see me, sweetie."

"Are you?"

"Of course. I always like to see my old friends. Especially when I think they're going to be generous," she said, giving him a smile that was just a little too broad. Her teeth were even worse than before. Valfierno told her to get to the point and asked her what she wanted. Valérie said money, of course.

"Or did you think it might be something else, Marqués?"

He thought: I could kill her. She was right—he did want to kill her. He tried to push the idea away, but it kept coming back. She talked on and on, the wine disappeared, and he couldn't stop killing her.

He had never before believed that killing someone could be

a solution, that the problems it caused could be less than the problems it solved. Fear of the law and the police didn't count for much in someone who had spent so many years living with them already. Of course, forgery and fraud were not the same as murder, he thought. A good con was elegant, and popular, whereas killing someone was dirty, and people didn't like it. The public loves art forgers like us because we are all brains, we use our wits and cunning to get what everyone wants anyway. And we take advantage of people whom they don't like anyway because they're too rich, or because they're also trying to take advantage—you can't be conned unless you are also trying to con. And they like us because we mock the supposed value of things whose value they don't understand.

Murder, on the other hand, is something else entirely. The public likes mass butchery, great battles, accidents with no one to blame, but murder?—not a bit. The simple murder gets very bad press, and too much of it. For centuries our leading voices have been preaching to us that life is sacred—the same voices of those who were always killing: kings, judges, priests. But the fools keep believing the nonsense; a million flies.

He tried to take stock: neither fear of the police nor the ancient prohibition against killing could shake him of this solution. Maybe their shared past would dissuade him—it would be easier to kill a stranger, after all—but that wasn't it either. If it had been, their relationship would have made the idea of killing her repugnant. And it wasn't.

If he could have been sure that he was doing it only for the security of the operation he would have killed her, but he was afraid it might also be malice, spite—all those feelings that appear when a woman won't do what a man wants. He was seized with fear—he might kill her without knowing exactly why, or knowing only too well.

"You know, we were about to escape with the painting . . ."

"Who is we?"

"Don't pretend, Valfierno."

"You and Vincenzo?"

Valérie said nothing and looked at him hungrily. For a moment she was her old self. Valfierno looked away but then decided it was better to engage her.

"What happened?"

"Nothing. Some things are better when you don't do them."

They ordered another bottle of Sancerre. Just before the dessert, Valfierno handed her the envelope he had prepared. She asked for more, and he told her not to try her luck. Something in his face, his voice, some memory, made her not insist. Afterward, she offered—it was an offer rather than a suggestion—to spend the night together, and this time Valfierno didn't think he ought to refuse.

He has created art, he tells himself, and no one else knows it. He, the Marqués de Valfierno, is not—could never be, would hate to be—one of those charlatans who, realizing that they were terrible painters and negligible poets, declared that their life was their art. No, he would never have chosen art; it had just appeared one day, suddenly.

The first thing I asked that morning in his hotel room at the Fillmore was why he had chosen me to tell his story to. He smiled. It was not the right question to ask, but it didn't matter; Valfierno did not mind my questions. He had a very definite idea about what he wanted to say, and he said it. The fact that I was there was almost incidental. He needed me to be there and to be listening, though for most of those two days I had no idea why. I do know that it bothered him that he needed me there; he made that quite clear.

"Tell me, Newspaperman—I imagine you've masturbated before?"

"I assume we're not here to talk about that."

"You assume wrong. A jerk off, if you'll pardon my French,

is a kind of fake sex, wouldn't you say? Until it becomes its own kind of sex. It's the same with every forgery—it always ends up becoming the thing itself. You ought to know that."

The hotel room's blinds were closed; Valfierno had not wanted them open. He said we couldn't let the present interfere with our story. Later it occurred to me that what he was really keeping out was reality, but I didn't say anything. His recounting was exhaustive; we spent endless hours in there. He began the story of his life at the beginning, in Italy, and spared me no detail—I couldn't say if these were true, but he supplied many details of all kinds—in the telling, all the way through to the theft, and the ending.

He showed me papers, clippings, photographs. He was scornful, warm, anxious, conscientious. Those two days were endless. Little by little, almost without meaning to, I began to realize that this Marqués was different from the other. That he would say things so that his interlocutor would think the opposite. He would tell me that he needed me there, but very sarcastically, to make it seem as if this wasn't the case, to neutralize that need with his irony. But he did in fact need me. And of course I understood very well how extraordinary his story was—I was overcome with the excitement of knowing how it would change my life.

"So, Newspaperman, you are now the only one who knows the truth. Or perhaps not. Sometimes I think they also know . . ."

"They?"

"The ones who can't not know. The thing is, they don't want to say anything. The story of the little idiot Perugia, a dumb thief who represents no threat, serves them well. They much prefer that story to mine, which could inspire copycats. So they keep it going. I don't know, I'm not sure about that."

I was amazed that he told me this; in those two days I had also learned that uncertainty was not comfortable for him.

"In any case, I know that if no one ever hears my story, then they will have won."

No, he tells himself, unsung glory works for a while, but we are not really that strong. The moment comes when we reach for the mirror, for others to learn that it was me, he tells himself. He has lived all these years with that knife in his flesh.

He tells himself that he is a fully grown man. He doesn't want to think of himself as old already, but he's almost fifty now; if all goes well he could have another ten or fifteen good years.

He often remembers something that Don Simón, that unlikely con man, had said to him, so long ago now. Don Simón had told him—twice, three times, more—that after a certain age, it no longer paid to boast: the truth would either disprove you and make your boasts look pathetic or it would bear you out, and they would be unnecessary. And that this was called maturity, according to the old Galician, and could be quite pleasant.

It must be, thinks the Marqués. He thinks that it really must be, but that he never managed to learn it.

Though he might have been close once. It was when he had the accident, just over two years ago. He was in that little hospital bed, completely shattered—he was immobilized, entirely in their hands, while a doctor with a fearsome expression poked around in his wounds. He knew that he couldn't do anything, and he felt a profound relief: he didn't have to make any more decisions. He had done all he could and could do no more. He thought that day that he had learned something. Then he got better, and it left him, so in truth, he hadn't learned.

Though he knows he created something that no one else could, that no one could have imagined: his life. He knows—tells himself—that he has created art. Everyone talks about art—the dandies, the salon revolutionaries, the weekend painters who boast about using colors their mothers would have forbade them, the avant-garde "musicians" who arrange dissonant chords reminiscent of schoolyard farts. They all talk about it, but he really did it, made art; the rest is just playing around.

He has created art, he tells himself, and no one else knows it. He, the Marqués de Valfierno, is not—could never be, would hate to be—one of those charlatans who, realizing that they were terrible painters and negligible poets, declared that their life was their art. No, he would never have chosen art; it had just appeared one day, suddenly.

But he had known how to grab hold of it. He doesn't want to be one of those pathetic fools who believes he's created a masterpiece that no one else can see, who skulk in the corners and badmouth everyone who can't appreciate them, who are gradually poisoned by their failure, which they persist in regarding as genius.

No—he tells himself—unsung glory works for a while, but we are not really that strong. The moment comes when we reach for the mirror, for others to learn that it was me, he tells himself. He has lived all these years with that knife in his flesh. Not all the time, of course, not every minute, or even every day, but it was there nonetheless. Always there.

And now he didn't know how to get rid of it. The whole success of his plan—his great plan, his work of art, he thinks—depended on no one knowing about it. As long as everything went well it would remain a secret. Only if the plan failed would an even greater failure be avoided: that the world would never get to know of it. But in that case, his masterpiece could not be perfect: if it is not discovered, if I remain free, unpunished, then no one will ever come to know who the Marqués Eduardo de Valfierno was. And if they discover me then it will not have been a masterpiece—and I will no longer be Valfierno.

He has spent all these years with this wound, with the knife. And now Valérie has found him again and he cannot give her what she is asking, or rather, he just no longer wants to.

The afternoon of the second day stretched on. In the next-door room, a couple made love in a profusion of noise. More than once I detected—or thought I did—a wistful smile on Valfierno's face. I had more questions, but I didn't ask them. Interviewing is a strange business. Somehow, you think you have the right to ask a perfect stranger what you wouldn't ask your best friend. This time, in spite of that, I kept quiet.

We had reached the point where there was not much left to say, when Valfierno called down to have them bring us a bottle of champagne. It was his way of marking the end. We had just been through two days that had felt like two years. I could no longer see in his face the majestic features I had seen at the beginning. His greying mane was in disarray, his eyes were tired, and he wore a kind of grimace I could not decipher. His slightness of frame was now more noticeable. He had just entrusted me with the story of his life, and yet he continued to keep an unbridgeable distance between us. We toasted. Then he reminded me that I had asked him, on the first day—to say "yesterday" would have been improbable—why he was telling me all this.

"Yes, I remember. Although I think I'm starting to understand."

"I doubt it, Newspaperman. I'm telling you all this because tomorrow Valfierno is going to die," he said, and he gave what he meant to be a dramatic pause, which it was. By now I had learned: I didn't want to seem ridiculous by asking what was sure to be the wrong question. He proceeded to play with me, going on a detour:

"That rascal Don Simón was wrong. Age is knowing that there are things you are doing for the very last time. You don't know this yet; you're too young, but I know. I have eaten kidneys, which I will not eat again, as my body will not let me. I have been in places that I know I will not see again. I have enjoyed the company of women who are now dead. I've given up all hope of seeing certain parts of the world. This is the last time I will tell the story of

Valfierno. It might even be the first, but it is without doubt the last. Starting tomorrow I will have to have a new history or I will be finished. And I will have to forget what it was I did so that my life would have meaning."

These were very hard words—hard more than sad—and so they were accompanied by his brightest smile. I didn't know what expression to have as I listened.

"Tomorrow I will no longer be Valfierno. I don't know yet who I will be. I do have a passport which I will use for a while, as you might imagine. I know what I will call myself, and where I'm going to live, but these are small things. It saddens me, but I have no option. The truth is, Newspaperman, I liked being Valfierno."

Valfierno's specialty was words, concocting grand phrases, but this time there was something very serious behind them. Valfierno—or whoever he was by this time—spoke in softer and softer tones, as if to himself only.

"If I had been consistent, if I had really been making a work of art of my life, I should have died—should have been seen to die—seven years ago, when I finished selling the *Joconde*s. Valfierno has already lived too long, certainly longer than was a good idea. But I'm not happy about it. I had become used to it, I liked it," he said, and fell silent. He seemed to be very far away. He had another sip and went on, not looking at me.

"Now of course it's necessary. Valérie is hard at my heels, so I have no choice but to disappear. This revenge is much greater than anything she could have planned. She will have gotten rid of Valfierno. It's funny, isn't it?"

And then, suddenly, as if it had just occurred to him:

"What do you think about Bonaglia as a name? Now that would be a great joke, don't you think?"

Whenever I think about the story of my life I always look for the moment when everything changed, when everything turned around. And I find that there wasn't one. That even though I changed my name and my story many times, that was never it. And that for me, for him, for us—for the one who survived—that was the key: the hope that one day we would become another. But it never happened. I don't know why, I can't explain it—it just never happened.

"Excuse my asking, but why did you choose the name Valfierno?"

"Didn't we agree that you would limit your questions to matters of fact?"

"Yes, of course. Isn't that a matter of fact?"

"My dear fellow . . ."

It was now very late. With the last of the champagne, Valfierno moved on to detail his instructions.

"Of course, you're not going to be able to tell this story, Newspaperman."

"What?"

My face must have looked a sight. For the first time, Valfierno let out a huge guffaw.

"It's not so bad! I didn't say never. I'm just telling you that you cannot tell my story until I say that you can."

"And when do you think that will be?"

"It's not that I think—I'm ordering it. You may not think I can do that, but you'll see that in fact I can. I realize I've put myself in your hands, but not in the boring way you imagine. It's true that you could publish all of this tomorrow, and I'd have a bad few days of it, but it would be much worse for you."

Valfierno stood up and began to pace the room. I could only think of that old image of the caged lion. He told me it would not be difficult: that if I were to publish early, he would be able to deny the entire story categorically, and that I would be found, not long after, with a bullet in my head.

"A suicide, of course. You would not have been able to bear the shame of such an enormous lie."

It didn't seem that simple to me, but from where I stood, nothing he said seemed all that implausible. I believed him. Valfierno opened the blinds. It was the middle of the night.

"No, the reason I'm in your hands is because when the time comes, if you don't print my story then I will vanish forever. It's up to you: if you remain quiet, my entire life will be a resounding failure. I'll be like the castaway who writes a magnificent book on his desert island. Or the blind man who conceives a brilliant sculpture that no one will ever see. Or the great ruler who stepped down in a friend's favor in order to avoid the war that would have destroyed his country. If you remain silent, then an artist of genius will have disappeared from the face of the earth, disappeared without a trace. But you won't do that. You couldn't stand that silence. That is not what you are made of."

"How do you know?"

"Don't you worry—I know. Or do you think I chose you without knowing anything about you?"

He stopped talking and stared at me, and I could not return his gaze. He went on to give me his specific instructions:

"Every year from now on, on the twenty-second of August, you will receive a letter from me. It will not, of course, say who it's from, but you will know. This annual letter will be what tells you that I am still alive; it will be the affidavit of my existence. Don't look for me—you would regret it. When I die; then, yes—then you can tell my story to the world."

I thought about what he was describing and then said, without thinking:

"But, Marqués, that could be a long time."

"Are you disappointed?"

"No, no, please—that isn't what I meant. Forgive me, but how will I know when you are dead?"

"You will know, don't trouble yourself. You will know when I die. The person who won't know, of course, will be me," he said, attempting a smile which was pure melancholy.

"That is when you will tell my story. This is another reason why I have told you all of this—so that I can die in peace. I don't want to have to remember it all on my deathbed. It would be horrible if what occupied my life were to occupy my death as well."

I didn't want to offend him, but there was one question I still had to ask. I had learned his very own lesson:

"Forgive me again, Marqués, but how can I be sure that you are not lying, that your whole story is not another forgery?"

"You can't know. But don't worry. You'll see that it's true. When you tell the story, there will be certain old fools who will appear, bleating that Valfierno sold them one of the paintings. Nothing will please these old leftovers more than to have been hoodwinked by someone widely acknowledged to be their better. It's a simple fact. If it weren't for this, modern democracy could not exist."

"Never mind all that, Marqués. I'm asking you if it's true."

"It is, but you will never be able to be sure. You could ask Perugia, but you would still never know if he was lying. You could look for the others, but you might never find them. Or you might— who knows? But you will not know. These are the terms on which you tell the best story of your life—the story of mine."

I don't believe I have made a mistake: Becker will tell the story. Then I will have the answer to the question that haunts me so much now: who is it that will die when I die? At one point I came to believe that no one would. That just in the strength of changing who I was over and over again, I could cheat death itself. I now know that that is not true; that someone has to die.

But I would like to know who. Who will die when I die? Which one? The one who walked the earthen streets of Rosario? The one who loved Marianita without knowing who she was? The one who made art of a plan? The one who didn't want to be one? The one who wasn't one of the others? The one who never smoked that opium in Malacca, who tried all those delicacies, who didn't see his father, who let himself be touched by that priest, buggered by that prisoner, loved by those women who never wanted him. Bonaglia, Juan María, Perrone, Eduardo—the one who tomorrow, in telling his story, would die. Not all of these—so many deaths in one would be an injustice! But nor had they all been lives—just intentions.

No doubt for Becker it will be Valfierno who dies. For many people it will be Valfierno. There is no one for whom it will be Bollino who dies—Bollino died a long time ago. Sometimes I think that you could prevent an old man from dying if you were to call him by his first nickname—if someone were to address him by the name his mother first used, and if he were to believe it. But someone has to die. Where will they bury me? And under what name?

Becker will tell the story; he will answer my question. Of course, it's also possible that he won't. I hope that he does, but I will never know. I could tell it myself, first, but who knows what price I might pay? Perhaps one day I will decide to pay it. It's an interesting thing to decide one is going to pay a price when one doesn't know what that price is. I've done it so many times; it's the only way to really pay. It's quite possible that he will never tell the story. Many years ago I read a sentence which I have never forgotten: "Now, in the room, all that's left is what is left when there is nothing else left."

Me.

Valfierno.

About thirteen years went by after that meeting. I moved to Baltimore, and his letters continued to find me. They would arrive every year in late August, containing the same fragment of a poem, in Spanish. After a few years, I had it translated so I could discover its message:

> I shall die before you, and my spirit
> In its tenacious resolve
> Will sit there by the doors of death
> Awaiting you.
> There, where the enclosing tomb
> Opens, in turn, an eternity
> Everything we've both so long kept quiet
> Now we must begin to speak!

I have to confess that I did not quite understand it.

From time to time he also sent me gifts: an expensive book, opera tickets, a three-day vacation in New York, even a silver service for my wedding. He was in my hands as he had said, though in fact I held nothing. I must admit that I found it difficult, knowing that I had a story that would change my entire career and not being able to use it. More than once—in fact hundreds, thousands of times—I was tempted just to go ahead and publish it. But I resisted, or rather, I didn't have the courage not to resist. That night in San Francisco, as we were taking leave of each other, Valfierno smiled:

"Who can say for sure that the painting that Perugia returned is in fact the real *Mona Lisa*? That I don't have it in my house, for example. That I didn't burn it, or sell it to J. P. Morgan? Can you, Newspaperman?"

I, too, tried to banish my own doubt. It served me to do so.

In October of 1932, I learned of the death of Eduardo de Valfierno. As he had promised, I received a very formal letter announcing his decease. It was not signed, and the style of it made me think he might have written the letter himself before he died. There was a poem, but a different one this time. I had it translated that very day:

I'd gladly give the best years
of the little life I have left
to know what you told them
when you spoke of me.

The letter went on to inform me that in his last years he had
called himself such-and-such and had lived somewhere, which I was
asked not to reveal—and I won't; it doesn't change anything. The
letter told me—and authorized me to reveal—that in his last
months he had again taken the name of Valfierno, and that death
had finally visited him on a *finca*—a ranch—near Buenos Aires. He
had told me once: that to have lived as Valfierno he would have to
die as Valfierno.

This news caused me unparalleled excitement. It never even
occurred to me to wonder if indeed it was true. I quit my job at that
Maryland newspaper and invested everything I had in completing
the story. In those months I met Perugia, and Chaudron—and I
convinced myself that the Marqués had not been lying. Valérie, on
the other hand, I was never able to find. I don't know if she is even
alive now, and I don't like to think that he might have killed her. I
also tried to get in touch with the buyers. Valfierno had not given
me any of their names, which was understandable. I never found
any of them, which is also understandable.

So now at last I can write the story of the most ingenious
theft of the century. And while I can't be sure this is exactly how it
happened, that can't prevent me from telling the story—journalism
does not allow such indulgences. In any case, all that is left now is
for me to write.

About the Translator

JASPER REID WAS BORN IN MADRID, and has lived in Spain, France, the United Kingdom, the United States, and Latin America. This is his second work of translation. He lives in Massachusetts with his wife, Deb, and children, Ian and Ella.